Lured

The Doms of Genesis, Book 6

Jenna Jacob

Lured by My Master
The Doms of Genesis, Book 6
Jenna Jacob

Published by Jenna Jacob

Copyright 2016 Dream Words, LLC
Edited by: Blue Otter Editing, LLC
ePub ISBN 978-0-9864306-9-5
Print ISBN 978-0-9864306-3-3

If you have purchased a copy of this eBook, thank you. Also, thank you for not sharing your copy of this book. This purchase allows you one legal copy for your own personal reading enjoyment on your personal computer or device. You do not have the rights to resell, distribute, print, or transfer this book, in whole or in part, to anyone, in any format, via methods either currently known or yet to be invented, or upload to a file sharing peer to peer program. It may not be re-sold or given away to other people. Such action is illegal and in violation of the U.S. Copyright Law. If you would like to share this book with another person, please purchase an additional copy for each recipient. If you're reading this book and did not purchase it, or it was not purchased for your use only, then please purchase your own copy. If you no longer want this book, you may not give your copy to someone else. Delete it from your computer. Thank you for respecting the hard work of this author.

This is a work of fiction. Names, places, characters and incidents are the product of the author's imagination and are fictitious. Any resemblance to actual persons, living or dead, events or establishments is solely coincidental.

OTHER TITLES AVAILABLE BY:

Jenna Jacob

The Doms of Genesis Series:

Embracing My Submission: (Book One)
"I have read my share of BDSM but this book was unlike the others as in I get an even CLOSER look inside the relationships."
Twinsie Talk Book Reviews

Masters Of My Desire: (Book Two)
"THANK YOU for pulling me in to this world. This world full of love, lust, and intrigue. THANK YOU for creating such a powerful connection with these characters and their lives."
Shayna Renee's Spicy Reads

Master Of My Mind: (Book Three)
"From the very first pages of Master of My Mind, Jenna Jacob had me emotionally riveted, pulled into a story so intriguing, so enthralling, so spellbinding, that I tuned out the rest of the universe in order to fully immerse myself in Leagh and Tony's story."
Sizzling Hot Books

Saving My Submission: (Book Four)
"Simply beautifully written as I have come to appreciate and expect for Janna Jacob!"
The Book Fairy

Seduced By My Doms: (Book Five)
"I loved everything about this story. It had suspense, sizzling romance, and decadent scenes that will have you BEGGING for more."
Marie's Tempting Reads

The Passionate Hearts Series:

Sky Of Dreams (Book One)
"Jenna takes all the colors of life and paints them into a true masterpiece."
Nikki's Book Addiction

The Doms Of Her Life Series:
Shayla Black, Jenna Jacob & Isabella LaPearl

One Dom To Love: (Book One)
> "Buckle your seatbelts for the start of a yummy new BDSM series, The Doms of Her Life, in One Dom to Love."
>
> Two Lips Reviews

The Young And The Submissive: (Book Two)
> "I found myself lost in the story ignoring everything that was happening around me."
>
> Sizzling Hot Books

The Bold And The Dominant: (Book Three)
> "These three authors continue to blow me away with what they bring to these characters and the storyline. They bring out a reader's emotions so gently, so vividly, you feel like you are on the same level as one of their characters."
>
> Shayna Renee's Sexy Reads

Dedicated to my bestie, Cindy.

There is no one on earth I'd rather be with to:
Get roofied at the bar.
Dodge cougars and log trucks.
Hide beneath the bubbles in a hot tub.
Break hotel beds, windows and ashtrays.
Witness the aftermath of Lucky, the one-eared wonder rabbit.
Survive monsoons, frostbite, sunstroke, and endless miles on Harleys.
Drink in the beauty of Spearfish Canyon, over and over again.
Reminisce about hurricanes and beads on Bourbon Street.
Administer first aid for insect stings and other painful things.
Share—Hot flashes, laughter, tears, hopes & dreams.

I love you with all my heart.

CHAPTER ONE

Rushing through the ER doors of Highland Park Hospital, the newly appointed faculty physician, Dr. Metcalf—who I lovingly referred to as Dr. Dipshit—bellowed my name. Dread spilled through me as I forced a plastic smile and turned toward the five-foot-four asshat with a raging Napoleon complex.

"Nurse Noland," he repeated in his usual scathing tone. With his face contorted in a scowl, he marched into my personal space. "As charge nurse of this unit, it would behoove you to arrive a few minutes, not seconds, prior to the start of your shift. Allotting time to acquaint yourself with the patient load might enable you to run this unit in a more professional capacity. Don't you agree?"

I agree that a couple cc's of propofol injected in your ass would give this entire unit a well-deserved break, you pompous, egotistical prick.

Being dressed down by the little bastard wasn't how I envisioned the start of my day. Neither was finding my gas gauge hovering on empty when I left my apartment this morning.

Gritting my teeth, I kept my feigned smile in place while mentally cursing Dr. Reynolds—the former faculty physician—for accepting a position with a competing hospital across town. Unlike Dipshit, Reynolds bestowed his warm and compassionate side to patients and staff alike.

"As you well know, I never fail to evaluate the patient load," I began, wanting to vindicate myself. "This morning I had to stop and—"

"Spare me your boring personal dribble, Miss Noland. I'm not interested in your excuses. Either do your job or I'll find a charge nurse who will," he barked before storming away.

Kiss my ass you nasty little troll, I inwardly huffed, then marched to the nurses' station. As I scanned the patient board, I heard the coffeemaker gurgle behind me. I tossed a glance over my shoulder and thanked the nameless coffee fairy for making the fresh pot. Striding over to the nurses' station, I poured myself a cup of liquid fortification.

"Good morning, sunshine," Liz Johansson—my best friend and fellow nurse—cheerfully greeted as she rounded the corner.

"Is it?" I grumbled before taking a sip of the steaming brew.

"Oh, my. Sounds like somebody woke up on the wrong side of the bed." She frowned before a mischievous grin speared her lips. "What's wrong, did Dr. Brooks keep you up all night playing head nurse?"

I wish. Samuel Brooks, the drop-dead-gorgeous, ob-gyn surgeon who I'd been dating for the past three months, had been too busy lately to call, let alone come around to play hide-the-meat-thermometer. My insecurities had started bubbling to the surface and I couldn't quite find a way to tamp them back down.

I waved her comment away as I tried to ignore the sated sparkle in Liz's eyes. No doubt her *two* lovers, Ian and James, were the ones responsible for that glowing look of contentment on her face. A few months before Sam and I started dating, Liz had become immersed in an unconventional relationship. She now had two men rocking her world on a nightly basis. *Lucky little bitch.*

"You know…I'm getting real sick and tired of you showing up every morning wearing that just-fucked glow," I chided with a mock scowl.

I was both envious and curious about her kinky love triangle, but mostly I was grateful that she'd found Ian and James. The duo had somehow brought Liz back to life after her brother, Dayne, committed suicide. They'd taught her how to forgive herself and move past the perpetual mourning she'd been mired in—something I'd tried to accomplish for years but failed.

"Hmm, sounds like the good doctor isn't examining your girly bits the way he should. Is that the problem?"

"I need to go to work."

"Wait." With a frown, Liz grabbed my arm. "I was only joking. What's wrong?"

"Dr. Dipshit ripped into me this morning. If he catches me talking to you, it'll give him yet another reason to crawl back up my ass. Once was enough, thank you very much."

"Screw him. He's a disgusting little toad," she said with an absent wave of her hand. "I mean, what's going on with you and Dr. Brooks?"

"Nothing. Well, nothing I have any proof of yet."

"Proof? Whoa, slow down. What are you talking about?"

"I think Sam's seeing someone else."

"What?" Liz's eyes grew wide. "You caught him with another woman?"

"Well, no. Not exactly. I think he is."

"That's crazy, Cin. Sam's head over heels about you." Liz shook her head. "What makes you think that he's seeing someone else?"

"The past few weeks, he only works me into his busy schedule on Sunday. He's obviously doing something or *someone* he doesn't want me to know about."

"Maybe he's just"—she shrugged—"really busy."

"Oh, give me a break. I've been down this road before. I was blind the first time, but now I know the warning signs. There are red flags flying all over the place in my head."

Something odd flashed over Liz's face before she quickly banked her reaction. Turning, she grabbed a cup and poured herself some coffee.

She ,too, was hiding something from me. A sick feeling rolled through my gut.

"He *is* seeing someone else, isn't he? And you know it." I somehow managed to push the words past my constricting throat.

"Cindy, I—" Spinning to face me, Liz blanched, then swallowed tightly. "Good morning, Dr. Brooks."

"Morning, Liz."

From behind me, Sam's familiar, buttery voice spilled over me like thick, warm syrup. As I darted my attention his way, my pulse quickened at the sight of his chiseled features. No man had the right to look as sexy as Sam did. And when he flashed me his patented panty-melting smile, my pussy clutched as if he'd been hardwired to that particular place. Every nerve ending in my body revved to life and started warring with my unruly suspicions.

"And how are you this morning, Cindy?"

"Fine," I replied curtly.

As the warm smile fell, Sam cupped my chin and forced my gaze. His wheat-colored brows slashed in concern as he delved deep into my eyes. "You don't sound fine, sweetheart. Something's bothering you. Let's talk."

Hell no. If he got me alone, I'd break down like a weak, stupid kitten. "I can't. I'm on Metcalf's shit list this morning. I need to get to work."

Frowning, Sam studied me for several long seconds before darting a glance at Liz. A blind man couldn't miss the silent dialogue the two quickly shared, and it only served to reinforce my worst fears. My heart plummeted to my knees. I began breaking out in a cold sweat as tears stung the backs of my eyes.

Shit. To think I'd been the only woman warming Sam's sheets over the past three months had been stupid…foolish. How could I be so damn naïve?

But why hadn't Sam grown a pair and at least talked to me if he wanted to see other women? A little voice inside my head scoffed. I already knew the answer…me.

I'd told him from the start, I didn't share my lovers with others. Obviously, Sam had only agreed to exclusivity in order to get inside my pants. He'd even vowed that he didn't want anyone but me. Who knows, maybe he really didn't…at least not until some snag-nasty bitch came along, wiggling her tits and ass in his face, and made him change his mind.

Fucking men.

And what the hell was wrong with me? Did I have some fucked-up personality disorder that made me attracted to man-whores who couldn't keep their dicks in their pants? Or were there really no honest ones left?

Fucking men.

Anger at myself for being so trusting, and fury at Sam for cheating on me, bubbled within like a cauldron of witch's brew. I knew if I didn't get out of here, I'd rip into his cheating ass or fall apart like a spineless wimp. Both would only paint me as a complete fool.

"If Metcalf gives you trouble, I'll take care of it," Sam assured. "You can spare a couple of minutes to talk to me."

As he stepped in closer, the air seemed to begin sizzling. But that wasn't anything new. The chemistry between us was always unlike any I'd ever experienced. If the man so much as touched my skin, I'd squander all my dignity and beg him to pick me over the other woman.

How pathetic was that?

Zigzagging around Sam, I snagged the nearest patient chart and scurried away. I could feel the burn of his gaze boring through me as I fled down the hall. I prayed he didn't know what I was thinking, but the man had an innate ability to read my mind. A part of me thought he was possibly psychic. But the pragmatist within me wagered I'd simply opened myself up far more than I should have.

Fucking men.

Glancing at the room number on the chart in my hand, I sucked in a deep breath and slid past the curtain. A wrinkled old man flashed me a wide toothless smile as he propped himself up on one elbow. A mischievous twinkle danced in his eighty-something-year-old eyes.

"Did the doc send you in to help me get rid of this?" the old geezer asked, whipping back the bed sheet, proudly displaying a purple, blood-engorged hard-on. "I had no idea taking two of those little blue pills would keep this soldier standing at attention *this* long."

The old man stared at his erection with an enamored gaze.

Stunned speechless, I blinked, then quickly pinched my lips together to keep from groaning. There wasn't enough bleach in the world to scrub this sight from my eyes or clean it from my brain.

"Ah. Let me check with the doctor," I stammered, forcing a level of professionalism I didn't feel.

"If he can't do nothing about it, that's okay. I'll just go back home. There's another lady friend I can call. Maybe she can convince this old one-eyed trouser snake to finally lie down and take a nap."

Shoving down the visual of wrinkled balls, saggy boobs, and matching medical-alert necklaces slapping in tandem, I held up my hand and shook my head. "Wait right here. I'll be back."

Ducking out of Great-Grandpa Boner's room, I closed my eyes. *What. The. Fuck.* This day had already turned into a nightmare of biblical proportions. I didn't know if I had the courage to see what would happen next.

Glancing at the nurses' station, I felt a burst of relief—both Sam and Liz were gone. As I made my way to the drug room, I began making a mental list of items needed to alleviate Father Time's erection. Just as I rounded the corner, I heard Sam and Liz. The two were engaged in a nasty argument—based on the tone of their voices—inside the supply room. Pausing, I pressed in close against the wall and inched toward the partially open door.

"What do you mean, you're not going to tell her? You have to tell her, Sam," Liz scolded.

"Don't tell me what I *have* to do, girl. You're stepping over boundaries you're forbidden to cross. Don't force me to discuss your behavior with Ian and James."

"Really? You're throwing that in my face? This had nothing to do with those types of boundaries, and you damn well know it. Cindy's my best friend. She knows something's up. You have to tell her. You have to, Sam. I can't be trapped in the middle of this any longer. It's not fair to me or her."

My heart hammered wildly. My mouth went dry. When I'd first voiced my suspicions to Liz, I'd wanted her to tell me I was crazy. That my insecurities were coming into play, but now...like the concrete crumbling under my feet, they were all too real. I could no longer ignore that Sam was cheating. That realization leveled me with a brutal blow, but debilitating was the fact that Liz knew and hadn't warned me.

Dual betrayal stabbed my heart like well-honed knifes.

I felt too much for Sam to pretend he was just another lover. And it was equally impossible to diminish the friendship I shared with Liz. We'd shared a bond, like sisters, for years. A bond that superseded men—chicks before dicks, and all that. At least that's what I'd believed. How many months had we spent commiserating about our nonexistent love lives? Too many. Hell, I'd spent months trying to convince Liz that her ex-asshole boyfriend, Ryan, who was nothing but a worthless scumbag, long before he kidnapped and nearly killed her. Why? Why hadn't she tried to save me from Sam's lies...from the heartbreak that now consumed me?

"I'll tell her when I'm damn well ready. But now isn't the time," Sam stated sternly. "My relationship with Cindy doesn't concern you. Understood?"

The tone of his voice told me he was pissed. Good. That made two of us. It took all the strength I had not to burst into the supply room and slap them both. Instead, I clenched my teeth, swiped the tears that spilled down my cheeks, and continued to listen like a stupid, sick martyr.

"I respectfully disagree, *Sir*," Liz spat. "It *does* concern me. Cindy's my best friend. I get the feeling that your time spent with Destiny means more to you than being with Cindy. If that's the case, then you need to end it now. Choose one or the other, but I won't keep your secret any longer. I'm through."

Destiny? Sam was kicking me to the curb to fuck some skanky stripper named Destiny? A shiver of repulsion raced up my spine along with relief for Sam always gloving up before we made love.

Made love? Ha, I scoffed with an inward snort. *Fucked would be the proper term now.*

"For the love of…Nurse Noland," Dr. Metcalf barked from behind me.

Startled, I jumped and screamed as I snapped my head in his direction. A wicked scowl lined his mouth.

"What in the world are you doing loitering in the hall when we have patients needing treatment/ Is it too much to ask that you consider actually working today?"

His condescending tone raked over my flesh like alcohol poured over thousands of paper cuts. From the corner of my eye, I saw Sam and Liz dart into the hall. Turning, I took in their matching expressions of guilt mixed with shock.

Liz's shoulders slumped as she pinned me with a look of apology before turning a caustic glare toward Sam.

"Nurse Noland," Metcalf barked once more. "Are you deaf? I'm speaking to you."

"Cindy, let me explain. It's not what you think." Sam's expression was wrought with regret as he reached a hand toward me.

"No." I shook my head and stepped back. "Don't touch me."

I wanted to ask how long he'd been fucking the slutty stripper, but my self-esteem couldn't handle the blow. Had he been deceiving me the whole time we'd been together…the whole time he made me feel as if I were the most adored and tempting woman on the planet? He probably made Destiny feel that very same way.

"Noland? Are you deaf as well as incompetent?" Metcalf thundered.

Incompetent? Yes. That pretty much summed up my entire life. A suddenly surreal and foreign existence that now mimicked a shoddy carnival ride, spinning disastrously out of control.

Without warning, Sam grabbed Metcalf by the throat and slammed him against the wall. "If I hear one more derogatory comment about Nurse Noland roll off your tongue, you're going to need the services of this ER unit. Am I clear, you weasely little prick?"

"Oh, shit," Liz whispered in fear.

Metcalf's eyes bulged from their sockets. His face grew an increasingly deeper shade of crimson, yet he somehow managed to nod.

"For heaven's sake, Sam. Stop," I cried, tugging at his rock-hard forearms. "What the hell do you think you're doing? Have you lost your damn mind? Let go of him this instant."

Sam blinked at me as if coming back from the throes of insanity. With a shove, he released Metcalf, who nearly stumbled to the ground, coughing and wheezing.

Pinning Sam with a glare, Metcalf's lips peeled back in a sneer. "I'll see you brought up on assault charges, Brooks."

"Go ahead, you pompous little prick. I'll file a few charges of my own," Sam countered. "Starting with the prejudiced, racial slurs you constantly make behind Cindy's back. Either you start acting like a professional or I'll rain down a shit storm so hard on you, you'll hand your medical license back on a silver platter."

Metcalf paled as he darted a guilty look my way.

"Now get the fuck out of here. I need to speak to Nurse Noland alone," Sam snarled.

Turning his back on the man, he dismissed Metcalf altogether. Like a scolded dog, tucking its tail between its legs, the evil doctor coughed once, then skittered away.

Sam's furious expression vanished, replaced by a look of apology. "I'm sorry, Cin. I don't know what you heard of my conversation with Liz, but I need to explain some things to you."

"I heard enough," I bit out. "You don't need to explain." Turning, I settled a scathing glare on Liz. "In fact, I'd rather not hear anything from either of you again."

Spinning on my heel, I stormed to the employee lounge. After snatching my purse out of my locker, I punched out at the time clock, then headed toward the door. Sam stood leaning against the frame. His thick arms, folded over his wide chest, made me want to whimper. Especially when I saw the sorrowful expression settled on his face.

"So you're going to just walk out the door without even giving me a chance to explain?"

"What I do is none of your business. If you want to talk to someone give your little fuck-toy stripper Destiny a call."

Sam's nostrils flared. His eyes narrowed and his jaw clenched. "You have no idea what you're talking about, Cin."

"That's where you're wrong. I'm not an idiot. She's the reason you haven't been spending time with me lately, and we both know it."

He exhaled a heavy sigh as he dragged his gaze to the wall behind me. The guilty rat bastard couldn't even look me in the eye. "I have been spending some time with her lately, but I had other obligations to take care of, as well." The confession pouring from his lips tossed me into a bottomless pit of revulsion that I hadn't visited in years. "But it's not what you think. She's not a strip—"

"Spare me. I don't give a shit if she's the goddamn queen of England. You lied to me. You went back on your promise. You told me you wanted an exclusive relationship and like a hopeful moron, I believed you."

Struggling to push down the flood of tears rising inside me, I lowered my head and charged the exit like a bull. Without a word, Sam reached out and grabbed me. He pressed his lean, sinful body against mine, then pinned me to the wall. Like a brushfire, his formidable command blistered my skin. His potent dominant mien dragged my thoughts back to the spine-bending pleasure he always unleashed in bed.

"I've never lied to you, Cin. Never once did I stand you up or bow out of a single date," he stated. "Regardless of what you *think*, I'm not sexually involved with anyone but you."

"Correction, you *were* sexually involved with me. Not anymore. That ship has sailed, mister. And your big, fat cock is onboard the boat."

The corners of his mouth twitched as if fighting back a smile. "My big fat cock is right where it belongs," he murmured in a familiar deep, velvet voice that instantly made me wet.

Sam arched his hips, driving his ready erection deeper between my legs.

My pussy clutched in demand.

My brain screamed in protest.

"Get off me," I spat. "Don't you get it? We're over…finished. We had some fun, shared a few laughs, and fucked like bunnies. And now we're through."

His brows arched in disbelief. "No, we're not, sweetheart."

"Oh, yes, we are. I'm done with everything. You. Liz. Dr. Dipshit. My job. I'm done with the whole damn mess. Because that's all my life is right now, one big, fat, ugly mess. I'm not some desperate, needy woman you can play booty call with while you're sticking your dick in some crack whore stripper." My voice rose to the point of hysteria.

Sam tensed. Anger flared and danced in his eyes. While my heart shattered into a million pieces, the heat of his body and masculine scent wrapped around me like a blanket of perfection. Fury and lust fused with a powerful throbbing that coursed through my veins, the sensual zing so compelling I could practically taste it. And all the while, Sam's rock-hard cock—nestled all nice and cozy against my pussy—made me wetter by the second. My caustic rage soared even higher.

"Get off me. I'm leaving," I hissed.

"Not so fast. You're telling me the time we spent together meant nothing to you?" The steely, cold edge of his tone made me shiver.

"Pretty much." I shrugged, fibbing through my teeth.

Sam narrowed his eyes, dissecting deeply with his piercing stare. "Now who's breaking promises? We promised we'd never lie to one another, yet you're doing that now. What we share is far more than casual, and you damn well know it. You *think* I've been unfaithful, but I haven't. I won't let you pin a man-whore label on me, because I'm not one."

As Sam spoke, I couldn't tear my eyes off his mouth…couldn't stop remembering how incredible the soft, firm texture of his lips felt.

"You're wrong, sweetheart…oh so wrong," he murmured before dipping his head to capture my mouth beneath a tender kiss.

The familiar lure of his command pulled me helplessly under as he disarmed and laid waste to my fury.

No, my head shrieked in rage.

Yes, my body moaned in delight.

"Um, I'm sorry to interrupt," Liz mumbled from the doorway. Sam grudgingly eased back but kept his smoldering gaze locked on me. "Metcalf sent me to find you two. Cindy, the Life Wings chopper is en route. ETA: five minutes. Sam...err...I mean, Dr. Brooks, the EMTs are pulling in now with your patient."

"We'll be right there," he replied, still holding me prisoner with his stare.

Liz darted out of the room while Sam caged me with his steely frame.

"Clock back in, Cin. This department doesn't run the same without you. If Metcalf looks at you sideways, I want to know about it immediately." Sam arched his brows, pausing until I gave a little nod. "Thank you. One more thing, meet me back here after your shift. I'm going to take you someplace quiet so we can talk this out."

I wanted to refuse him. Tell him not to waste his breath, but he'd used that uncompromising tone that brooked no argument. The same one he used when we made love and he commanded me to hold back my orgasms until he granted mercy and growled for me to come. Did the man have any idea how his unyielding control turned me inside out?

Of course he does, you fool. That's why he talks to you that way, my conscience taunted.

"We'll see," I hedged, not wanting to readily succumb to his edict.

"No. You'll wait here for me, Cin. Seven o'clock."

Like Kryptonite to Superman, Sam's authoritative tenor melted every ounce of my resolve. "Fine." I exhaled a heavy sigh. "I'll meet you here at seven."

"Good girl." He smiled, then kissed me once more before pushing off the wall and striding out the door.

The loss of his blissful body heat only served to reinforce how difficult it was going to be to walk away from the glorious bliss Sam never failed to bestow.

"Yeah, well, he shouldn't have started bestowing it on that bitch, Destiny," I spat as I shoved my purse back into my locker.

After clocking in again, I hurried back to the ER unit. Several hectic, stressful hours later, Liz plopped down next to me at the nurses' station and began updating patient charts.

The air between us was with thick with tension.

After several awkwardly silent minutes, Liz turned toward me. "I'm sorry."

I dismissed her apology with a cold stare.

"I haven't been the kind of friend that you've been to me. I never meant for any of this to happen. I'm sorry I hurt you."

Jerking my head in a nod, I started to glance away.

"There's extenuating circumstances involving Sam that I'm not at liberty to divulge." A pleading expression lined her face. "I want to. I want to tell you everything, but I can't."

"Oh, please," I scoffed bitterly. "I didn't want to tell you Ryan was a bastard, but I did. Because I cared enough to tell you the truth…risked our friendship to try and save you heartache in the end."

Liz's face wrinkled in regret. "I know, and I appreciate you trying to do that for me. Honestly, I do. But until Sam talks to you. I—I can't go into details and it pisses me off."

"*You* have nothing to be pissed about. Your actions clearly declare your allegiance is with Sam and not me. Let's drop—"

"That's not fair," Liz interrupted, clearly distraught. "I've never sided with Sam or tossed you under the bus. It's not like that. There are personal things about him that I know but can't discuss with you or anyone."

"So the fact that he's sharing secrets with *you* and not me is supposed to, what…make it better?" I chortled humorlessly as the knife in my back twisted in deeper still. "Look, don't sweat it. He and I are going to talk tonight. Whatever he wants me to know, he'll tell me. I'm sure he's thinking he can sweet-talk his way into my life and bed, but he's in for a rude awakening. Fool me once, shame on me. I don't plan to stick around for him to fool me twice. We're through."

"What? No. You can't," Liz gasped. "Don't jump to conclusions, Cindy. Listen to him. He'll explain every—"

"I don't have to listen to you take his side anymore," I snapped. "You don't get to try and sew my fucked-up love life back together. I know how to handle players like him. I've done it before, remember?"

"Aw, Cin. Sam isn't anything like Darnell," Liz began, ignoring my words. "You can't compare—"

With a raise of my hand, I cut her off. "Don't say a word about my personal life…past, present, or future. Got it? I should never have confided about Darnell to you in the first place. I just hope Sam knows how lucky he is to have you in his corner. Now, if you'll excuse me, I have patients who—"

"Dammit, Cindy. I said I was sorry," Liz barked.

"You think this is a boo-boo you can just kiss and make better?" I railed. "You betrayed me, Liz. Betrayed our friendship over some two-timing worthless fucking man. How could you do that to me?"

Tears swam in Liz's grief-stricken eyes. With a strangled sob, she bolted from her chair and raced out of the unit.

"Shit," I hissed. The sight of Liz's tears was burned into my retinas long after she'd gone. Guilt sluiced through my veins as the puckered scars of my heart split open. A piercing ache thrummed through me as a wave of self-loathing consumed me in its fiery blaze.

I had no business talking to Liz about Sam. Not when my emotions were stampeding all over the damn place. I should have simply accepted her apology and waited until the gaping wounds inside me started to heal.

"Nurse Noland?" Metcalf's abnormally soft tone pulled me from my thoughts. "I could use your help in room six if you have a minute, please?"

His timid request ricocheted through me like a bullet in a steel chamber. Obviously, Sam's threat had made quite the impression. Still, I didn't trust Metcalf's new demeanor and remained guarded as I followed him into trauma room six.

The remainder of my shift seemed to drag on forever. No doubt worsened by the fact that Liz was deliberately steering clear of me. That, coupled with the kicked-puppy-dog expression lining her face, told me I'd been much too harsh on her. Still, her siding with Sam wasn't a wound I could dismiss or erase in a few hours, or days. When I finally managed to pull the knives from my heart and super-glue the damn thing back together, I hoped Liz and I could mend our riff. We'd had spats before, though none this brutal. I truly hoped a permanent wedge hadn't been driven between us. In the end, one of us would swallow our pride, and if it had to be me, fine. I simply couldn't wrap my head around Liz being gone from my life. I loved her like a sister.

As I glanced at my watch for the hundredth time, anxiety climbed higher. The closer to seven p.m., the harder it became for me to tamp down the trepidation within. When Liz walked past me, I realized how badly I'd cut off my nose to spite my face. If there was a time I needed my bestie to talk me off the ledge and pry the icy hands of uncertainty from my neck, it was now.

In a matter of minutes, Sam would be here, expecting to work things out. Hopefully, the flames of jealousy burning inside me would make short work of ending our relationship. The last thing I wanted to do was talk about Destiny. I didn't buy for a minute Sam's claim that they weren't having sex. Did he take me for a total fool? Obviously.

With a heavy sigh, I stalked off to the nurses' lounge. Sam wasn't there and a glimmer of hope ignited inside me. If I hurried, I could sprint to the garage, drive home, open a bottle of wine, and draw a hot bubble bath. Then I could finally purge and purge the tears I'd been shoving down over the past twelve hours.

"That sounds like heaven," I sighed out loud, anxious to find my zen again.

"Something might sound like heaven, but I'm looking right at it," Sam drawled.

His deep voice startled the beejeebers out of me, and I jerked my head up to find him standing in the doorway, wearing a sexy smile. My heart leapt to my throat. My body trembled. Though I wasn't sure if that was from being startled or the instantaneous cravings zipping through my body.

In an effort to mask how easily he aroused me, I lifted my chin defiantly.

I knew he saw right through me when he shook his head and chuckled. "Are you ready to go?"

"Go? Go where?" Before he could answer, I marched into his personal space. "If you think I'm going home with you, you're out of your mind."

Because the minute you have me alone, you'll try to seduce your way out of this, and I'll end up naked beneath you. Which will make me feel more damn pathetic than I do right now.

Sam leaned in close to my ear. "Oh, I'd love to take you home and fuck the sass right out of you, baby," he growled, then lifted his head and stared down at me. "Where I'm taking you is a surprise. But I promise I'm not going to take you home and cuff you to my bed."

A strange little smile curled over his lips.

Two other nurses ambled in, then headed toward their lockers. I didn't want to make a huge scene, so I bit my tongue and slung the strap of my purse over my shoulder.

"You're damn right you won't, because I won't let you," I hissed lowly. "Go ahead. Lead the way."

"Oh, I fully intend to." He softly chuckled.

In the parking garage, Sam held open the passenger-side door of his sleek red Audi R8 as I slid down onto the buttery-soft leather seat. Buckling up as he closed the door, I inhaled the scent of his musky cologne still lingering in the air. I could almost taste the heady flavor of his skin on my tongue. A melancholy sadness filled my heart.

God, I was going to miss the magical way he drew the passion from deep inside me. He was an amazing lover, both tender and commanding. Sam never failed to drive me to the point of powerlessness, and I loved breaking free from every inhibition that had been drilled into my head since birth.

I closed my eyes and sucked in the surrounding scent of him one last time. I knew that telling him good-bye wasn't going to be easy, but I began to question whether I had the courage to snuff out the light he'd brought to my life. I didn't want to slide back into the lonely, dark single life again. But I was strong. I'd learn how to live without him…somehow.

Sam opened the door and settled in next to me. The heat of his body surrounded me like a warm caress. As he pulled out of the parking garage, I watched him grip the steering wheel and studied his hands…hands that knew every curve and crevice of my body. The same hands that could set me ablaze with the slightest touch. As my mind began to spool through the happy memories we'd shared, I knew that strolling down memory lane would only make my heart hurt more. But try as I might, I couldn't keep the happy times at bay. Like wine and cheese picnics in the park beneath the shade of a big oak tree. Walking down the street, holding hands, and eating ice cream as we laughed at silly nothings. Or stealing to the back row of the movie theatre to kiss and grope like a couple of teenagers.

Tears pricked the backs of my eyes. This was definitely going to be a lot harder than I'd imagined. Especially when Sam turned and glanced at me with those erotic sapphire eyes. I didn't miss the flicker of lust and adoration twinkling there before he turned his attention back to the road. My heart sputtered and my nipples hardened. And for a moment, I wanted to believe that Sam hadn't been unfaithful, and that the connection we shared wasn't short-circuited beyond repair.

But he had and it was.

"How open-minded are you, Cin?"

Open-minded? My stomach lurched.

Surely he wasn't suggesting what I thought he was…or was he? No. Maybe? My heart rate tripled. *There was no way in hell I would ever participate in some kinky threesome with him and Destiny.*

Anger thundered through me.

Slashes of rage ignited like lightning, coalescing into a violent and unrelenting storm that rocked me to the core.

"Take me to my car. Right now. Turn around and take me back to the hospital," I snapped.

"What the hell?" Sam jerked a worried glance at me. "Why are you freaking out?"

"Open-minded? Just what kind of woman do you think I am, Sam? If you think I'm going to take part in some depraved ménage with you and that trashy stripper, you're out of your fucking mind."

Sam's eyes grew wide. A wicked laugh rumbled from deep in his chest. "I wasn't asking you to..." He paused and darted me a quizzical look. "Are you sure? I mean, I hadn't thought about that, but since you mention—"

I interrupted him with an unladylike growl.

"Okay, okay," he chuckled. "I confess. I *do* have some wonderfully twisted fantasies about you, Cin, but trust me...in each and every one of them, I have you all to myself."

"Well, you can shove your *wonderfully twisted fantasies* right up your ass. In case you weren't paying attention earlier...we're through."

Sam braked hard at a red light, then cupped my chin. "No. We're not, gorgeous."

The silky edge of authority that laced his words flipped the switch on my libido to high.

What the hell had I been thinking, letting him get me alone?

Dammit, it was too late for second chances, and I was only making this harder on myself.

The light turned green. Sam accelerated, zipping through traffic like a race car driver, yet I wasn't afraid. I'd never been afraid when I was with him. Unlike other men, Sam always made me feel safe, protected, secure. I was going to miss that, too.

Headlights from oncoming traffic flashed across his handsome face. God, he was gorgeous, but my attraction to him was more than physical. He called to me on some primal level and touched my heart in ways I'd never known possible. Sam was kind, gentle, considerate—always considerate, especially when we made love. He was hands-down the most passionate and capable lover I'd ever known. Only Sam could finesse every last drop of pleasure from my body. But he was also giving and compassionate, and treated me as if I were as precious as gold. And that was just the tip of the iceberg of all the reasons I loved the man.

But he's fucking around on you. Hello? my consciences scornfully reminded.

That insurmountable fact ripped me in two.

The silence in the car was all but deafening. Never before had we suffered a lack of words…until now. And the awkward emptiness and undertow of tension filling the air only seemed to widen the gap between us.

Anxiety bubbled and churned in my stomach as Sam pulled into a dimly lit alley. Slowly making his way past a nondescript brick building, he whipped the car into a vacant parking space and turned off the engine.

"We're here."

Peering out the windshield, I scanned the nearly empty lot. "What is this place?"

"It's a private club."

"What kind of private club?"

"You'll see. I'll explain everything to you once we're inside."

"If you have something to tell me, say it here…in the car."

"No. I need to do this the right way. I don't want to run the risk of fucking it up and losing you."

Too late. You already have. The words of finality lay poised on my tongue, but I couldn't find the courage to push them past my lips. My heart wouldn't stop balking at the thought of ending things with Sam. But the jaded, jealous, insecure woman within wanted nothing more to than call it quits, lick my wounds, and move on.

CHAPTER TWO

With his hand pressed against the small of my back, Sam led me up a flight of industrial stairs. Pausing before an imposing metal door, he whipped out his phone and shot off a text. Seconds later the door opened. Standing in the portal was a perky, petite, buxom blonde wearing a fiery-red corset, tiny black leather miniskirt, and impossibly high red stilettos.

A sour taste lay on my tongue as I wondered if this woman might be the infamous slut, Destiny.

"Thank you, Sammie," he greeted. "This is my Cindy, the woman Mika spoke to you about."

Okay, so this bitch wasn't Destiny. Then who the hell was she, and why was she dressed like a fucking Madame? Fear, like spiders, crawled up my spine while panic surged through my veins. Sam had brought me to a whorehouse?

"It's a pleasure to meet you, Cindy." Sammie smiled.

I didn't reply, simply stared at the woman in horror.

She darted a look of concern between Sam and me before

inviting us in with a wide sweep of her hand. He took a step forward, but I remained frozen on the stoop. My legs had turned to concrete.

Still wearing a wary expression, the woman addressed Sam. "If you need any help, let me know. I'll do whatever I can."

Help? Help with what? A fresh wave of dread consumed me, stealing all rationale from my brain.

"Thank you. I appreciate your offer," Sam replied.

Pinning Sam with a look of sympathy, and me one brimmed with pity, Sammie turned and retreated down a long, dimly lit corridor. It was then I noticed several doors lining the hallway. I knew they were private rooms where hookers fucked their nightly quota of Johns. Which room was Destiny's? Was she flat on her back letting some sweaty bastard pound his dick in and out of her pussy?

There were so many rooms. How many rooms had Sam visited, and how many hookers had he fucked? A dizzying wave crested through me, and I swallowed down the bile rising in the back of my throat.

Casually—as if he were escorting me inside a restaurant or museum—Sam cinched his arm around my waist and led me past the threshold.

"Come on, Cin. I'd like to introduce you to a couple more of my friends."

Friends? He meant hookers, to be sure. Numbness invaded my body. Confusion sullied my mind.

Why would Sam want to introduce me to a bunch of whores? Maybe this wasn't a brothel after all. Maybe it was a swingers club. My brain was immediately assaulted with images of some strange man fucking me while Sam did the prick's wife. My stomach pitched.

When the metal door slammed behind me, I nearly jumped out of my skin. Hookers or swingers, didn't matter which, both were light-years out of my comfort zone.

"Wait." Digging my heels into the carpet, I tried to wriggle free of Sam's hold. "I want to leave. I'm not comfortable here. Take me to my car. Take me, right now." My quivering tone bordered on hysteria.

"Whoa. Calm down, sweetheart. What are you freaking out about?"

"I know what this place is, and I don't want to be here."

Sam arched his brows in surprise. "You know what Club Genesis is?"

"Not exactly. But I have a damn good idea," I challenged with a lift of my chin. "It's either a swingers club or a whorehouse."

Sam softy shook his head. "No, sweetheart. It's neither of those. Come on. Let me show you."

Suddenly unable to find my voice, I gave him a curt nod. Sam bent and kissed the top of my head while my stomach churned and my pulse thundered.

"That's my girl."

I was unnerved by my strange surroundings, and Sam's reassurance didn't even scratch the surface of my anxiety. But I let him tuck me against his side and lead me toward the light spilling from beyond an open archway at the end of the hall. The spicy aromatherapy fragrance that filled the air gave way to a pungent scent of leather, while the sturdy beat of my heart rapped against my ribs like a war drum.

As we breached the archway, Sam turned and watched me with a guarded expression. The room that lay before me was lined with dozens of polished wooden crosses, strange standing frames, and misshaped benches covered in padded leather. Paddles, floggers, and other chilling implements of pain hung from individual hooks along the walls.

My throat went dry. My tongue stuck to the roof of my mouth. A blast of adrenaline sent my already pulsating heart to skip like a flat rock over a placid pond.

The only normal-looking furniture in the massive room was hundreds of chairs surrounding dozens of tables—a vast seating capacity for voyeurism.

A cry of alarm lodged in my throat. Genesis wasn't a whorehouse or a swingers society. It was a fucking BDSM kink club. A cold, clammy sweat popped out over my lip. Like the Wicked Witch of the West, I'd been flattened. Not by a house but by Sam, who had landed me smack-dab in the middle of Fetish Oz.

Turning in a slow circle, I took in my surroundings. Near the archway, Sammie stood behind a long, brightly lit bar, studying me with a pensive expression.

Whipping my gaze to Sam, I clenched my jaw. "Why did you bring me here? You didn't honestly think that I'd let you…?" My voice quivered in rage and fear. "Oh, hell no. Take me to my car. Now."

Worry lined Sam's face as he cupped my cheeks and shook his head. "Breathe, sweetheart. I didn't bring you here to scare you. I brought you here to talk—"

"Talk?" I shrieked. "There's not a *damn* thing to talk about."

"Cin," Sam began in a placating tone.

"No," I interrupted, shaking my head adamantly. "Whatever kinky shit you're into is fine, but this…this… jesus, Sam. What made you think I'd be okay with this kind of… No. Fuck no."

Putting some much-needed space between us, I stepped back.

The icy chill filling my veins grew even colder at the loss of Sam's body heat. Darting a furtive glance toward the hall, I wanted to run as fast and far as my legs would carry me.

Sam had no trouble reading my thoughts. With a disapproving scowl, he quickly closed the distance between us and gripped my arms. "I know you don't want to believe this, but there's a submissive woman hiding inside you."

Unadulterated shock sent air to explode from my lungs on a whoosh. Anger, like a snake, uncoiled with a venomous strike. Slapping my hands on my hips, I cocked my head and narrowed my eyes.

"You are higher than a kite if you think there's a single submissive cell in my body."

Sam held up his hands in surrender, but the challenge in his eyes said he was far from giving up. "Don't jump to conclusions, Cin. Before you arbitrarily reject what I'm saying, hear me out."

"You can say anything you want, Sam. Hell, you can talk till you're blue in the face, but you're never going to convince me that I'm some weak-minded, malleable submissive."

"You're right. You're not a submissive."

"Ah-ha. Thank you. Now take me back to my car."

"I wasn't finished," Sam replied. "You're not a submissive *yet*."

"Not ever," I spat. "At least not in *this* lifetime."

"I know this is hard for you to hear…even harder to believe, but you've revealed your submissive tendencies, over and over…more times than I can begin to count."

I pinned him with an incredulous stare. "That's the biggest crock of shit I've ever heard. Submissive tendencies, my ass," I scoffed. "I'm a successful, independent, self-sufficient woman. There's not an ounce of subservience in my body."

"You're wrong. Not about the self-sufficient parts, but... Okay, think back on all the times we've made love, Cin. You yield to me in every way. You let me take control. Take command. You surrender to me like a natural-born submissive. Don't try and deny that."

I snorted derisively. "Just because I let go of my inhibitions doesn't make me a submissive."

He shook his head. "It's more than letting go of your inhibitions, and we both know it. Look, Cin. You can lie to yourself all you want, but if you're willing to be brutally honest, you can't deny that letting me take control drives you wild." A devilish smile tugged the corners of his mouth. "I see it, hear it...hell, I feel it every time. And it's spectacular."

"Stop saying that," I screeched. "I'm not some spineless robot or blow-up doll that lacks a fucking brain."

"Ah-hem." A bald man with skin a shade or two darker than my own and muscles that seemed as if they might explode from beneath his flesh interrupted my rant. Captured by his unique amber eyes, I blinked before noticing the fair-complected woman with crimson corkscrew curls and bright green eyes standing beside him.

"Good evening, Cindy. Welcome to Genesis. I'm Mika LaBrache and this is my slave, Emerald."

I blanched. *Slave? Slave!* A sickly wave of disgust crested through me, followed by a flash fire of outrage. Every muscle in my body tensed as I sent the man a caustic glare. "Evidently you didn't pay attention in history class. Slavery was abolished in 1865. And trust me. If there were any lily white girls like her"—I nodded toward the man's *slave*—"working the plantations that owned my great-great-mammy, I would have certainly heard about it."

My hateful chiding sent a rush of pink blossoming over Emerald's cheeks. She quickly cast her gaze to the floor. Sam let out a disapproving grunt while Mika simply held me with his golden eyes. Ever so slowly, a smirk crawled across his toffee-colored lips.

"I wasn't referring to that type of slavery," he explained in a calm, velvety tone. "Our similar pigment corroborates the fact that a generous portion of cream has been added to our lineage. Though my ancestors were brought here from Jamaica as slaves, the term—at least inside these walls—holds a totally different meaning."

Duly chastised, I nervously tucked a strand of straight hair—a genetic gift from my Filipino mother—behind my ear. A palpable awkwardness hung in the air.

"Like I said," Sam stated pointedly to Mika, "we're starting from ground zero."

"Yes, I can—"

"We're not starting from anywhere," I argued. A flash of irritation flittered over Mika's eyes. Evidently the man didn't like being interrupted. So sad. Too bad. I didn't give a rat fuck about his feelings at that moment. My nerves were stretched to the point of breaking.

"Stop trying to pick a fight, Cin," Sam scolded. "I asked Mika and Emerald to join us, hoping that if you met the owner of Genesis and his girl, it might ease some of your fears."

Owner? So Mika wasn't just a fellow pervert, he was president of Kink Central.

Priceless.

"Fears? You think I'm scared of all this?" I defiantly asked as I waved my hand around the room. "Scared doesn't come close to what I'm feeling right now, Sam. I'm fucking terrified that you think you're going to make me into some gutless plastic doll."

"First of all, I don't want to make you into anything. And secondly, submission is neither gutless or plastic," Sam replied with a hint of exasperation.

"My apologies if my club makes you uncomfortable," Mika offered in the same smooth, welcoming tone as before. "You're perfectly safe here, I assure you."

"Uncomfortable? That's an understatement," I derisively mumbled under my breath.

Sam arched his brows, clearly unhappy with my rebellious attitude. What the fuck did he expect? That I'd fall to my knees and beg him to play degrading Master/slave games? He was in for a rude awakening. The urge to tell him to go fuck himself burned like acid on my tongue. But I knew the longer I stood here fighting his delusions, the longer it would take for me to escape this dreadful place.

A low chuckle rumbled off Mika's lips, but stark intimidation danced in his eyes. "You've got yourself a feisty one, Sam. But then, a strong-willed sub is so…invigorating."

Emerald lifted her head as a saucy smile tugged her lips. "How would you know, Master?"

I held my breath waiting to see what method of torture the *Master* would choose to put his taunting *slave* back in line.

Instead of yanking her by the hair, chaining her to the medieval furniture, and beating her senseless, Mika simply laughed and swatted Emerald on the butt. "Because I have a spirited, sharp-tongued girl who needs my consistent firm hand."

"Can I beg you for that, Master?" Emerald purred with a seductive grin.

"Seems you already are, my pet." Mika chuckled.

Their lighthearted banter confused me. Outwardly, Mika appeared the quintessential big bad Dom…and then some. At Emerald's taunting, I expected him to puff up like a prizefighter and start pulling out whips and chains, not laugh. Strangely, he seemed to enjoy...even indulge the woman's cheeky remarks. I wasn't witnessing any of the kneel-on-the-floor-and-kiss-my-boots behavior that I associated with this heavy-handed lifestyle.

Still wearing a grin, Mika slapped Sam on the shoulder. "My office is unlocked. Go on up. I'll be along to monitor the private rooms later."

"Thanks, man. I appreciate it," Sam replied.

"Good luck." Mika smirked as he slid a hand to Emerald's elbow, and led her toward the bar.

Sam cupped my elbow the same way Mika had Emerald's. I couldn't help but wonder if it was some moronic Dominant caveat, like a secret squirrel handshake. Whatever. It really didn't matter.

As he led me back down the hall, I focused on the metal door. The damn thing called to me like a siren song with an offer of safety to the scared girl inside me. If I could make it out that door, I'd be able to purge the sickly sludge pressing in on my lungs, and draw in a deep breath.

The urge to choose flight over fight had me perplexed. I'd never purposely sidestepped any challenge. But then again, I'd never been thrust so far out of my element that I willingly grabbled for a foothold on sanity, either.

"Sam. Please. I don't want to stay here. I'm exhausted. I just want to go home."

He stopped in his tracks and frowned. "What's the real reason, Cin?"

"I...I don't like this place. It scares me."

Sam's expression softened as he wrapped me in his arms and pulled me tight against his chest. "I know it does, but if you'll let me, I'll ease your fears. I need to explain the dynamics of this lifestyle before you'll truly believe I'm not cheating on you."

I wasn't ready to banish my jealous rebellion any more than I wanted to succumb to the safety found in Sam's arms. Unfortunately, I could feel my rancor easing, my heart softening, and began to second-guess whether Destiny was truly a threat or simply a byproduct of my own insecurities.

Sam skimmed a feather-soft kiss over my lips as he pressed my back against the wall. "Close your eyes for me," he whispered.

My eyelids drooped shut as if cast under a hypnotic spell. The chaos dancing in my mind began to settle, then still.

"Good girl." The pride lacing his words sent a shiver through me. "I want you to clear your mind. Forget about this place. The dungeon. Your fears. Your insecurities. All of it, and focus only on the sound of my voice."

After brushing a sweet kiss over each of my eyelids and one to my forehead, Sam continued. "Think back on all the times we've made love. Feel my hands, my lips, my tongue nibbling and sucking on your milk-chocolate skin. Feel my fingers and cock stretching and filling your silky, hot pussy, stretching past the tight rim of your heavenly ass. Can you feel me…feel me driving deep inside your sinful body?"

His enticing words sent nectar spilling over my folds. "Yes," I whispered.

"Listen…you can hear your panted whimpers and moans filling the air. I hear them, too…all the time. I can see you writhing beneath me clinging so desperately to that orgasm blazing inside you. Can you see us, hear us, smell us, Cin?"

The erotic images he painted filled my mind. Every cell in my body ignited.

"Yes," I breathlessly whispered.

"Feel my hand wrapped around your wrists, pinning your arms above your head. You're flying high and hard. Fighting your own need…your own desire as you struggle and wait for my command. You'd do anything to hold back that sweet release for me because I asked you to. Helplessly you wait for me to say that one word. Knowing you're at my mercy…and that I'll grant your permission in my own time feels almost freeing, doesn't it? It feels as if I've taken the world off your shoulders. And you ache to release all responsibility…bask in a feeling of completeness like you've never known before. Am I right, sweetheart?"

"Yes," I groaned.

"And when I tell you to hold back for me, it's not simply because I want to shatter with you, explode to the heavens as your hot, tight cunt sucks the come from my balls. I tell you to wait because it feeds every dark, dirty fantasy crawling around inside me. But it's not just about me…it's always about you. The reason you fight that natural-born compulsion to come—because you want to please me. And that fills you with a sense of empowerment, doesn't it?"

His moist breath spilled over my lips as Sam brought every sinful sensation to life. My skin felt hot and alive, and I could almost feel his strong, naked body pressed to mine. Feel his thick cock stretching and thrusting inside my pussy…pressing past the tender rim of my ass. I could even smell the scent of our blending musk—thick and heady—as it filled the air, permeated my senses, and made me dizzy. But of all the imagery coloring my mind, I fixated on Sam's uncompromising fist, wrapped tight around my wrists and holding me in place.

"Yes," I whimpered pitifully.

"Giving me that control turns you inside out. I know, because I watch you…feel you clutch me tight inside you, hear you scream, and savor every fucking orgasm. You never knew giving me all that power had a name. It's called submission. You've been doing just that from the very start."

"Oh, god," I whimpered.

"Have you ever wondered what makes the connection between us so powerful? It's because you find the missing pieces of your soul when you submit to me."

My eyes flew open wide. My mouth gaped in shock. A wave of dread slammed through me. I wanted to call him a liar…force him to take back his words. But I couldn't, because everything he said was true. The spine-tingling pleasures Sam elicited when he turned all alpha in bed blew my mind.

Still, just because I enjoyed the things he did, didn't mean I was some lap dog who rolled over so he could get his dominant rocks off.

I was not a submissive!

At that moment, I wanted to take back every moan, scream, and orgasm he'd dragged out of me to prove that point. But the past was over. I couldn't go back and change my reactions.

And dammit, I felt as if he'd played me to the hilt.

A rolling blaze of resentment thundered through me. Fury spiked, right along with my blood pressure, as I shot him an angry glare.

"Don't you dare go there, Allisinda," he snarled. His jaw ticked, his nostrils flared, and his lips flattened to a thin, tight line.

The only time Sam called me by my given name was when he was buried balls deep inside me. But I'd never heard him say it in such a savage tone. Usually he called my name in a strained, husky, or reverently soft timbre.

Every muscle in my body tensed.

"Don't do this to me *or* our relationship. Everything I feel for you is real. Every kiss, lick, nibble, and caress I slide up and down your body turns you into an uninhibited dream. Everything I do to you is from my heart. Don't start painting me as some kind of villain."

Sam's cool, controlled veneer had cracked. Seeing this unfamiliar side of him should have frightened me, but it didn't. I found it sexy as hell—in a weird erotic way.

You are fucked up beyond repair, my conscience inwardly chided.

I didn't know what to say to the man. The logical part of my brain was mired in lust; everything else was swirling in a cyclone of indignation mixed with denial. I couldn't form a single syllable.

"Do you honestly think I'm playing some kind of game with you?" Sam asked incredulously.

Yes, my brain implored.

No, replied the embers of reckless hope smoldering in my heart.

"I'm not," he spat, then sucked in a deep breath. "I'm simply trying to open your eyes, expand your mind, and prove that, deep down inside, you crave my Dominance."

Did I? I had no idea. Sam had pried open a door inside me…a door I never knew existed. Questions spilled into my head in a deluge.

Why did I become so excited when he pinned my arms above my head? Was the chemistry between us so potent because I secretly craved his control? Or was it nothing more than pure animal instinct, some rogue genome that had failed to fully mutate over the millennia?

I needed facts…logic to disprove Sam's claims. Obviously trying to convince him that I didn't possess the DNA to morph into a spineless, robotic doormat was futile. And why should I have to convince him of anything? I didn't owe him anything. And I certainly didn't need to compromise my morals or beliefs to satisfy any man. Not even Sam.

The clouds of confusion parted, revealing an angry red sky. Either he accepted me the way I was—competent, strong, and totally kink-free—or not at all.

As I leveled him with a caustic glare, a part of me hoped he would turn to ash, like a vampire exposed to sun. When that didn't happen, I sucked in a deep breath and lifted my chin. "Listen, Sam. You may *need* a lifestyle where slavery holds some twisted, exalted meaning, but I have no desire to be strung up, tied, or chained to your bed and certainly not any of that weird furniture out there." I jerked my head toward the archway. "I won't ever let you strip me of my self-worth, or play victim to your kinky perversions."

A wicked smirk curled his lips. "I've already tied you up a million times in my mind. But I'd walk the fuck away from you before I tried to force you to do anything you didn't want to." An arctic expression lined his face. "Just so we both have our facts straight. Every time we made love, it was one hundred and ten percent consensual. I might be a pervert in your eyes, but I've never forced a woman to do anything she didn't want to, including you. Are we clear on that?"

His sharp, defensive tone told me I'd hit a button—a big hot one.

The dream of our break-up remaining civil flew out the window. This was going to turn downright nasty. That fact filled me with sadness. I didn't want this to end with some big, ugly fight. I had to work with the man, for crying out loud. Animosity would be obvious, and Dr. Dipshit would have the perfect excuse to fire my *incompetent* ass.

Things had been so perfect with Sam, but now it had all taken a disastrous turn.

"I said, are we clear?" he repeated.

I issued a tiny nod. Sam eased back, then cupped my elbow once again. As he led me toward the back door, I let out an inward sigh. *Finally.* We were actually leaving this horrific place. Near the blessed exit, Sam turned into an alcove and began ushering me up a flight of stairs. Freedom fizzled out like a faulty bottle rocket.

Clearly, he wasn't done convincing me of my *submissive tendencies.*

Wonderful.

I had to give the man credit, he was as stubborn and obstinate as me. Surely he didn't think I'd be receptive to his persuasion tactics, did he? Evidently, because Sam didn't blink an eye as he opened an ornately carved wooden door and walked into a normal-looking office. There wasn't a stick of barbaric furniture in sight.

"We have some time alone until Mika comes up to keep an eye on the private rooms," Sam stated as he nodded toward a wall covered in monitors. Most were blank, but a few fed images from outside the building.

Sam led me across the room, past a wide mahogany desk, to a leather couch situated in front of a wall of windows. Before I sat down, I peered through the glass. Below was the room with the weird furniture and torture devices on the walls. I noticed people had begun spilling into the room from behind a long red curtain. I assumed that must be the front of the club.

"You're looking at what we call the dungeon." Sam's calm, patient tone had returned. "I know you have a million questions. Let's sit down so you can ask them. I don't want there to be any misconceptions about me or what is done here."

Taking a seat beside him on the couch, I didn't think I had any misconceptions, but there were far more than a million questions rolling through my head. Of course, only one mattered to me.

"Is this where you and Destiny hook up?"

Sam frowned. "Not for sex, but yes. We meet here at the club."

"So, since you claim you two aren't fucking, what exactly is it that you do?" I couldn't mask the hurt in my tone.

"I help fulfill her submissive needs."

"Oh, I bet you do," I scoffed. "Without fucking her? Is that what you want me to believe?"

"I can't force you to believe anything, Cin. I can only tell you the truth. I don't have sex with Destiny. In fact, sex has nothing at all to do with this lifestyle. BDSM is an exchange of power. Submissives willingly hand over their control. They crave the boundaries, a known set of rules, a path they aren't allowed to deviate from. It makes them feel safe. Protected. Secure. A Dominant shoulders the responsibility for the sub's power—a duty not taken lightly, by the way. The Dom evaluates the sub's needs and finds individual ways to push their limits. Some can be as simple as giving them a list of chores to accomplish each day, some subs may have their free time and diet regimented. And sometimes Doms incorporate a sexual element to their exchange, like controlling orgasms. In a way, that's what I do with you."

"You don't control my orgasms," I countered with a humorless laugh. "I always come when we have sex."

"Yes, but you don't come until I tell you to, do you?" He smirked.

I opened my mouth to refute him, but there was no snappy comeback to be had. I was lost in visions of Sam controlling

Destiny's orgasms, too. My head was a swarm of jealous wasps. There was no place to hide from the stings of betrayal.

"I'm sure Destiny enjoys the hell out of that," I drawled derisively.

"I wouldn't know. I've never touched her in a sexual way, and I never will. I've not cheated on you, Cin. I only Top her because it's what she needs."

"Oh, how gracious of you," I replied dryly. "I'm sorry, but I have no idea what *Top her* even means."

"It means that while I'm not in a Master/slave relationship with her, I provide the dominance in order for her to achieve her submissive needs."

"And her *submissive needs* don't include an orgasm? Right."

"No, hers don't. I'm simply a facilitator of stress relief for the girl."

A ripple of revulsion rolled through me. "You make it sound sterile and impersonal. What exactly is it that you do to her?"

"Destiny is what we, in the lifestyle, refer to as a pain slut. Through pain, she finds a sense of inner peace. Sometimes I use a crop, or dragon tongue, but most times I use the whip...depending on how far she needs to go."

Sam...my gentle, loving, compassionate Sam, *beat* women? My stomach pitched in disgust. How? How could he purposely inflict pain on a woman? Did he like doing it? He must: he'd just fucking confessed. Bile rose in the back of my throat. Everything I thought I knew about the man had been wrong...way wrong.

He was nothing but a fake...a wolf in sheep's clothing.

"Everything we do here is consensual. There are rules that every member must adhere to. Safe words are always respected, and there are DM's—Dungeon Monitors—who make sure each scene is done in a safe, sane, and consensual manner. I'm not a monster, Cin. I've never taken a sub past their limit."

"How do you decide what their limit is?" I asked, managing to push the words past the bitterness in my throat.

"Before I begin a session, or a scene—you'll see some of those shortly—I talk to the sub, negotiate with them. Find out their hard limits, what they need. With Destiny, I determine if she's under more stress than usual, and plan my scene accordingly to ensure she purges the pent-up tension inside her."

"If she's so stressed that she needs you to beat it out of her, why doesn't she get a prescription for valium or something?"

He chuckled softly. "I suppose she could, but she'd rather decompress through submission. Drink in the rush of endorphins, dopamine, and serotonin released through pain than obtain relief with pharmaceuticals."

"So, you beat her in order to make her feel better?" I scoffed. "That's...that's messed up. I know a good psychologist. His name's Tony Delvaggio. He'd have a field day with that."

Sam tensed, then quickly relaxed, and I realized I'd insulted him. I'd all but called him mentally unstable and in need of a shrink. Oh, well, since I'd already stuck my foot in my mouth, there was no reason to stop now.

"How do you do it, Sam? How do you go from saving women and babies to inflicting pain here as a Dom? Do you have a split personality disorder or something? I mean, those are two extreme personalities. How do you balance them, or do you?"

"First of all, I don't *beat* women. I'm not an abusive prick," he railed before pausing to exhale slowly. "Believe it or not, my personal and professional lives are one and the same."

I flashed him a look of doubt. "They can't be. Your reputation would have taken more than a few hits if you were secretly chaining up your patients and smacking them on the ass."

Sam rolled his eyes. "Give me a break, Cin. You know I do nothing of the kind. Patients come to me so that I can make them better. It's the same with submissives. While my methods are on opposite ends of the spectrum, the end results are actually quite similar. I help them, both physically and mentally."

"Okay, so assuming you're not having sex with Destiny, what if she wanted it? Would you give it to her in order to *help her release her stress?*"

Sam grinned. "My, my. I never knew my little chocolate drop had such a jealous streak."

I shot him a bitter sneer, at which he simply laughed.

"No. I wouldn't have sex with her even if she needed it. I'd discuss the situation with Mika and he would find a Dom who could accommodate her needs. But I doubt that will ever happen because cuddling and coddling isn't what she—"

"Hold up," I interrupted. "Are you telling me that you Doms just pass her around like she's a plate of hors d'oeuvres?"

"No. Destiny is a free sub." I wrinkled my brow in confusion. "She's not formally owned or under the protection of any specific Dominant. As owner of the club, he pairs the free subs with Dominants he feels can provide guidance for their individual needs, just like he asked me to help Destiny achieve hers."

"But why you? Why can't Mika or some other Dom beat her ass? Why do you have to be the one?"

"I don't *have* to do anything, Cin. Neither do you, or anyone else here. I help her because as a Dom I have a responsibility to the free subs and Mika. I've also been in the lifestyle a long time and have the skills needed to deliver the kind of pain Destiny needs, without fear of injuring her."

The idea of Sam being skilled at something so violent sent a chill up my spine.

"So you're not only a skilled surgeon but a skilled ass whipper as well. That's good to know," I drawled sarcastically. "So how does Mika pair you up with pain sluts? Do they have to fill out a questionnaire, like Kink-Match.com or something?"

It was unimaginable to me that someone actually *needed* pain inflicted on them. I couldn't wrap my head around the idea of handing over my body to be beaten, degraded, or god knows what else.

Sam tossed back his head and laughed. The deep, rich timbre slid over me like sweet molasses and kicked-started sparks low in my belly. Damn him. Why did he always stir such a visceral reaction in me? I wanted to stay mad at the big oaf.

"You do have a wicked green-eyed monster lurking beneath those sexy brown eyes of yours."

"Stop dodging the subject," I scolded.

"I'm not trying to dodge anything," he murmured before brushing a kiss to my lips.

Sam was certainly doing his best to whittle away my defenses. Unfortunately for me, it was working.

Shit.

With a placid smile he trailed a finger down my cheek. "There isn't any magic formula or a bunch of yes-or no-questions. Mika simply uses his good judgment when aligning unowned subs to Dominants. Personally, I wouldn't want his job. There are a lot of free subs in the club."

"How many do you…do things to?" I stammered.

"Only Destiny, but I need to be honest with you, sweetheart. If

Mika decided that another sub needed my Dominance to help her grow, I'd have to take his request under serious consideration."

Well, fuck. That wasn't at all what I wanted to hear. My heart sank. Not only was I in competition for Sam's attention with Destiny but a whole horde of needy subs as well. At least he was honest. Though his honesty did nothing but drive another nail into our relationship coffin.

"Well, I hope Destiny doesn't get her panties in a bunch when Mika tosses another sub your way."

Ignoring my venomous tone, Sam simply bit back a grin. "She won't. Even if I were to scene with another sub, Destiny wouldn't be upset."

I arched a brow. "Oh really? I sure as hell would."

"I can see that," he said with a chuckle. "I'm not in a relationship with her. Nothing even close to the one I am with you."

You mean the one you were in with me.

"So where is she? Where is the mysterious Destiny?" I snapped impatiently.

I honestly had no desire to lay eyes on the woman, but the insecure and jealous parts of me needed to see what I was up against. Of course, if she was anything like I imagined, I'd only set myself up for a bigger heartbreak.

For all my years of education, there were times when I wasn't very smart.

Sam glanced down at the bar. "She's not here yet." Cupping my cheeks in his strong hands, he stared into my eyes. "Destiny isn't important. She has nothing to do with my feelings for you, or our relationship. Tuck your jealousy away, sweetheart. She's not a threat...not in the least."

Maybe not in your eyes, but she sure as hell is in mine. The bitch is nothing but a rabid dog who needs to keep her filthy paws off my man.

Biting my lips together, I simply grunted and issued a nod. When he released my face, I turned and peered into the dungeon. A few brave souls were migrating toward the crosses, benches, and tables. I watched as several stripped down to their skin. None seemed embarrassed or self-conscious to bare all in front of the growing crowd. Some of the naked ones knelt on the floor. Others stood like mannequins as they were cuffed or tied to various pieces of the polished furniture.

The idea of Destiny offering herself up to Sam—naked—pierced deep. Swallowing tightly, I sucked in a deep breath.

"So, when you scene with Destiny, does she get naked, too?" Bleeding insecurities poured from my lips before I could stop them.

"Using implements on a sub fully dressed kind of defeats the purpose, sweetheart." Sam slid a knuckle down my cheek, drawing my attention. A hint of sadness clouded his eyes. "What's it going to take for me to convince you that you're the only woman I need and want?"

Tears stung my eyes. I ached to believe him, believe the sincerity in his voice and the compassion glistening in his eyes, but too many doubts still swarmed within. With a weak shrug, I turned my focus back to the dungeon.

A man dressed in jeans and a leather vest helped a naked woman onto one of the long, padded tables. After she settled on her back, the man bent over and kissed her while gathering her wrists and drawing them over her head. A tremor rippled through me. Was the same erotic thrill pulsing inside her as it did me when Sam secured my arms in that manner? Did she feel helpless and small while at the same time content and secure, the way Sam always made me feel? I wanted to know what feelings she experienced, but at the same time, I was terrified they would be a carbon copy of my own.

Unable to peel my eyes off the couple, I watched as the man wrapped yards and yards of thin white rope over her body. Longing to be stripped of all social niceties and splayed out, immobile, for Sam burned deep. Instantly, the thought awakened the feminist inside me who began howling in outrage.

"I would love to tie you up like that," he whispered in my ear.

The radical suffragette within me snorted. "Never going to happen."

"Yes, it will. One day." His tone held a surety that made me tremble.

Studying the various scenes playing out before me was like watching a train wreck—gruesome yet so intriguing. I couldn't look away. Swimming in an ocean of visual overload, I couldn't compartmentalize the tsunami of unconventional input. These people and the things they did were light-years away from the proper social etiquette pounded into my brain since birth. Some of the scenes icked me out so badly I had to look away. Like the regal blonde woman, dressed in red latex, who snapped an evil-looking whip over the ass of a tall, buff man cuffed to a cross. The angry red welts that rose on his flesh made me cringe.

Still, other sights captivated me. Watching the face of a sub bent over a bench, I sighed inwardly at the look of bliss and her heavy eyelids as her Dom swatted her back and butt with a thick flogger. The woman looked as if she were at total peace. For a split second, I wanted to be that woman…feel such a level of serenity.

The idea of *me* submitting to such unnatural acts shocked me to the bone. I tensed.

Sam drew his fingers up my arm in a soothing sweep, then leaned in close to my ear. "Relax, baby. I don't expect you to grasp the dynamics all at once. I know I've tossed you into a raging river, but I promise...I won't let you drown."

"It certainly feels like I am."

Sam slid an assessing gaze over my face before inching his mouth to mine. His kiss started out soft and sweet before slowly morphing into one of raw and hungry passion. Desire ebbed and flowed between us on that familiar sizzling current we'd shared from the very beginning, that invisible fiber that melded us as one.

I wanted to believe our combustibility was special...a once-in-a-lifetime kind of thing. But worries that Sam and Destiny shared this indescribable fire all but crushed my heart.

Tearing my lips from his, I jerked my head and sucked in a deep breath.

Visibly affronted by my retreat, Sam frowned. I turned my head. I didn't want to see his disappointment. Scanning the members once more, I blinked back the tears that stung my eyes. My attention was drawn to a beautiful blonde with long, slender legs and a set of boobs that would make a centerfold model cry. The scantily dressed woman paraded through the dungeon, obviously in search of someone. Pursing her red lips in an unhappy pout, I watched as she sauntered to the bar and inched her perfectly shaped ass onto one of the barstools.

Darting a look at Sam, I saw he was dissecting me with a piercing gaze. My heart thundered in my chest. I whipped my head back to the woman at the bar who sat poised and wearing an air of sophistication like an obscene expensive perfume.

Destiny.

As if I'd been blindsided by a wrecking ball, my whole world suddenly disintegrated.

"Don't you dare try to compare yourself to her," Sam chided. "You mean a million times more to me than she could ever hope to."

Was he insane? Sam's little pain bitch was perfect in every way. Jealousy exploded through my veins like lava. And while Sam droned on trying to assure me that I had nothing to fear, my insecurities pulled me under like an alligator, suffocating me with a furious death roll.

There was no conceivable way Sam would ever choose me over her. No man would. I was convinced that every straight, red-blooded man in the club fantasized about riding Destiny into the sunset. Seeing the woman brought my worst nightmares to life. Panic rose inside me. I didn't belong in this club, and I certainly didn't belong with Sam—not anymore.

The embers of hope I'd been foolishly fanning flickered out. The finality that Sam and I were through turned my heart to stone.

Mentally reaching deep, I dusted off the cloak of indifference I'd used growing up to mask my emotions. Sliding it on once again felt awkward and foreign. Like a fool, I'd thought once I left New York I'd never need the damn thing. I was wrong.

Swallowing back the lump of anguish lodged in my throat, I turned toward Sam. "I—I can't see you anymore. Please take me to my car."

Storm clouds rolled across his face. "You're ending our relationship over a woman I have zero feelings for?"

"It's not just that," I replied as I allowed a chilly ice water to flow through my veins. "I can't do the kinds of things you need. I have no interest whatsoever in being a part of this…lifestyle."

Sam couldn't miss the haughty disdain in my voice.

"No, you're simply grasping for excuses. You're already are a part of it, Cin. I've been dominating you since the first time we made love." Pausing, Sam delved deeper with his steel-blue eyes. "You made up your mind we were done before I ever brought you here, didn't you?"

In an attempt to hide my guilt, I tore my gaze away from him.

"Well, isn't that fucking perfect? You found me guilty of a crime I never committed without judge or jury. You sentenced me...sentenced our relationship to death row. Tell me, Cin. How the hell can you throw away what we share so goddamn easily, huh?"

"It's not easy," I bit out as I leapt to my feet and raced toward the door.

No way could I explain that he'd ripped off the scabs of my past and plunged me into a cesspool of insecurities. If I showed him the broken parts I'd kept hidden for so long, he'd run...run straight into Destiny's arms and her fucking bed.

Before I could even touch the knob, Sam was off the couch. He stormed up behind me and slapped his palms against the door, thwarting my escape. As I turned to face him, Sam caged me in, fury and pain blazing in his eyes.

Filled with remorse and regret, I cast my gaze to the floor. I couldn't stand to see the hurt and anguish reflecting in Sam's eyes.

"Why, Cin?" he whispered, cupping my chin in silence until I peered up at him.

Every cell in my body screamed to take back my words. I didn't want to say good-bye to this man...turn away the only person on the planet who brought me to life. But I didn't have the courage to exhume the secrets I kept buried deep, either.

Focus on the obvious. Hopefully it will be enough.

"Look at her, Sam. I can't compete with someone like Destiny."

"I already told you there's no competition," he whispered

tersely.

"Oh, please. Everything about her is perfect. I'm not blind."

"Maybe on the outside," he conceded. "But I have nothing in common with her except this club." Sliding his thumb over my cheek, Sam's expression softened as he issued a heavy sigh. "I can't talk to her the way I do you. She has no way of comprehending the life-and-death decisions you and I make every day. She wouldn't have a clue how to comfort me—not the way you do—when I've had a shit-tastic case. She has no clue what it's like to deliver a brand new life into the world, then an hour later, lose a patient. Destiny is self-absorbed, focused on her career. She's a shell, and definitely not someone I would ever let inside my heart. But you? You're so deep inside of me I feel it when you breathe. Not only are you more beautiful than a rainbow, you're as succulent as a ripe plum. You're a treasure. You mean everything to me, Cin."

Tears slipped past my lashes and trickled down my cheeks.

Leaning in, Sam sipped my tears between his lips. While his heart-melting confession echoed in my ears, he bent and claimed me with a fiery kiss that compelled the war between my heart and head to end in a stalemate.

"Christ," he groaned, shaking his head. "You're the only woman I've ever felt this connection…this powerful chemistry with. I'm not about to let you throw it all away…not without a fight."

"I don't want to fight," I gasped.

"Good, cause neither do I. I'd much rather do this…"

He claimed my lips with a slow thrust of his tongue, retreating only to press deep once more. The surging energy passing between us made me dizzy. As I savored the sinful stroke of his tongue sweeping inside my mouth, sparks of desire ricocheted through my body. And when he pressed his hard erection against my pussy, hunger uncoiled, hot and ready.

When I slid my fingers through his soft-cropped hair, safety and relief settled deep. I wanted nothing more than to stay wrapped in his sublime splendor for all time. All too soon he slowly eased from my lips. I issued a whimper of mourning. Sam raised his heavy eyelids and stared at me with a look so raw it was as if he'd sliced his heart wide open. Met with his unchecked emotions, I not only saw the depth of his desire but also a powerful blinding light of love, pure and true.

My heart soared. Sparks of salvation sputtered up my spine. Without hesitating, I cupped his nape and pulled him in for another kiss. Opening for him, I met each sweltering sweep of his tongue with mine and tumbled in the landslide of perfection.

With a rumbling growl of approval, Sam cinched his fist in my hair. The commanding and seductive way he deepened the kiss sent shivers racing through me. Lost in the slick heat of his mouth, I surrendered my all as he greedily claimed every morsel of my being.

Skimming his hands beneath my shirt, he burnished his thumbs over my bra, igniting a desperate throb beneath the tight peaks. Teasing and taunting the sensitive tissue, I ached to feel his fingers on my bare flesh. Longed for the flick of his tongue. Hungered for the sweet burn of suction as he drew each nipple into his gifted mouth. His steely shaft nudged at my swollen, wet folds. I spread my legs to his incessant sexual call, offering myself wholly.

Sam tore from my mouth with a feral roar. He was panting, and his ragged breath blew across my tingling lips as he lowered his forehead to mine.

"Let's get out of here," he said in a raspy, impatient tone.

"Where are we going?"

"Someplace private."

CHAPTER THREE

After leaving Mika's office, we traversed the stairs. I was grateful for Sam's strong arm around my waist—he kept my wobbly legs from folding beneath me. Back in the long hallway once again, Sam stopped at one of the doors and fished a key from his pocket. Sam unlocked the door, then reached inside and turned on the lights as he ushered me through the portal.

Sam's room reminded me of the studio apartment I rented while in nursing school. Small and efficient, though his décor held a distinctively male flare. A bold oak armoire ate up the wall near the light switch, while a massive four-poster bed with thick balusters, and draped in a fluffy white comforter, sat poised in the center of the room. Staring at the bed, I tried to press away an annoying ripple of jealousy. How many subs had spent time, indulging Sam's mad skills, in that very bed?

Turning to face him, I masked my unfurling insecurities and watched as he closed and locked the door.

"This is my private suite," he revealed. Strolling across the room, Sam flipped on the light of a white-tiled bathroom. "Ever since we started seeing each other, I haven't stepped foot inside these walls, not even for aftercare."

While his caveat was considerate, the indication that he'd made some kind of sacrifice on my behalf confused me. "Aftercare?"

Tugging at the knot of his tie, Sam slid the fabric from his collar. "It means watching over a sub as they come back down from an endorphin rush." A lazy smile spread over his lips. "It has nothing to do with sex, so tuck away your jealousy and fears. BDSM 101 is over for the day."

Thank god.

With seduction written all over his face, Sam slid a heavy-lidded gaze up and down my body, leaving a tingling trail over my skin as if he'd physically touched me. As he began to unbutton his shirt, my mouth went dry. Dryer still when he peeled the material off his shoulders and tossed it to the floor. My stare traced the perfect lines of his chest, down his tapered waist, and farther still to the bulging erection straining beneath his trousers.

Spreading his arms wide, he whispered: "Come here, baby."

Unable to refuse his command, I hurried into his welcoming arms. Maybe it was wrong, but I couldn't deny myself the feel of his touch. After all, this could very well be the last time Sam and I ever made love. All my reservations faded when he rasped his tawny whiskers over my cheek. Then trailed featherlight kisses up my neck, over my jaw, until he settled his mouth on mine. With busy hands, Sam tugged at my clothing. He broke the kiss long enough to hoist my shirt and bra over my head before reclaiming me with a searing kiss.

Passion surged. Our tongues dueled, sweeping over each warm, wet crevice. Parting only to nip and tug at the plump flesh of lips before melding together again as one. His coarse chest hairs abraded my nipples, increasing the pulsing demand thrumming through my clit.

Grudgingly, Sam pulled away, then stared at me. A look of awe lay etched on his face as he focused on my breasts. He reverently cupped them in his hands, and my nipples tightened. Strained to meet the indulgent texture of his warm palms. Dragging the pads of his thumbs over each beaded tip, he smiled as I moaned. And when he extended his tongue, circling my dark areolas, I exhaled a sigh of delight as my pussy copiously wept.

"Such pretty puckered perfection," he murmured, staring at the glistening saliva he'd left behind.

As he bent and laved his tongue over each rigid tip, the air tore from my lungs on a quivering sigh. Opening his mouth, Sam engulfed one nipple, then the next. His wet heat and gentle suction sent shards of lightning exploding through me. I rocked my pussy against his crotch, anxious for him to put out the inferno building inside me.

In answer to my plea, Sam scraped his teeth over each sensitive crest, then explored each puckered ridge with lips and tongue. The sinful heat of his mouth made my whole body seem to crackle and thunder.

Peppering kisses down to my stomach, Sam hooked his thumbs in my waistband, dragging my pants and underwear off as he knelt before me. Kicking off my shoes, I breathed in the scent of my spicy arousal. The cool air met my sweltering folds and I trembled.

Sam leaned back on his heels, then reached out and petted the inky curls between my legs.

"I'm going to shave you bare here soon. Then I'm going to slide my tongue over your velvety flesh before I sink my teeth into your pretty pouty mound. Mark you with my brand."

Inching his face in closer, he inhaled deeply, then exhaled, spilling his moist breath over my folds. "The scent of your intoxicating spice makes my cock hard as stone."

I was unable to form words, and the sounds of helplessness bubbled from the back of my throat. Clutching his head, I tried to force his mouth to my center. Pulling away, Sam tsked, in mock reprimand, before rising to his feet.

His gaze held me with a look so bold and daring he seemed to steal my soul. Then he tenderly brushed the hair from my face and cocked his head. "You're not in charge here, sweetheart. I'll give you everything you ache for…eventually. So just relax, and let me take care of you."

I licked my lips and trembled as I nodded ever so slightly.

"That's my girl."

He picked me up, cradling me against his naked chest as he walked toward the bed. With an intense stare that stripped me to the bone, he lowered me to the mattress. I wanted to believe that nothing, not even his dark desires, and or no one, namely Destiny, could tear Sam and me apart.

With rapt attention, I watched as he toed off his shoes and kicked out of his slacks. I drank in the perfection of his body, the rippling muscles bunching and flexing, and the golden hue of his flesh.

Suddenly Sam launched to the bed. Unceremoniously, he gripped my thighs, spreading my legs wide open. Parting my folds with the pads of his thumbs, he let out a raspy growl before bending in close to draw a flat tongue up my center.

Crying out, I arched at the sinful swipe. My stomach muscles bunched and quivered as Sam focused on my clit. Laving and lashing my sensitive button, Sam wrapped his lips around the nub and pulled as if striving to suck the pleasure from me. Gone was his usual slow, methodical seduction, replaced by a seemingly harsh and primitive need. With each stab of his tongue, I could feel his urgency to conquer, claim, own. And when he filled me with his fingers, strumming my g-spot with the perfect stroke of pressure, stars pulsed and flickered behind my eyes.

Holding tight to his scalp, I cried out for more. Every ending sang in bliss while ecstasy hummed and ricocheted inside me. In a matter of minutes, Sam soared me to the heavens—fast and hard.

I was more than desperate to hurl myself into the dazzling abyss, and keening cries of need tore from the back of my throat.

Sam lifted from my cunt, his eyes narrow, his mouth and chin shimmering in my slickness, a feral smile curled on his lips. "Beg for me, Allisinda."

Shivers slid up my spine. Demand pressed in around me. Sam had used that same command dozens of times. But knowing the significance of his request, I wasn't sure I had the courage to degrade my dignity and give him the power to control me now.

"Say it, sweetheart," he instructed, then gently scraped his teeth over my clit.

With a jerk and a gasp, I writhed and whimpered. "Please, Sam. Please." Despite my reservations, the words tumbled effortlessly off my lips.

Triumph blazed in his eyes. Blinking rapidly, I fought the tears of defeat and focused on the slow velvet stroke of his fingers still buried inside me.

"Not yet, gorgeous," he denied on a raspy growl before clasping his mouth over my sex once more.

I was drowning in desire. Sam obliterated my defiance and fears while I began to slip past the point of no return.

"I...I can't hold back. It's too...too much," I panted, gripping his scalp in desperation.

Inching from my pussy, Sam gazed up at me. "Yes. That's it. Suffer for me, sweetheart."

The satisfaction illuminating his face was all but blinding. "I am," I mewled.

"More, baby." His voice dipped, sliding over my flesh like warm caramel. "I want all you can endure."

"I can't...hold back," I gasped, writhing beneath his masterful touch.

"You can...you will," he challenged in a buttery-soft whisper.

Forcing down the quickening tide, I panted and whimpered as Sam resumed his blissful onslaught. Sliding one hand beneath me, he lifted my hips off the bed, ravenously feasting on me.

My body bowed in search of more friction. More suction. More...everything.

Pressure built as my soul lifted to the heavens. The decadent sensations Sam compelled set my nerve endings to swell. Tighten. Desperate to burst beneath his onslaught of pleasure.

"Sam!" I screamed. I was going to come with or without his command.

The motion of his body blurred as he clamored to his hands and knees. Hoisting my legs even higher, he drove his cock inside me with one feral thrust. Incoherent words spilled from my lips as he angled in deeper to drag his swollen crest over my g-spot as demand spiked and surged. Consumed in an annihilating white and blinding light, I issued a helpless moan, then screamed his name and shattered. Spasming around his cock, I gripped his arms as ripples of rapture engulfed me.

Sam hissed, then grunted. His body grew taut. His muscles strained and quivered as he gripped my hips in a vice-like hold. As he plowed through my clasping tunnel, his face contorted. Then, with a rumbling shout, he followed me over.

His hot seed splattering my wall only intensified my release. And after several long minutes floating in sublime liquid peace, Sam gently lowered my hips to the mattress before crumpling over me.

With his head nestled in the crook of my neck, our ragged breathing filled the air, while my tunnel involuntarily fluttered and throbbed around him. Lifting a heavy arm, I softly scraped my fingernails through the sweat-soaked hair at his nape, boneless and quivering in sated perfection.

My sluggish brain slowly stirred back to life, and I realized he hadn't verbally told me to come like he always did. Yes, he'd asked me to beg, like usual, but before he could sanction my release, I had already come. Even more confusing was that Sam hadn't pinned my arms above my head this time, either. Was there some underlying message he wanted to convey? I didn't know.

I also didn't know why he hadn't stopped to sheath himself with a condom. Sam had always gloved up in the past. Because I was on the pill, I was unconcerned about pregnancy, and we were both clean. Had he been so caught up in the moment he'd simply forgotten? Or was Sam pulling some alpha caveman shit to ensure our relationship remained locked up nice and tight.

Tinges of guilt wormed their way into my brain. I struggled to analyze my feelings of regret and the notion that I'd somehow failed him.

"I can hear your thoughts swirling, Cin." He lifted his head and stared at me with a crooked smile. "Tell me. What's going on in that beautiful head of yours?"

"I'm sorry I came so fast…before you could tell me to."

A slow smile crept over his lips. "No apology needed. I wasn't going to tell you to come for me this time."

"Why not?" I blinked, more confused than ever.

"Don't get me wrong. I enjoy the hell out of controlling your release. But I wanted you to grasp that you're always going to be your own woman. In charge of your own body. BDSM isn't about me trying to steal your identity or spirit or any of your self-esteem. It's not about whips and chains and pain. It's simply the willingness to trust…to put yourself in my hands with the belief and faith that I will do whatever it takes to keep you safe, both physically and emotionally. That's the kind of freedom I ache to show you."

Sam's words painted a dreamy illusion, like the soothing muted colors in a work by Monet. But I'd seen the various implements of torture in the dungeon with my own eyes—everything in that room screamed imprisonment instead of freedom.

"I'm not sure I can do that," I whispered.

"Listen, I don't expect you to comprehend all you've been exposed to tonight in a matter of minutes. But dammit, Cin, I don't want to lose you. I want to own you."

Own me? Every muscle in my body turned to granite, but my eyes nearly popped out of my skull.

Sam scowled and shook his head at the sight of my mortification. "Not like an object. Dammit. That's not what I meant. I want to cherish you…treasure you, because that's what you are to me…a treasure."

Cherish…treasure? His words were nothing but oxymorons. It was as if he wanted me to believe owning me was somehow romantic.

"You can't own anyone, Sam. Christ, that's…that's insane."

With an exasperated sigh, he scrubbed a hand through his hair. "Look, all I want you to do is open your mind. Give me a chance and taste my Dominance before you decide that the power exchange isn't for you."

"What if I can't do that?"

"You'll never know until you try, Allisinda," he murmured in a whiskey-soft drawl.

Then he brushed a kiss to my lips, as if he could magically wipe away my fears. I wasn't going to let that happen, but when his kiss grew urgent and hot, they began to lift. I wanted to stay mad at the man, fight for my morals. But most of all, I wanted to convince him that he wasn't a Dominant. Sam was loving and kind.

You seriously think you can change this man? my conscience mocked.

Blocking out the tide of uncertainty rising inside me, I nibbled the plump flesh of his lip. Sam sucked in a hiss of approval before claiming my mouth with another arduous kiss. His cock grew hard inside me once again as our tongues dueled for supremacy.

"I want you, Cin…I want your surrender, but most of all, I just want *you*."

Before I could respond to his heartfelt plea, a knock came from the door.

"Someone better be dead," Sam grumbled as he begrudgingly eased from inside me.

As he stood and snagged his trousers off the floor, a second knock—louder and more impatient—sounded.

"I'm coming. Give me a damn minute to get my clothes on," he barked, tucking his erection beneath the fabric and carefully drawing up the zipper.

Sam yanked the door open with such force I thought it might fly off its hinges. Clutching the comforter around me, I sucked in a gasp. Tony Delvaggio—the highly respected psychologist who gave regular lectures at the hospital—was standing in Sam's doorway.

"Sorry to disturb you, man. But we've got an emergency. Kerr's been shot."

"What? Where?" Sam barked, jerking on his shirt.

"Someone outside shot him. He staggered into the club and collapsed when he reached the dungeon," Tony explained grimly. "Sammie's calling an ambulance, but Kerr's in pretty bad shape. We could use your help."

"Yes, of course. Cin and I will be right there," Sam assured.

As if suddenly realizing Sam wasn't alone, Tony glanced my way. His eyes grew wide as recognition set in. "Nurse Noland," he greeted tightly before pinning Sam with an unhappy expression. "She knows the rules, right?"

"I hadn't gotten around to that yet," Sam replied. "I'll tell her now."

"Make sure she signs a waiver," Tony grumbled as he turned and stomped away.

"What waiver? What rules?" I asked.

Sam hastily tossed my clothes on the bed. I flipped back the covers and began to quickly get dressed.

"There are a number of rules here, but one is vital to the safety of the members."

"Go on," I pressed as I slid on my shoes.

"What you see here, but more importantly *who* you see, doesn't leave the club. Anonymity is paramount. Outing a member is…well, it can ruin people's lives. Protecting each other's identities is a must."

"I understand." I nodded, rising from the bed and walking

toward him. "My lips are sealed about this club and any people I happen to see here. I promise."

"Thank you." Sam gripped the knob and opened the door. "Let's go see if we can help Kerr...the slimy motherfucker."

"I take it you don't like the man."

"No. I don't. He's a player. And if the circumstances were different, I'd tell you to steer clear of him," Sam snarled as we made our way against the flow of members streaming into the hallway from the dungeon.

"A player? You mean, like, a man-whore?"

"No. A player, as in someone who doesn't take the lifestyle seriously. Pretends at it. Thinks it's a game. Kerr tries to slap his collar on every unowned sub, not because he wants to help them grow in their submission but because he wants to put another notch in his bedpost."

More members poured into the hallway and began entering the numerous rooms. Sam and I fought our way through the surge of bodies as anxious voices filled the air. Once we entered the dungeon, the buzz of loud voices and movement charged the air around me. Doms were hurriedly releasing their subs from the equipment and wrapping them in blankets or their arms before guiding them away from the commotion near the big red curtain.

Someone bumped into my shoulder, nearly knocking me off my feet. As my body twisted, I caught sight of Drake, a big, burly biker-looking dude, and his young, thin, blond-haired lover, Trevor—a former patient of the ER. Drake held Trevor, who wore a look of total panic, in his arms as he charged toward the private rooms.

Sam jerked to a halt so suddenly that I nearly plowed into his back. Peeking around his body, I saw Destiny. Terror marred her flawless face as she gripped Sam by the arm.

"Help him, Master Sam," she begged with tears in her eyes.

"I'll do all I can for him, girl," Sam answered in soft reassurance.

A jolt of jealousy seized me. The tender exchange between the two was a visceral slap to the face. Even if they weren't sexually involved—which I still wasn't completely convinced—Destiny and Sam shared a visible, intimate bond that excluded me altogether. Even if I somehow managed to accept his Dominant desires, I suspected that Sam would still feel obligated to help the subs here. The idea of him touching any other woman made me see red, while my heart ripped in two.

"Make some room," Sam barked before tucking his arm around my waist and drawing me in close beside him.

Dragging me with him, he shouldered his way through the crowd hovering over the victim. Focused on Kerr and the copious amount of blood oozing from beneath his prone body, I could tell the man's injuries were critical. Someone was applying pressure to his chest and abdomen. The cloths being used were turning crimson far too rapidly. We'd be lucky if we were able to save him. Dragging my gaze to the woman aiding the man, I nearly swallowed my tongue.

It was Liz kneeling beside Kerr, trying to stem the flow of blood.

A startled look flashed across her face when our eyes met, before she turned her attention on Sam. "I feel like I'm losing the battle here," she mumbled.

Ian and James stood behind Liz, watching over her like a couple of bodyguards. I was still reeling with the onslaught of jealousy prickling my veins, when a new wave of emotions poured over me, mixing with the already bubbling cauldron within. I didn't have the luxury to process my feelings of jealousy, anger, betrayal, disbelief, and sadness invading me. Kerr needed help. The kind of help that Liz, Sam, and I could provide. Welcoming the professional instinct that suddenly kicked in, I prayed it would be enough to keep my messy emotions at bay.

Dropping to the floor, I grabbed a couple of clean towels stacked near the victim before moving in alongside Liz.

Jerking her head up, she issued a tight smile. "Thanks. Grab some gloves."

Liz shoved at a box of latex gloves with her knee. I grabbed two pair, handing off a set to Sam as he settled on the floor opposite Liz and me.

"Vitals?" he prompted as he rolled up his sleeves and donned the protective gloves.

That calm, controlled professional voice of his seemed to center me as I, too, covered my hands.

"Pulse is thread, but he still has one. Blunt trauma to the head and face. It looks like someone worked him over with a crowbar," Liz stated grimly. "Bullet wound to the abdomen, another to the chest."

She didn't have to say more. The amount of blood growing beneath Kerr's body proved it wouldn't be long before he'd code. Another stack of towels was placed on the floor beside Sam. I glanced up to find Destiny staring at him with a look of worry and devotion.

"Thank you, girl," Sam replied in a tone suffused in affection.

What the fuck am I doing here? Doing with Sam? I didn't belong in a BDSM club, and I certainly didn't belong with him. I had nothing to offer him, at least not the kind of things he obviously craved. But his spank slut or pain whore or whatever the hell he called her did. The bitch was right by his side, catering to his every need, just like a proper submissive should.

If it hadn't been for Kerr, bleeding out in front of me, I would have walked out the fucking door.

Sucking in a deep breath, I mentally shoved my insecurities and everyone—especially Destiny—from my mind and focused on the victim. Shutting off all emotion, I flipped into autopilot and found the familiar rhythm Liz and I shared at work. As Sam assessed Kerr's wounds more thoroughly, I kept a finger pressed against his carotid. His pulse was weakening at an alarming rate. A pall of death hung heavy in the air, and the tight line on Sam's lips confirmed what I'd already known—Kerr was running on borrowed time.

"Where's the fucking ambulance?" Sam snarled to no one in particular.

"It's on the way," Sammie called back, visibly distraught.

"That's not soon enough," he murmured grimly.

Kerr's heartbeat fluttered twice on my fingertips, then stopped.

"I've lost his pulse," I stated quietly.

"Fuck," Sam hissed. Rising to his knees, he began chest compressions.

The crowd gathered around us fell deathly still.

"Shit," Liz mumbled. "We've got to get him back."

"I'm working on it," Sam grunted.

Grabbing one of the clean towels Destiny had delivered, I pried open Kerr's jaw and sopped the blood from inside his mouth. Just as I tilted his head back to begin resuscitations, a man cried out that the ambulance had arrived.

"About fucking time," Sam spat.

Staring off over my shoulder, Sam curled his lips. A wry look of resignation settled over his face. When I glanced over my shoulder, my mouth went dry as I watched Jeb and Freddy—EMTs who regularly delivered patients to the ER—hurry toward us with a gurney. When they saw Sam, Liz, and me working on Kerr, both Jeb's and Freddy's brows rose in surprise.

My face grew hot in embarrassment for being caught inside a BDSM kink club. To my surprise and relief, both men slid on a professional veneer without any awkward comments. I prayed they'd remain as tight-lipped once back at the hospital. If not…I could kiss my career good-bye. I closed my eyes and exhaled a long-suffering sigh.

"How long's he been flat lined?" Freddy asked as he set up the portable defibrillator on the other side of Liz.

"Couple of minutes," Sam huffed, still pumping Kerr's chest.

"You can all move back. Jeb and I will see if we can get his ticker started again," Freddy announced in his familiar unflappable manner.

James leaned down, wrapped his arms around Liz's waist, and plucked her off the floor. Ian sidled in next to her possessively. Sam stood, extended his hand, and helped me to my feet. But he didn't let go: he simply laced his latex-and-blood-covered fingers with mine. We stood in silence, watching as Freddy injected an atropine/epinephrine cocktail while Jeb continued CPR. Like paste, tension hung in the air, and I held my breath as Freddy readied the paddles, then sent a low current of joules to Kerr's heart.

I darted a glance up at Sam, but his stony expression remained fixed on the busy EMTs. Next I skimmed a glance over the members and was instantly stabbed by Destiny's hateful glare. The reminder of her association with Sam landed with a solid kick to the stomach. Self-consciously, I slid my hand from his. How could such a beautiful woman be jealous of me?

Turning away from her surly stare, I noticed long, red drapes had been drawn around the kinky furniture, masking the true nature of the club. Most of the members had vacated the dungeon, leaving only a handful clustered around Kerr. Mika stood in a sea of empty tables and chairs, talking to several police officers. I knew then the others had opted to hide out in the private rooms to keep their identities from being compromised.

A curvy dark-haired woman, with big blue eyes and a thick leather collar adorning her neck, approached us carrying a trashcan. "For your gloves, Master Sam," she softly explained.

"Thank you, Raven's Song," Sam replied with a gentle smile. "You honor your Master with your willingness to help, girl."

The regal tone of Sam's voice made me shiver. As we peeled the soiled latex from our hands, I watched a crimson hue crawl across the girl's cheeks. Sam's praise had suffused her with pride. A low vibration hummed within me. What would it feel like to be steeped in his approval to such degree?

"We've got a rhythm back," Jeb announced triumphantly. "Let's pack up and transport, stat."

"You got it," Freddy replied.

As they loaded Kerr onto the gurney and began to wheel him away, the remaining members began to disperse.

Darting a glance at Liz, I found her staring at me with a look of apology and regret. Sam's lecture about anonymity echoed in my ears. My stomach twisted as it dawned on me that Liz hadn't tossed our friendship under the bus to side with Sam. She hadn't purposely kept his secret, or this aspect of her relationship with Ian and James, from me because she wasn't a true friend. She'd kept the secrets in order to honor the rules of the club. While that knowledge didn't wipe away all my anger, it definitely lessened the fire. I couldn't hold a grudge with Liz for keeping confidences, not when that was just one of the reasons I admired her as a friend.

Easing away from Ian and James, Liz nibbled her bottom lip as she made her way toward me.

"I owe you an apology," she softly offered.

"No. I owe you one...many, in fact. I acted like a bitch today. A spoiled, bratty bitch. I'm sorry."

"Don't. You didn't know, and I...I couldn't tell you what—"

"I understand *now*," I explained, interrupting her. "I should have trusted you more. I wasn't a very good friend today."

Tears started to pool in Liz's eyes. "Don't say that, Cindy. You're an amazing friend. I know how hard it is for you to trust, and though I didn't mean to, I gave you every reason to doubt your trust in me." Her voice cracked. "Keeping all this a secret tore me up inside. There were so many times I wanted to say fuck it and tell you everything, but I couldn't. This isn't just about me."

Tears slipped down both of our cheeks. I felt horrible that she'd been putting herself through hell. Leaning in, I wrapped my arms around her and hugged her tight.

"From now on, screw the rules." I sniffed on a soft laugh. "You tell me any and everything you want. I'll keep all your secrets locked up like Fort Knox."

Pulling back, she choked on a sob, then flashed me a watery smile. "Deal."

A ray of hope blossomed inside me. If felt good to mend fences with Liz. At least one relationship had been salvaged tonight. Sliding a gaze across the room, I saw Sam engaged in a discussion with Destiny. Though their conversation was hushed, I could tell it was a wildly heated discussion—based on the angry fire shooting from her eyes. She was up in Sam's face, and I wanted to bitch-slap the little tramp into next week. Instead, I clenched my teeth and fists in tandem.

"Retract the claws, kitty," Liz whispered softly. "She's not a threat. Trust me on that."

"I'm not so sure," I mumbled.

She issued a derisive snort. "I am. You don't need to be jealous of her."

"Right. Just like he's never had sex with her."

"He hasn't. Ever."

"How do you know for sure?"

With an explosive exhale, Liz's cheeks puffed out. "Destiny is...needy. She tends to sink her claws into any Dom who works her."

"Oh, she's possessive, huh?"

"Not in the usual way. She's not here for sex, unlike some of the Doms who have slid under Mika's radar, like Kerr. I understand why she's like she is, but that's another story. But trust me, Sam has never once encouraged her in a sexual way."

Pondering Liz's words, I watched Destiny. Her pinched angry expression and limbs as rigid as marble said she didn't like what Sam was saying. His posture, on the other hand, appeared normal. Relaxed and in charge, he wore his command like a finely tailored suit.

Suddenly, Sam reached out and snagged the pissed-off woman by the elbow. With wide eyes, I watched as he marched Destiny to the end of the bar, then pointed to the floor. She sent him a pleading expression before bowing her head and dropping to her knees. Reaching inside his pocket, Sam pulled out a coin and pressed it against the wooden panel in front of her. Slapping her hands behind her back, Destiny lifted her chin defiantly, then leaned in and pressed her nose to the coin.

"What the fuck is that all about?" I whispered.

"Oh, hell. She's pissed Sam off, royally," Liz replied with a strangled chuckle.

"What is he doing?"

"Punishing her."

"Why doesn't he just chain her to a cross and beat her ass?"

Liz smirked. "Because that wouldn't be punishment for her. She'd like that."

"I'm never going to grasp all this shit," I mumbled.

As I watched in fascination, Sam bent, obviously talking to Destiny, who willfully kept the coin in place. The jealous bitch inside me wished the woman would sneeze or cough so I could see what bizarre punishment Sam would dream up next for her. Maybe he'd make the prissy little pain clean all the toilets in the private rooms. Maybe she'd break a couple of nails, have a total meltdown, and be banned from the club.

"I won't lie," Liz stated soberly. "The learning curve for this lifestyle is pretty steep, but once it all clicks"—she let out a low whistle—" it will blow your mind, in a magical way."

I grunted skeptically, watching as Mika approached Sam with a friendly slap on the back. After the two exchanged a short conversation, Sam turned and walked back toward me. His expression was sullen.

"We'll talk more later," Liz whispered, then scampered back to her lovers.

"I'm sorry, Cin," Sam began. "I had to deal with Destiny's disrespect. Unfortunately she crossed the line."

"I assume she's pissed at you because of me."

"In a way. She's angry that all the Doms she's counted on to help her achieve relief have basically left her for other subs. I think informing her that I would no longer be working her was the last straw." He shook his head. "She was wrong to keep her animosity about the other Doms locked inside her."

"Sounds like she needs a session or two with Tony."

Sam cringed. "Actually, Tony *is* one of the Doms who used to work her."

"Oh." That was an interesting tidbit of information. "I saw him with a cute little blonde when the EMTs arrived."

"Yes." Sam nodded. "That's his wife, Leagh."

"I knew he got married, but… So she's his submissive, too?"

"She is, but again, that information isn't for public consumption."

"I understand. I do. When Jeb and Freddy came waltzing in…well, so much for anonymity, right? Do you think they'll rat us out?" I asked, trying to tamp down the anxiety rising inside me.

"No. They won't say a word," Sam assured as he slung his arm around my waist and led me back down the hall.

I didn't share his confidence. Instead I let myself imagine the fallout if Jeb and Freddy decided to talk. The subsequent chain of events could only lead to the demise of my career. I wanted to throw up.

As we entered Sam's room once more, he plucked his cell phone from his pants pocket. "It's almost one in the morning. Would you like spend the night here with me?"

What I wanted was to be on my own turf with Sam in *my* bed. To snuggle against his rugged body and feel his arms around me and pretend clubs like this only existed in books and movies.

If I stayed with him here at the club, he might take that as a sign that I could embrace this kind of lifestyle.

Could I?

That was the ten-million-dollar question.

What I needed was time…time away from Sam's compelling charisma so I could sort out the onslaught of emotions pinging through me.

"I can't," I replied with a weak smile. "I need to be at work early so Metcalf doesn't—"

"If he talks to you again like he did today," Sam interrupted with a smoldering murderous look in his eyes, "it will be his last mistake. I won't allow that arrogant prick to stroke his own ego at your expense."

"I appreciate you sticking up for me today, but don't do it again. I won't have you risk your job or reputation for me."

"That's a promise I can't keep," he countered before moving in close.

Cupping my nape, Sam pulled me tight against his firm chest, then slanted his lips over mine. The kiss was deep, erotic, and steeped in desire. It would be so easy to succumb to his passion. To drown in all the spine-tingling pleasures he'd bestow, but it wouldn't change the crossroads I now stood at. It would only blind me, in a shroud of sexual fog, from seeing which path I should choose.

"I think you'd better take me back to my car," I whispered, taking the cowardly way out.

CHAPTER FOUR

Before Sam had even pulled out of Genesis' parking lot, a myriad of emotions circled my brain. The entire day had been surreal, like the hallucinations of a crack whore in detox. Well, all but making love with Sam… That had been spectacular, as always.

I'd spent most of my day in a schizophrenic twist thinking that Sam had been unfaithful. While trusting men was never going to be my strong suit, it'd taken Liz's corroboration to Sam's claims he hadn't slept with Destiny before I'd been truly convinced. My continual lack of faith in men lent little hope at finding a lasting relationship. But a part of me wanted something more than just a casual fuck with Sam. If only I could find a way to stop projecting that every man was capable of a crippling betrayal, I might possibly find my happy ever after.

My subconscious scoffed. *This is the real world. Not some stupid fairy tale.*

Why couldn't I have both?

Because Sam wants a submissive woman.

His allegation that one resided deep inside me still had me bewildered and confused. And while I felt in some ways Sam knew me better than I did myself, he should know I wasn't the kind of woman who would strip off her pride and fall at his feet. Yet no matter how vehemently I wanted to deny it, the curious parts of me wanted to delve deeper into his dark desires. Take a taste of the strange allure that beckoned him, Liz, Ian, James, Tony, and the other members of the club to embrace such an alternative lifestyle.

Could I find a compromise that would extract enough acquiescence to fulfill Sam? Was there a way to ride the edge of submission without slicing myself into pieces, and keep us together?

Probably not.

Sam wasn't the kind of man to be content with only the parts of myself I wanted to dole out. He'd want all of me.

If only he'd told me about his kinky desires from the start, maybe…

You mean like how you've been so open and honest with him? my conscience mocked.

I couldn't point a finger at Sam when three guilty ones pinned back at me. There was a big, ugly ghost in my closet as well. Not a kinky one like Sam's, but horribly embarrassing, nonetheless.

People in glass houses…

"You're awfully quiet, Cin," Sam regarded, pulling me from my thoughts.

Turning, I issued a weak smile. "I know."

Sam sat silently brooding over my short response. "Don't shut me out, Cin. Tell me what's going on inside your head. I can't help you get a handle on anything if you run and hide."

When he glanced at me, I couldn't miss the rejection in his eyes any more than I could miss how he wanted to crawl inside my brain and dissect my emotions.

"I'm not trying to shut you out, Sam. I'm tired, overwhelmed, and more confused than I've been in a long damn time. I just need to sort everything out."

"Nothing has changed between us."

I snorted. "You're wrong, Sam."

"No. I'm not. The only thing that's transpired today is you now know why I enjoy controlling you in bed."

"Yes, but before you took me to the club, I thought you wanted to take charge because of some doctor-god-complex-ego issue."

"A doctor-god-complex-ego issue?" he repeated with a slight grin. "I hope to hell you're not suggesting that I have something in common with Metcalf, sweetheart."

"Heavens no." Mortified at his assumption, I shook my head. "I was referring to the way you doctors waltz into the trauma room and take over. I just assumed you were all hardwired that way and it simply spilled over into the bedroom for you."

The sound of his rich, deep laugh acted like a balm, soothing my frazzled nerves. "Oh, I'm wired that way for sure, but I doubt it's a universal professional DNA twist." Sam smirked as he pulled into the hospital's parking garage. "When you give me control of your body and you're writhing, panting, and screaming my name, like earlier tonight, it flips every hardwired Dominant switch inside me. Whether I'm holding you down or not."

Flashbacks of Sam soaring me past the heavens made my nipples grow hard and my clit begin to throb. Though he'd thoroughly sated me a short time ago, the sexual hunger he bred within only proved how much of my heart and soul he already owned. I'd given him the power to hurt me, either generously or erroneously.

Stop making so many foolish mistakes, Allisinda. We have a reputation to maintain, and a woman of your stature must remain above reproach.

From the far recesses of my brain, the reproving voice of my mother clanged in my ears.

Every tendril of arousal instantly died and turned to ice.

Pulling into the vacant parking spot next to my car, Sam turned and gave me a weary smile. "Go home and get some sleep. We'll talk more tomorrow."

Nodding, I moaned affirmatively.

After escorting me the few yards to my car, Sam settled a toe-curling kiss over my mouth, then grudgingly pulled back. As I stared at the moisture glistening on his lips, he cupped my chin, drawing my focus to his compassion-filled eyes. "When you get home, I want you to shut off your brain, climb into bed, and get a good night's sleep. Questions and doubt will try to crawl inside your head. That's completely normal. But I will be by your side the whole way through this, Cin. You're not alone. Understood?"

"Yes." I nodded.

"Text me so I know you're inside your apartment safe and sound."

"I will," I promised as I shut my door and started the engine.

Glancing in my rearview mirror as I drove off, I saw worry etched on Sam's face. Unfortunately, I couldn't turn back and offer him any reassuring words—I didn't have any. My emotions were bobbing up and down like the balls of a circus juggler.

When I arrived home, I sent him a text, then climbed into the shower. I'd hoped that the hot water might pelt away some of the chaos in my brain. No such luck. Though utterly exhausted, I tossed and turned, unable to turn off my brain. Sleep was nothing more than an elusive fantasy. Finally, I gave up and tossed back the covers before climbing out of bed.

Long before dawn peeked over the horizon, I was dressed and swilling coffee at the kitchen table. As I'd done all night—ad nauseam—I weighed the pros and cons of my relationship with Sam.

The idea of dipping my toes into submissive waters brought visions of alligators with razor-sharp teeth latching onto me and dragging me under the murky depths of no return. While the thought of being alone again wasn't nearly as violent, the waters were still as dark and dank.

Even trying to compare my courage—or lack thereof—to Liz and her fearless foray into the lifestyle with Ian and James did little to bolster bravery.

"What is keeping me from hiking up my big-girl panties and taking the plunge?" I asked the walls. "What's the worst that could happen?"

That list is long, my goading conscience snorted.

Actually, it wasn't. The number one horror holding me back was having my heart broken…again. But before I'd let myself start strolling down memory lane with its unnerving spoils, I shook the thoughts from my head.

Instead, I focused on the reservations plaguing me about the lifestyle but realized I couldn't make any rational decision based on assumptions. Assumptions that had been proven wrong at the club. I wanted guarantees, but I needed more facts.

Jeb and Freddy had seen me inside the kinky club. In a way, I'd already committed professional suicide. If I were to be shit-canned from work, I couldn't fathom an explanation I could give my parents.

My parents… "Oh, god," I moaned.

The refined, dignified socialite Natia Noland—mistress of ceremony for multimillion-dollar fundraisers and hostess of pretentious gallery openings at New York's famed Chelsea art district, along with my father—the Revered Professor Rufus Noland, MD, MS, ScD, EdD. would shit bricks. They'd never be able to wrap their tiny little minds around my involvement with such lewd and immoral acts. Why, the very thought would shatter their perfect, aristocratic façade.

A shudder of shame wracked my body.

I could disgrace my family or I could live a cold, empty life without Sam. Choosing one or the other filled me with sadness and an overwhelming sense of failure. Either way I'd lose.

Failure isn't in our repertoire. We Nolands never fail. We rise above adversity, dust ourselves off, and forge ahead. Like a mighty gong, my father's motivational battle cry reverberated in my head.

"No, Daddy. We Nolands *do* fail." Or rather *I* was about to.

Despair gripped my heart in a tight fist. Tears slid down my cheeks and dripped onto the cotton placemat beneath my elbow.

Growing up with overachieving parents, the pressure for both my brother, Matatino, and me to perform—not only academically but also socially—hung like a weight around our necks. My brother, Matti, seemed to take it all in stride, but not me. To this day, I wore my own perverse expectations of perfection like a dysfunctional straightjacket.

I'd already crushed my parents dreams by *settling* for a career in nursing instead of achieving my doctorate in neurology and adding an alphabet train behind my name, like Daddy.

I don't understand why you waste your talent in the trenches of an ER, Allisinda. You're much too bright to settle for that lowly position. Refusing to further your academia shows a lack of ambition that is totally unacceptable, but then you've always been a frustrating child. Your father and I raised you better. It's time you put away your foolish notions and obtain a profession deserving of your stature. One day you'll want nice things.

Cringing, I shoved my mother's sanctimonious lecture from my head. There was a time when I had aligned my future in accordance to their plan. But I'd ditched my doctorate when my ex-future husband became threatened by my success. And when the earth crumbled out from under my feet, I realized I never possessed the desire to be a clone of my father. Packing my bags, I left New York and chose the career *I* wanted. A career that wouldn't keep me perched on a pedestal, meant to impress their inner circle of pretentious friends. I'd committed the ultimate in *elite society* suicide, and it felt really damn good. Unfortunately, neither my mother or father stopped trying to revive their dreams that I'd assassinated.

For years I tried to convince them that my charge nurse duties were just as vital and important as anyone else in the medical profession. That working in those *trenches* filled me with pride and satisfaction. Still, their palpable displeasure never waned. If I wanted their approval, I merely had to inform them that I was dating Sam. While that encouraging tidbit might placate my parents, nothing short of reinventing myself would change the epic failure I'd become in their eyes.

Fortunately, I'd never use Sam as a tourniquet for my shortcomings.

"Sam," I muttered on a bittersweet sigh.

He'd done such an admirable job of mending the fragile pieces of my heart. Though we'd only been together three short months, his tender adoration made me want to try and love again. Right now, I couldn't imagine my life without him. The invisible web of happiness he'd spun around me had brought sunshine to my dark existence...at least until yesterday.

I'll be by your side the whole way through this. His vow tumbled through me, like a lifeline. I grabbed hold and held tight. Somewhere along the way, between the laughter, romantic dinners, late-night conversations, mind-blowing sex, and post-coital cuddles, I'd lost my heart to the man. I wasn't sure I possessed the strength to purge him from my life, or if I even wanted to.

That in itself was a huge red flag. I'd learned how to pick up the pieces of my heart and move on since third grade. Bobby Pope had kissed me on the cheek in art class and told me that he loved me. But two hours later, at recess, I saw him kiss Pamela Marker near the monkey bars. Of course, Bobby's betrayal paled in comparison to walking in on my boyfriend, L'Vaught Parsons, fucking the prom queen in a back room at our high school graduation party.

Why on earth, with such a stellar track record, had I put an ounce of faith in my ex-fiancé, Darnell's promises of love and devotion? I'd always been a hopeless idiot when it came to men and love.

But I'd never been weak—even through the darkest days of rejection, I'd found my spine and held my head high. Though now, when it came to Sam...I didn't feel the least bit strong. If he'd been fucking Destiny, I wouldn't be trapped in this endless loop of indecision. I'd have cut my losses and moved on.

Why was I so fucking torn when it came to Sam?

Because you love him...truly love him...more deeply than anyone else in your whole life.

Yes, I did. But if I couldn't accept his frightening desires...

A tidal wave of defeat-laced self-pity swallowed me whole. I slumped to the table and sobbed. My gut-wrenching cries echoed off the walls and rang through my ears, mocking my weakness.

As I crumbled beneath the onslaught of emotions, my heart felt buried in ruins. I ached to feel Sam's strong arms around me, hear his whiskey-soft voice assuring me that everything would be all right.

"Oh, god. What am I going to do? I don't want to lose him," I wailed pitifully.

Filled with unsettling panic, I bolted from the table. Coffee sloshed from my cup, but I ignored the mess as I began pacing my apartment. Arms clutched around my waist, I tried to keep from unraveling even further, but it was no use. My stomach swirled in a sickening pitch as I raced down the hall. Dropped to my knees before the toilet and purged the coffee I'd consumed. After retching violently, I lay on the cold, hard tile as tears streamed down my face. Several long minutes later, I gripped the sink and heaved myself off the floor. Trembling, I rinsed my mouth with cold water and blew my nose. With shaking fingers I dialed HR and feigned the flu, then shuffled back to my bedroom. Crawling beneath the covers, I cried myself to sleep.

I woke hours later feeling as if I'd been hit by a train. Feeling drained and depleted, I rolled out of bed, then padded to the kitchen where I brewed myself a cup of tea. After curling up on the couch once more my brain engaged again. Thankfully sleep had aligned my thoughts a bit, but the internal pressure to make a decision about Sam rode me hard. Instead of falling victim to my emotions, I decided to dissect this clusterfuck in a clinical way...or at least attempt to.

Would I have any inkling to pursue the BDSM lifestyle if I weren't involved with Sam?

No.

Were my fears of submission reason enough to end things with him?

Maybe. I wasn't sure.

Do you think you have the power to change him?

Never. Nor did I want to.

If we remained together, could I come to terms with what he wanted?

Who the hell knew? I certainly didn't, and that was the crux of the whole damn mess.

The feminist within reared her head.

Why should I sacrifice my independence and morals for any man?

I shouldn't, any more than I should toss aside my convictions and embrace a degrading and demeaning lifestyle. I didn't need that kind of misery in my life. I was happy, dammit. Content even. I was self-sufficient, liberated, and successful. I didn't need a man in my life to make me complete—I had the fortitude to do that on my own. Besides, I'd never be some spineless, codependent submissive.

Filled with self-righteous indignation, I launched off the couch and stormed into the kitchen. Snagging a bag of potato chips from the cabinet, I sat down at the table and began munching away. My body might very well revolt at the intake of fat and rain down a load of hail damage all over my thighs, but they were *my* thighs, if that happened, *I'd* deal with the aftermath…at the gym.

"Oh, to hell with the gym," I snarled. "I might just let myself go. Blimp out so no man will look twice at me. Besides, I've got a drawer full of toys that are tons less hassle than a fucking man."

After consuming half the bag of chips, I scrolled through the television channels. Scarfing down all those wasted calories, I'd tossed off a layer of propriety. I might not have my course fully charted, but putting the focus back on me had certainly filled my sails.

Still clicking through channels, I paused on an old seventies movie, my heart clutched double time. A young Robert Redford appeared on the screen. I never realized the actor bore such an uncanny resemblance to Sam. Both shared the same wheat-colored hair, rugged jawline, and the eyes... Oh, the look of longing in Redford's eyes as he gazed at Barbara Streisand sent a chill down my spine. Sam had blessed me with that exact gaze time and time again. Mesmerized, I sat staring at the actor as the camera panned out and the music came up—a tune I remembered my mom listening to when I was young.

Memories. Light the corners of my mind. Misty water colored memories, of the way we were. The lyrics assaulted me like a punch to the gut. And the sad, melancholy expressions the actors portrayed as they parted and went their separate ways slammed through me like an apocalyptic prophecy.

That would be us if I said good-bye to Sam.

As my vision blurred and a lump of regret lodged in my throat, I clicked off the television, threw the remote across the room, and curled into a ball on the couch. All the butterflies and rainbows I'd been blowing out my ass flew right out the damn window. My heart filled with pain, annihilating every one of my brave intentions. Closing my eyes, I let the sorrow pull me under and dissolved into a sobbing, hot mess.

Though I cried all the tears I could muster, I remained on the couch, wrapped in a heavy blanket of depression. When a loud knock came from the front door, I ignored it. I didn't have the energy to get off the couch, let alone deal with some overzealous magazine solicitor. As I burrowed deeper into the cushions, another knock rang out, louder and more insistent.

"I know you're in there, Cin. Open up," Sam bellowed from outside the portal.

"Shit," I cursed as I leapt to my feet, quickly palming away the tracks from my tears.

"Go away, Sam. I'm sick. I don't want you to catch this bug." My words came out thick and laced with remorse.

"Open the door. Open it now, or I'll kick the son of a bitch in," he roared.

"Okay. Okay," I spat. Flipping the lock while keeping the safety chain engaged, I opened the door.

Sam eyed the chain with a quizzical expression before turning a hard stare on me. His brows pinched together in concern. "Let me in, Cin."

"Sam," I stalled. "You don't need to catch this flu."

"Open the fucking door. Now," he barked in a tone that brooked no further argument.

With a heavy sigh, I closed the door and unlatched the chain. Before I could even drop my hand back to the knob, he burst through, causing me to stutter-step backward.

"Why have you been crying?" he asked…no, actually more like demanded.

"I-I was cutting onions in the kitchen," I stammered. "Going to make some soup."

Turning, I began walking away. Before I'd even taken half a step, Sam gripped my arm and spun me around to face him.

"Don't. Don't ever lie to me again," he warned. "Now what the hell is wrong? Why are you crying? Do I need to take you to the ER?"

"No. I'm fine. I told you that. What are you doing here?"

"Stop evading my questions, girl. Answer me."

"I...I..."

Tell him you're through. Do it now. Get it over with, the voice in my head beseeched.

"Fuck," he spat as he clutched me in his arms so tight I couldn't breathe. "Don't say it, Cin. Goddammit, don't even think it. If Liz had only kept her fucking mouth shut, I could have explained the lifestyle to you...gradually introduc—"

"Don't you dare blame this on Liz." I bristled, jerking out of his grasp. "If you'd have leveled with me from the start, we wouldn't be in this...this mess." Angry tears pricked the backs of my eyes, but I blinked them away.

"I was waiting for the right time to tell you." He glowered. "I took the risk last night and look where it's gotten us."

"And that's Liz's fault?"

"No. It's mine. I simply wish she'd talked to me about her concerns at the club, not at the fucking hospital."

"Well, it's too late to change that now. She did me a favor. She made me open my eyes and take a good hard look at myself."

Sam lifted his chin. Challenge was written all over his face. "And what did you discover, Cin? Did you finally unearth the scared little girl inside you? The one who's decided to tuck her tail between her legs and run away screaming before you've even had a chance to learn the basics of the lifestyle?"

"Don't try to psychoanalyze me," I hissed, slapping on my bitch wings. "If I need a kink shrink, I'll give Tony Delvaggio a call. Personally, *you* need to see him far worse than me. Maybe you should schedule a few appointments...find out why you can't have a normal relationship without needing to tie up your women and beat their asses."

A fiery blaze ignited in his eyes before he slowly closed his lids and clenched his jaw. Sucking in a long, slow breath, Sam exhaled, then looked at me once again.

Calm.

Centered.

In command.

That pissed me off even more. "Oh, for fuck's sake, Sam. The world's not going to implode if you lose control for five damn minutes. Let it out…say what's on your mind. It might do you some good to vent once in a while."

Before I could draw in a breath, Sam was on me like a lion taking down a gazelle. Driving my back to the wall, he pressed his hard body against me, then pinned my arms high above my head.

All at once, a white-hot surge of desire lit up inside me.

"You really want me to lose control, Allisinda?" he purred with a feral gleam in his eyes. "If that's what you want, I can give it to you, sweetheart. But you won't sit right for a month. Don't tempt me, girl. Once I start, I won't stop…not even if you beg."

"I'll never beg…never give you the satisfaction of breaking me." The hateful words spewed from my mouth before I could stop them.

Like a balloon, Sam's entire body deflated. Releasing my wrists, his shoulders sagged as he backed away. Resignation and regret were written all over his face before he slapped a façade of control in place. He began erecting a palpable arctic barrier between us.

"So you've made your decision." His voice was but a whisper.

Unable to look him in the face, I issued a barely perceptible nod.

"I never pegged you as the kind of woman who gave up on anything. At least not the things you truly want. I guess that means you weren't in this for the long haul. Tell me something, Allisinda. Did you make your choice before or after we made love last night?"

The accusation in his tone frayed the last of my frazzled nerves.

"If you're trying to manipulate me with some kind of ridiculous guilt trip, save your breath."

A humorless smirk kicked up one corner of his mouth. "If I wanted to manipulate you, I'd have your sweet, innocent mind wrapped around my little finger. Tell me something. Why the need for an exclusive relationship if you were only using me to scratch your itch?"

"I...I wasn't using you, Sam. It was never like that."

"Oh, really? It certainly feels that way to me. I have to give you props. I haven't let a woman play me for over a decade. But you? Well, you pulled the—"

"Stop saying that," I screamed. "If anyone was being used, it was *me*."

"How do you figure that? Because I didn't tell you I was a Dom until last night? What about your secrets, Cin? Were you ever going to tell me what fuck-nut obliterated your ability to trust?"

"That doesn't have anything to do with you and me."

"The hell it doesn't. It has everything to do with us," he spat. "Because whatever scars you're hiding are bleeding into our relationship. Your secrets are just as important to this relationship as my Dominance. The only difference is I'm not afraid of your secrets. Not like you are of mine." Folding his arms over his chest, Sam pinned me with a taunting stare as if waiting for me to deny his accusation.

"Not all of us are as confident and sure of ourselves as you," I countered derisively.

"True. But I know one thing—you're as cute as a button when

you're all riled up." He chuckled.

His glib comment sent a flash fire of rage singeing through me. Grabbing the first thing in reach, I heaved a stone coaster toward his head. Ducking, Sam cursed, then rushed me like a linebacker, tackling me onto the couch beneath him.

Struggling, I fought for freedom, but the weight of his beefy body made it impossible for me to escape. Swearing like a sailor, I slapped at his chest and tried to ignore the masculine scent of his skin. Dismiss the enticing heat pouring off his body and leaching through my clothes that distracted, infuriated, and aroused me. If I let the son of a bitch know how easily he melted my defenses, I'd be toast.

"Get the fuck off me," I hissed.

"No." His one-word command vibrated through my rib cage.

"Goddammit, Sam. I said get off."

"I'll let you up. Once you convince me you're not giving up on us." Conviction, concern, and a glimmer of grief swam in his eyes.

Staring at his lips, I wanted to bite them…draw blood…make him physically suffer for putting me through this shitload of mental anguish. But mostly, I wanted to kiss him. Drown in the texture of his mouth and tongue and let him wash away all my fears and insecurities.

I opened my mouth to rail on him, but he quickly covered my lips with his finger. "Search your heart, baby. Do you really want what we have to end?"

No, I didn't. But I couldn't tell him that, at least not yet. Not until I stopped waffling and made up my mind, because this indecision was driving me batshit crazy.

"I don't know, Sam. I'm just confused right now," I confessed on a sigh of resignation.

"I know you are, baby. But shutting me out isn't the answer. Give me a chance to peel back the layers of the woman hiding inside you. Let me grant you a taste of freedom you've never known."

"How?" I asked. My voice cracked with trepidation.

"Trust me. Trust me unconditionally with your heart, mind, body, and soul."

Trust him? Unconditionally? Right. He might as well be asking me to scale Mt. Everest in a bikini while mixing Mai Tais.

"I...I'm not good at that, Sam."

"I knew that the second you accused me of sleeping with Destiny. What I don't know is why?" Settling a finger under my chin, Sam tilted my head back. "Tell me, Allisinda. Tell me who broke your heart."

Humiliation and apprehension congealed in a ball at my throat. Liz was the only person, besides my parents, who knew my humiliating secret. If I told Sam what had been done to me, he'd only shower me with pity. The sordid details needed to stay in the past, where they belonged.

"Sam, it's—"

"Important. Important for me to know everything about you," he interrupted as he stroked his thumb across my bottom lip. "I need to know your secrets, your fears, and your fantasies. Along with all your hopes and dreams so I can take care of you the way I should...the way I need to."

"You already take care of me...good care of me," I whispered, unable to tear my gaze from his.

A slow smile slid over his lips. "But I want to do much more...take all this to a deeper level." Turning sober, he frowned. "Stop stalling. Talk to me, sweetheart."

Exhaling a ragged breath, I worried I wouldn't be able to push the words past my lips. Closing my eyes, I blocked out Sam's face. I couldn't stomach watching his reaction when I revealed my ugly past.

"Four and a half years ago, my father walked me down the aisle of St. Patrick's Cathedral in New York," I began, speaking softly. "It was a big wedding…very big. My dress alone cost over a quarter of a million dollars." I felt and heard Sam's astonished intake—I kept my eyes shut. "Waiting for me at the altar was my fiancé, the prodigal neurosurgeon Dr. Darnell Willingham Edmonton the third."

Even saying his name aloud left a bitter taste on my tongue.

"Edmonton? Fuck," Sam whispered. Obviously he knew or had heard of my former fiancé.

"When we announced our engagement, the *Times* called our impending nuptials the *event of the year.* Thousands of guests crammed into the massive cathedral to witness the children of two revered physicians exchange vows. When I was getting dressed, Mother informed me that several members of Britain's royal family were in attendance. Of course, so was the cream of the social elite from New York and other US cities."

"Noland…Rufus Noland? Is he your father?" Sam's question was rife with awe and shock.

"Yes," I confessed.

"And you've kept that little secret from me…why?"

"I didn't want any preferential treatment or someone deciding to advance my career simply because of my father. My reputation is my own, good or bad, thank you very much."

"That doesn't surprise me in the least." Sam chuckled. "Go on."

"As soon as my father led me up the steps to the altar, the smile on Darnell's face faltered. He grew as stiff as a board. His skin turned an ashy grey. Fear danced in his eyes like some kind of caged animal. He took a step toward me, cleared his throat, then apologized. He nodded at my father and explained that he'd be right back."

"Except he didn't come right back, did he?" Sam asked in an angry tone.

"No," I whispered. The memories rolled through me on a bitter wave. I was reliving each sight, sound, and smell that stabbed my heart and forced the same debilitating embarrassment to pump through my veins.

Sam's warm breath fluttered over my lashes as he sipped the tears spilling from the corners of my eyes. Sliding a warm hand to the back of my neck, he massaged the tense muscles knotted there.

"Finish your story, Allisinda," he coaxed, pressing a sweet kiss upon my temple.

"The longer we waited, the more rigid my father became. With our elbows locked together, he held me tight, forcing me to face the front of the altar while anger rolled off him in powerful waves. It seemed as if we stood there for hours before Calvin, Darnell's best man mumbled something to the priest and darted away.

"I stood there, humiliation pumping through my veins like acid, and stared at the golden crucifix, praying that Calvin would bring Darnell back. I kept hoping that his bout of cold feet was nothing but a bump in the road of our new beginning. God, I was so naïve and stupid."

A bitter scoff slid from my lips. "I later discovered that cold feet was the least of our problems. No, Darnell never came back. After another twenty minutes, the bridesmaids, who I thought were my friends, decided the embarrassment of standing alongside me—the poor, pitiful, discarded bride—was simply too much for their shallow egos. Every one of them, all sixteen, bailed without me."

Sam muttered something that sounded like a curse.

"The groomsmen soon followed, leaving me, my father, and the priest standing at the altar alone. The buzzing voices of the guests behind us grew louder and thrummed in my ears. Thankfully, the priest raised his hands and instructed everyone to bow their heads in prayer. By then, a full-fledged war had ensued inside me. It took every ounce of strength I had not to break down, sink to the ground, and dissolve in a puddle of tears.

"Somehow, I managed to keep my shit together and hold on to the last few threads of dignity. A short time later, one of the groomsman appeared and whispered something to the priest. With a look of regret, the man slowly approached my father and me. He apologized and informed us that Darnell had left the cathedral and that there would be no wedding."

Sam gently caressed my cheek as I continued.

"With a nod, my father thanked the priest, then darted a glance behind him. Seconds later, my mother was at my side. Unchecked tears spilled down her cheeks, but she held her head high and painted on a painful smile. Then, without a word, she and my father escorted me to a private room behind the altar.

"Mother wiped her tears, then led me to a long couch, where she pulled me down beside her. She patted my hand, but I don't remember a word she said. I was too busy watching my father pacing back and forth while cursing under his breath. He was uttering words I didn't think he even knew. But even alone with my parents, I refused to come undone. I didn't want them to see..." Pausing, I swallowed tightly. "See how weak a man had made me."

Sam's body tensed. An anxiety-inducing silence stretched between us before he brushed a feathery kiss over my lips. "Did you ever find out why Darnell chose to run out on you?"

"Yes," I scoffed acridly, wishing I could escape revealing the bitter ending to my story. "Darnell was a golden boy in most everyone's eyes. From the outside, he was confident, poised, and seemed to have it together. But inside he was an emotionally stunted adolescent. Maybe he didn't get enough attention from his über-rich mommy and daddy. But then again, who did? We were both raised by what I penned the Social Elite Circus. Neither of us had been permitted to be kids. Hell, from the time I could walk, my parents began grooming me to behave just like them. Every word and action was scrutinized, analyzed, and judged to be socially acceptable or not. Much to my parents' dismay, my behavior usually ranked in the unacceptable category."

Sam remained silent while I spewed my animosity. Still, I kept my eyes shut tight. Reliving the memories made my skin crawl. A blanket of claustrophobia closed in around me. I wanted to slide out from under Sam's body and pace…work off the nervous energy singing inside me. But I knew he wouldn't let me. Not until I finished purging.

"Three days after the wedding debacle Darnell came to the house where he nearly polished off a fifth of father's coveted Irish Whiskey. My unscrupulous ex confessed that he'd set up—not one, not two, but three mistresses—in various parts of the city. To, and I quote: *'help relieve the insurmountable stress'* he was under."

"That's a piss-poor excuse for not being able to keep his dick in his pants," Sam drawled derisively.

"Isn't it?" I chortled dryly. "Evidently he was content screwing his harem while we were engaged, but he said that once he saw me walk down the aisle, he realized that one day I would find out." A sarcastic scoff rolled off my lips. "He had no intention of getting rid of the other women; he was simply worried that his reputation would eventually be marred by an ugly public divorce. I guess he weighed his options and chose minor embarrassment over an eviscerating scandal down the road. Of course, he wasn't the one left standing at the altar looking like an absolute idiot."

When I paused, Sam pressed a tender kiss to my cheek. "Open your eyes, Allisinda. I need you to look at me. Now."

Begrudgingly, I lifted my eyelids, expecting to encounter a look of pity. Instead, I was met with a look of searing rage, or rather, a tightly controlled fury etched over Sam's face.

"Darnell is the idiot. He's also a fucking tool and a piss-poor excuse for a man." Sam's expression softened. "But if I ever meet the son of a bitch, I'm going to buy him a drink."

"You're going to what?" I asked, stunned at his remark.

"I'm going to buy that prick-faced son of a bitch a drink."

"Why would you do that?"

A gentle smile settled over Sam's mouth as he brushed his fingers along the hollows of my cheeks. "Because if he hadn't left you, I wouldn't be here holding you in my arms like this."

CHAPTER FIVE

Sam slanted his lips over mine, claiming my mouth with a spine-tingling kiss. My head swam and my blood surged. And all the slick, oily regret sluicing through me vanished like smoke. He drew me in with the warm texture of his lips and a slow, thorough swipe of his tongue. Without even trying Sam stirred my embers of desire into a flickering, hot flame. I could feel his heated erection grow thick and hard against my folds, making me wetter by the second. His kiss turned savage. Still, I wanted more, wanted to peel away the barrier of clothing separating our flesh and feel his steely, hot shaft sink deep inside me…one glorious inch at a time. Wanted all of him…all but his disturbing Dominant cravings.

"Thank you for being brave enough to tell me all that, sweetheart. I know it wasn't easy."

A tiny frown pinched my lips while his comment pressed through the lust clouding my brain.

"I understand now why submission frightens you."

At least one of us did, because I was totally in the dark about all of it. "I'm glad you realize why it's not for me."

"I never said it wasn't for you. I said I understand why it *frightens* you." A knowing smirk played on his lips. "It's my job to help you get over those fears."

His self-assuredness set me on edge. When I opened my mouth to dissuade his lofty goals, Sam pressed a finger to my lips. "Give it a chance. Let's see where this leads us."

Like an anvil, reality crashed through my bubble of bliss. We shared so many similarities, yet we were light-years away from finding a common ground with all this BDSM crap. Tensing, I pushed at his shoulders, attempting to sit up.

"Easy, Cin," he murmured as he kept me fixed beneath him.

"But what if I can't give you the things you want?"

"What if you can't?" He shrugged dismissively. "You already give me everything I need."

"Maybe for now, but what about…" *Shit.* I'd never once broached the subject of a long-term relationship with Sam. Two days ago, it was all I fantasized about, but now? A happy ever after simply wasn't in the cards for us.

"Down the road?" Sam finished with a quirk of his brow.

"I was going to say…what about tomorrow," I lied.

What about tomorrow? I hadn't been able to keep my emotional shit together for one damn morning. How was I supposed to make it through a long-term relationship with the man? I didn't know, and at that moment, I didn't really care. All I wanted was his anxious cock, still nestled against my pussy, to fill me, obliterate me with as many orgasms as I could endure.

"For now, let's take it a day at a time," he suggested in a lustful drawl. "In the meantime, since you're already playing hooky, why don't we go out and grab a late lunch?"

Lunch? Was he serious? I didn't want food...I wanted him.

"Uh, okay. But my refrigerator is stocked. I can whip us up some—"

"Go get dressed, Cin," Sam interrupted. "I'm taking you out."

After slowly inching off me, he held out his hand. I instantly mourned the loss of his decadent heat but took the hand he offered before rising from the couch.

"Oh, and wear something sexy for me, sweetheart," he added with a wolfish grin.

"What?" I asked, irked that he'd even suggest such a thing. I always tried to dress sexy for him. Had he honestly not noticed?

"You heard me." Sam smiled.

"Don't I always?" I challenged, not totally sure why I wanted to argue with the man. Ever since he'd taken me to the club, I'd been an emotional hot mess.

"Stop trying to bait me into an argument. I'm not biting." He chuckled as took me in his arms and pressed his lips close to my ear. "You always look stunning, but scrubs aren't exactly the tantalizing outfit I want to see you in today, sweetheart."

Sam's low, hungry growl took the confrontational wind from my sails.

Striding to my bedroom, I let lose an inward curse. Where had my spine gone? I should have told him I wasn't hungry and asked him to leave.

"Who the hell are you trying to kid?" I scoffed to myself as I stood in the closet searching for something *sexy*. Sadly, I wanted to spend as much time with Sam as I could before it all fell apart at the seams.

Spying a silky red blouse, an evil plot hatched in my brain. "You want something sexy? I'll give you something so sexy you'll never forget."

Wiggling into a tight, tiny black skirt, I slid the filmy blouse over my head, then stepped into a pair of red patent stilettos. Strolling back to the living room, I bit back a laugh when Sam's eyes all but popped out of his skull. The hungry look of approval dancing in his eyes told me my little plan was going to be a breeze.

Flashing him a flirtatious smile, I snagged my purse off the coffee table. "I'm ready."

"So am I, but definitely not for food," he grumbled as he caressed another long gaze up and down my body. Sam exhaled a heavy sigh fraught with frustration, then pressed a palm to the small of my back before leading me from my apartment.

As he pulled out of the complex, I decided to test the waters. Turning my attention out the passenger window, I slowly inched one leg up before seductively drawing the point of my stiletto down the calf of my other leg.

The sudden sound of a car honking had me whipping my head toward the windshield. Sam tore his eyes off my legs, cursed, then gripped the wheel before jerking the car back into the right lane.

"Better keep your eyes on the road," I chided with a saucy smirk.

"You're making that awfully difficult, sweetheart."

"Me?" I gasped with feigned innocence. "I haven't done a thing."

"Right."

"So where are we going for lunch?"

"A little Italian place I enjoy. They have the best lasagna on the planet."

"Good. I'm starving," I replied, then slowly licked my lips.

"You wicked minx," Sam groused in a low growl. "Keep it up.

I'll make sure you get properly stuffed, sweetheart."

I planned on it.

Tossing my attention out the window once again, I half-assed listened to Sam while he sang the praises of the restaurant's food. Of course, I acted as if I were interested, but my mind was a million miles away, plotting ways to make our luncheon as sexually stimulating and painfully uncomfortable for him as possible.

If the restaurant's décor held true to its Italian roots, I imagined red gingham tablecloths hanging low enough to shield me while I wiggled off my shoe and slid my foot to his crotch. And if we were lucky enough to be seated in a secluded booth, I'd have a teasing good time arranging for my blouse to slide off one shoulder and tempt him with a peek of my nipple partially exposed by my lacy demi bra. By the time our meal was done, Sam would learn a lesson or two about ever asking me to dress *sexy* for him again.

"So, you're okay with that?" he asked, drawing me from my schemes.

"I'm sorry, I zoned off. Okay with what?"

"I said I need to stop by the club and get some things."

"The club?" I choked on a blast of panic. Both my appetite and my plans to torment him out of his pants instantly evaporated.

"No one will be there except Mika," Sam assured as if trying to assuage my anxiety. "It won't take long, I promise."

"Oh. All right. I'll…I'll just wait for you in the car," I sputtered.

"You will not," he thundered. "I'm not leaving you alone in the parking lot. In case you forgot, Kerr was shot outside the club last night."

"I haven't forgotten," I replied, attempting to push the disquiet from my system. "But it's broad daylight, for crying out loud."

"I don't care. You're not staying in the car."

I rolled my eyes at his caveman dictate, then exhaled a piqued sigh. "How is he doing, by the way? Have you heard if he survived?"

"He did. Even made it through surgery. He'll be in ICU for a while. I heard his brother is coming to town today. If the man's anything like Kerr, don't wander up to ICU for a few weeks, all right?"

"You mean he's at Highland Park?" I gasped.

"Yes, I found out this morning. Why does that upset you?"

"Jeb and Freddy...Did they...did they say anything about seeing us at the club?" I asked before swallowing down the additional fear rising inside me.

"No, of course not. I told you last night they wouldn't say anything."

"How can you be so sure?"

"Because they've been called to the club before. I spoke with them both privately the first time they saw me there. Neither one is going to spill our secrets. Trust me."

"You don't know that for sure." The idea of losing my job or tarnishing my reputation swelled to a pinnacle of panic.

"Baby, if Jeb or Freddy wanted to out me, or any other member, they would have done it by now."

Sam's calm and reassuring explanation couldn't keep a shudder from sliding through me. Bringing the car to a halt at a red light, Sam turned and faced me with a frown. "I'm not ashamed of being a Dominant."

Dominant. The word still conjured images of whips, chains, and blood.

"It doesn't diminish who we are because we enjoy living an alternative lifestyle."

"Maybe not for you, but I don't want Jeb and Freddy thinking I'm a freak."

A scowl pinched Sam's face. The driver behind us honked. Noting the light had turned green, he silently continued driving. A palpable wave of irritation rolled from Sam's body.

Dammit.

"I...I didn't mean I think *you're* a freak," I explained, trying to ease the sting of my insult.

Sam quietly scoffed. "Yes, you do. You think we're all freaks. One day I'll change your perception of that." He flashed me a devilish wink followed by a wide grin.

Relieved that he'd taken my faux pas in stride, I still wasn't out of the woods yet. Sam had every intention of changing my opinion about the lifestyle.

Great.

I'm not ashamed of being a Dominant. His words rolled in my mind. *Why not?* I wondered. He had as much if not more to lose if his secret ever got out. Sam could lose his license altogether if he were found guilty of unethical behavior. What would persuade him to take such a risk with his livelihood?

"What do you get out of dominating women? I mean, what does it do for you on a psychological level?"

Pursing his lips, Sam pondered my questions for several moments. "The power exchange between Dom and sub is a glorious connection all its own. The depth of trust, honesty, and communication far exceeds that of most vanilla relationships. For me, Dominance is like blood, air, and food...it's my sustenance. Protecting and nurturing feed me on a deeper level than I've ever known."

"But don't you achieve similar satisfaction taking care of your patients? I mean, you heal and bring new life into the world."

"Yes, but with Dominance, I'm restoring the submissive soul. It's far more potent than anything physical."

Sam's words were pretty, but they still lacked a tangible blueprint. Evidently, bewilderment marred my expression, because he continued his explanation.

"Imagine a baby bird tossed from its nest. She needs my help…craves it actually. But before I can approach her, I have to gain her trust, let her grow accustomed to my scent, my voice, and my mannerisms. After reassuring her that she's safe, I can gently pick her up and place her in the palm of my hand. Once there, I can feel her heart racing. She's frightened, so once more, I take my time and calm her fears.

"An unspoken comprehension exists between us. She's placed herself in a vulnerable position; she knows I could readily squeeze my fist and shatter her bones, steal the life from her fragile form. But the ineffable beauty is that she knows I won't. The trust she gives me is so absolute, so fucking priceless, it drives the need within both of us for me to protect, pamper, and nurture her all the more. While at the same time, I am validating the inner strength that she possesses as I teach her how to spread her wings and fly. Within the protection and cherished safety of my hands, she finds a different kind of freedom than she ever thought possible, beneath my command. Liberating a submissive is…well, it's indescribable."

I wasn't prepared for the conflicted emotions Sam's moving explanation evoked. He made submitting to his Dominance seem almost ethereal.

"I've only given you a small taste of that freedom, but I want to give you more…so damn much more."

Basking in the fantasy world Sam's words painted, I longed for an even bigger taste, but reality reared its ugly head. In order to experience that glorious world, I had to give up my will. And no matter how much I loved Sam or ached to reach some middle ground, I couldn't let another man reduce me to rubble the way Darnell had. That was one life lesson I wouldn't willingly repeat.

"I know you do, Sam. I'm just not sure I can give you what you want."

"Maybe not. Who knows?" He shrugged. "Trust me, Cin. I'm a very patient man."

"And stubborn." I smirked.

"Yes," he chuckled. "A trait we both share, my little sparrow."

My little sparrow. Sam's endearment brought a soft smile to my lips. I could easily relate to his analogy and wondered if such thing as a part-time sub might exist. Wondered if I could play the part to fulfill his needs yet still maintain my identity.

The sounds of gravel crunching under the tires ripped me from my thoughts. The familiar brick building and subsequent parking area behind Genesis sent my stomach to swirl. My body tensed. Sam reached down and squeezed my hand in silent reassurance. Still, an uneasiness continued to thrum inside me. He swung the car into a vacant parking space next to a gleaming black Escalade. The big metal door of the club swung open and Mika appeared wearing a welcoming smile.

Sam shoved the vehicle in park and switched off the engine. He turned toward me. "Are you good?"

"No," I answered honestly as a cavalry of anxiety marched through my system. "Look, just run in and get what you need. Mika is standing right there. He can protect me from all the mass murderers hiding behind the trees over there."

"No. I texted Mika when you were changing into that sinfully skimpy outfit. He told me he'd wait and let us in but had to leave right away to spend time with Emerald and their son before opening the club tonight."

A son? They had a child? How the hell did that work? Hopefully they hid all the Master-slave crap around the innocent boy.

"Oh," I mumbled as Sam climbed out from behind the wheel.

Rounding the vehicle, he opened my door. I couldn't move. It was as if my ass had been super-glued to the seat. He extended his hand, waiting patiently as trust and reassurance oozed off him. Finally, I slid my fingers into his palm but found it took an immeasurable amount of strength to leave the safe fortress of his car. My legs felt like rubber. Thankfully, Sam slid his arm around my waist to keep me from tripping up the stairs.

"Good to see you two back again," Mika remarked. Still smiling, he slapped Sam on the back.

I knew the proper response was: "It's good to be back," but then I didn't like to lie.

"I appreciate you waiting for us," Sam stated.

"No problem at all. By the way, we're having Drake and Trevor over for dinner, and whoever else Julianna has invited. I know she'd love to have you two join us. Come by around five-ish or so if you want to eat."

"Who is Julianna?" I asked, wondering if Mika had a harem of submissives at his beck and call.

"That's Emerald," Sam explained. "Her real name is Julianna, but she goes by Emerald here at the club. A lot of members have aliases. It's just an added layer of anonymity."

"Do I need to have some other name?"

"Not unless you feel you need one," Mika replied.

"So I have a choice?"

Sympathetic smiles tugged their faces, forcing me to scowl.

"You have a choice about everything. Always," Sam assured.

"Safe, sane, and consensual is strictly enforced here," Mika added with a nod, then paused. He looked as if he wanted to say more, but instead turned and punched in a code to unlock the big metal door. Flashing Sam and me a mischievous grin Mika chuckled. "Enjoy yourselves."

"Thanks, man, and thanks for the dinner invite. We'll talk it over, and I'll text you if we can make it."

Sam's ambiguous response, and the fact that he intended to discuss the invitation with me and not run roughshod over my wishes, lightened my spirits…a little. Reaching up, Sam gripped the door as Mika dashed down the stairs and jogged to the Escalade.

Peering down the dimly lit hallway, I swallowed tightly. Being aware of what lay beyond the doors and at the end of the hall sent a prickly sensation to invade my system.

"I'll wait here while you grab what you need," I volunteered.

"The club is empty, and I promise I won't bite," Sam teased. Cinching his arm tightly around my waist, he led me toward the dungeon.

"It's creepy in here all alone."

"But you're not alone. You're with me," he challenged.

The scent of leather lay heavy in the air before we breached the archway. "What is it that you need to pick up here?"

A flicker of guilt flashed across his eyes. My head screamed danger. My heart clutched and the air in my lungs constricted. "Why are we here, Sam?"

"To help you face your fears."

"Oh, no," I cried, planting the heels of my shoes into the carpet.

"You are not tying me up and whipping my ass."

"You're right. I'm not," he replied.

"Then tell me what you plan to do," I demanded.

"Nothing *to* you. I simply wanted a chance to give you a private show-and-tell. I figured without any members here you might feel less intimidated."

I eyed him warily. "Is that all?"

The grin he flashed me made my stomach flip-flop in an entirely different way than it had minutes before. "That's all. Unless you're not willing to learn."

His tone reeked of a dare. "Go ahead," I replied skeptically.

"Good girl," he whispered, skimming a kiss over my lips before leading me into the dungeon. "The area around each piece of equipment is called a station. Last night, you saw how the St. Andrews crosses, bondage tables, and spanking benches were used. But over here"—he directed me to the opposite end of the dungeon, near the velvet curtain—"we have the medical, fire, and electrical play stations."

"Fire? You mean subs actually let their Doms set them on fire and electrocute them? I thought you said that subs were treasured and—"

"Whoa. Take your imagination down a couple notches. Fire and electrical play can be as soothing as a day at the spa. In fact, everything in this room can be as innocuous as velvet or wicked as fangs. It all depends on the sub's needs."

"I'd prefer cotton over fangs, thank you very much."

"I sense a bit of progress there. At least you didn't automatically reject both." He smirked.

"Don't get your hopes up, mister," I chided. "I'm not doing any of this stuff, so the point is moot."

With a non-committal grunt, Sam led me through the stations, explaining how each piece of equipment was used. His demeanor had changed, and I noted an air of authority vibrating off his body. Even his posture had grown straighter. His chest expanded, making him seem taller…more commanding in an alluring and erotic way. This bolder, more disciplined, and capable side of him set my girl parts tingling. This was bad…very bad. Not only because I wasn't wearing any panties—part of my torment-the-hell-out-of-him lunch plans—but because my pussy was already dripping wet. If Sam realized showing me the tools and trades of his Dominance secretly turned me on, I'd be fucked—and not in a way I enjoyed.

Anxious for him to finish his tutorial, I nodded and smiled, feigning interest when all I wanted to do was go the restaurant and turn the tormenting tables on him for a while.

"Touch the leather on this bondage table, Cin. Feel how soft and thick the padding is?" Sam urged as he swept his hand over the shiny black hide.

Following his lead, I quickly pressed my hand to the surface before turning to him with a nod.

"Mika spared no expense to ensure the subs are comfortable during a session."

"I can tell." Nervously glancing around the room, I turned back to Sam. "Are we done now?"

"No." A hint of humor tugged the corners of his mouth. "Hop up on the table so you can feel for yourself."

"I don't think so," I replied, shaking my head. "I know what you're planning to do."

"Oh?" Both brows shot up on his forehead. "What's that?"

"Not a damn thing. Because I'm not about to let you tie me up and do kinky things to me."

Moving in fast, Sam gripped the back of my nape and leaned close to my ear. "When I tie you up and do kinky things to you, it'll be because you've begged me to, sweetheart," he whispered in a hungry purr. Arching his hips, he pressed his steely erection against my mound. As he inched away, a sober expression lined his face. "Give me a sliver of trust, Cin, just one tiny sliver. That's all I'm asking."

Oh, mercy.

His tone held that same authoritative edge as it had last night, sending a surge of lust to uncoil in my belly and tingles to race up my spine. My body wanted all the nasty, dirty things he could give, but my brain balked, wanting a throwdown with my hormones like a couple of prizefighters. Squaring my shoulders, I lifted my chin. "If you even think about trying to tie me up, so help me Sam, I'll—"

"Don't threaten me, sweetheart," he warned with a grin. "Or I'll do a whole lot more than tie you up and spank your ass."

Something wicked sizzled inside me…something that told me I might like that threat. Swallowing the panic rising inside me, I jerked my attention toward the table. If I stopped being flippant, Sam would wind up this little tour and we could leave. What harm could there be in placating him for a minute or two?

Possibly a shit-ton.

Against my better judgment, I scowled, then crawled onto the thick leather surface.

Stealing a glance up at Sam, I saw pride twinkling in his eyes as a smile of joy stretched across his lips. It melted my heart that this small act of yielding had done that for him. Easing onto my back, I continued to gaze at the glowing approval in his eyes. Still, I felt naked and raw, and strangely aroused by the commanding mien surrounding him.

"You've never looked more gorgeous, sweetheart," he whispered as he skimmed his fingers down my arm. "Are you comfortable?"

"Under the circumstances, yes," I replied tartly, trying to resurrect a wall of indifference.

As if seeing through my ruse, he smirked, then plucked a thick leather flogger off the wall. I sucked in a startled gasp as panic slammed through me.

"Uh-uh," I cried as I sat up to launch myself off the table. "You are *not* using that on me."

Splaying a wide hand over my chest, Sam shook his head before pressing me back onto the table. He arched a brow and cocked his head. "I need that slice of trust now, baby."

Trust. Easy for him to say, and probably equally easy for him to give without reservation. Me, on the other hand? Not so much.

"I simply want you to feel the softness of the falls. Let me prove that not everything here inflicts pain." He brushed the tips over the back of my hand. It wasn't an unpleasant sensation. In fact, it felt rather soothing in a strange way. Still, I wasn't ready to climb onto all fours, lift my skirt, and tell him to fire away.

"See? It doesn't hurt. It doesn't bite. This is nothing more than a harmless caress." As Sam trailed the leather fronds up and down my arms, goose bumps erupted over my flesh. Though the sensation felt foreign, my muscles grew lax beneath the tranquil glide of leather. "This particular flogger, because it's thick and heavy, gives a thuddy kiss. It can be extremely relaxing, or so I've been told."

For a split second, I yearned to feel the sensation he described, but instead, I simply nodded and shoved my curiosity down deep. As he placed the flogger back on its hook, I swallowed down the tendrils of disappointment that suddenly sprouted inside me. Moving to the foot of the table, Sam sent me a wicked smile before reaching beneath the lip. I heard a snick of metal before he cupped his hands around my shins.

"I chose this particular piece of equipment with you in mind," he stated before shoving my legs apart.

The frame separated, spreading the bottom half of my body open wide. I let out a squeal of surprise and clutched the edge of the table, fearing I'd slip through the gap and land on my ass. Sam shoved my skirt over my thighs while his gaze remained fixed on my bare, wet pussy—totally oblivious to my temporary burst of panic.

"You've been keeping secrets from me. Normally I don't like surprises, but in this case, your glistening, plump pussy all splayed out for me is a welcome one."

A blush warmed my cheeks as Sam briefly closed his eyes and inhaled a deep breath. "The spicy scent of your pretty black orchid is intoxicating. I can't wait to devour you." His voice had turned ragged and rough.

Sam positioned himself between my legs, shoving my skirt even higher over my hips, then bent to draw a trail of silky kisses up my thighs. Aching to feel his mouth on me, I bit back a groan when he stopped just short of the juncture between my legs.

Lifting my head, I watched as he knelt on the floor, then inched his face toward my center. His warm breath wafted over my throbbing sex, and I jerked when he placed his thumbs on my folds. Slowly spreading me open, Sam dipped his mouth close to my core. I gripped his head, holding tight to his scalp as anticipation revved. Sucking in a deep breath, I held it as I waited for that first glorious swipe over my electrified tissue. Instead, he speared his tongue deep inside me before proceeding to eat at me like a man possessed.

A dizzying wave of demand ripped through me. Every cell in

my body pulsed in a kaleidoscope of heat and need. Making love to me with his tongue, teeth, and lips, Sam zapped all my control as he dragged me toward the stars.

Driving two fingers inside me, he circled my pebbled clit with his thumb, forcing me higher and higher. As I reached the brink of no return, Sam lifted his head. His mouth and chin glistened in my juices as he held my gaze with his blistering stare.

"Shatter for me." His raspy, feral command raked my flesh. "I want to feel that sweet explosion building inside you…taste your pleasure pouring over my tongue as it swallows you whole."

A rippling whimper slid off my lips.

"Just imagine how this would feel if I had you tied to the table," Sam taunted before lashing at me again with his maddening tongue. "Bound in soft, silky rope so tight you can't move…can't squirm."

Pausing, he flicked another wicked lick over my aching nub.

"Helpless to escape the tingling torment I give you. Pinned to this table…my sweet submissive prisoner. And the only salvation you'll find is at my mercy. Would you beg for me, Allisinda? Beg loud and long, my beautiful girl? Plead for me to set you free, both inside and out?"

His words sent a fire of intrigue igniting through me. Lost in the visuals assaulting my brain and the sensation of being defenseless against his dark desires, I felt a naughty thrill slide down my spine. Though I loathed admitting it, even to myself, Sam's suggestion unlocked something primal deep inside me. An unexplainable yearning to hand over my entire being and submit to him in every way.

Bewilderment and fear slammed through me. This couldn't be… I was as sick and twisted as Sam…as the other members of the club. Panic swelled, numbing from my toes as it spread through my limbs, twisting my stomach, and finally strangling my heart.

"Sam," I cried, unable to hide the terror consuming me.

Jerking his head up, he lurched to his feet. I tried to snap my legs shut, but Sam's sturdy body stood wedged in the V of the table. Wanting to bolt from the table, I sat up. Sam wrapped his arms around me, holding my trembling body as panic roared within.

His expression was marred with guilt as he studied me with a piercing gaze. I tried desperately to mask my unnerving revelation but knew I'd failed when understanding softened his features. The flicker of hope that danced in his eyes told me that Sam clearly saw through the frenzy of turmoil churning inside me.

I suddenly felt as if I'd unleashed a beast bent on destroying my life. I couldn't seem to slap a defensive wall up around me fast enough, so I simply dropped my head and held him more tightly.

"Sam. I-I'm scared." A fat tear slid down my cheek as my voice cracked.

Without a word, Sam tightened his grip, clutching me to his chest as if I might fragment and flutter apart. Then he placed a sweet kiss on top of my head. "It's all right, baby. Everything is going to be fine."

CHAPTER SIX

No. Everything was *not* fine. I was sinking into a sludge-filled pool of quicksand. Trembling in Sam's arms, I inwardly called myself a million kinds of stupid.

"Easy," he whispered before inching back to look at me. As he cupped his hands around my cheeks, his fingers rested on the thundering pulse points at my neck. I couldn't hide the crazy staccato of my heartbeat anymore than I could shield the fears clawing at me. "Take a deep breath and relax for me, sweetheart."

"I-I can't," I sputtered on a desperate sob. "What the hell is wrong with me?"

A sad smile tugged his lips. "There's nothing wrong with you, Cin. Not a damn thing in the world. You're perfect…at least you are to me."

"But why? Why did I… God, I can't even say the words."

"Say what? That the idea of me tying you down excited you?"

"Yes," I wailed.

Embarrassed by my confession, I buried my face in his chest

and wept. With soft, soothing reassurance, Sam tried to bring me back from the depths of despair. Nothing he could say...not even the heat of his erection pressed against my pussy could mitigate the chaos consuming me.

"Sweetheart, you may not want to hear this, but I suspected there was a bit of submissive in you before I ever asked you out. What do you think attracted me to you?"

"You're right, I don't want to hear it." I sniffed. "Besides, you're wrong. I'm not a submissive. I'm an indepen—"

"An independent, self-sufficient, woman. Yes, I know," he drawled with a hint of humor in his voice. "It will surprise you to know that most submissives are just as headstrong and independent as you."

"I doubt that. If they were secure with their own identity, they wouldn't feel the need to lower themselves in such demeaning ways."

"There is nothing demeaning about submission, unless one delves into humiliation scenes, but that's a different topic. Submission isn't about stooping to some lower level or giving up your identity. It takes a mighty strong person to hand over their control. But once they do, they usually find a new level of confidence and freedom. They ascend to a higher plane."

Pulling back, I sent him a scowl. "That makes no sense at all, Sam."

"No, I suppose it doesn't, at least not yet. I can help you Cin. Help you gain a better understanding. If you set aside your preconceived notions, I can unlock something magical within you. But it has to be something you truly want. It can't be for me; it has to be for you."

Silly man. Didn't he realize the only reason I set foot inside this club again was for him? Still, I couldn't ignore the visceral reaction that had assaulted me when Sam suggested tying me up. Nothing within me, not even a molecule, was ready to embark on this bizarre journey.

"I'm not sure I want to examine myself that deeply."

Sam's expression softened with understanding. "Don't be afraid, Cin. Bring your shadows into the light. Let me prove that the woman inside you is just as substantial and vital as the reflection you see every day in the mirror."

But fear was my only ally. The only power capable of supporting the walls around my soul. The walls that deflected the whispers and sympathetic looks from family and friends after Darnell left me in the lurch. They'd provided me strength to hold my head high and project an air of dignity when inside I felt crushed and defeated. I never had the luxury of visibly mourning my heartbreak. I was a Noland. I could attain anything I set my mind to…anything but indulging outward emotion. God forbid a slip of that social etiquette might make me human. The only time I allowed my impenetrable fortress to crack was alone in my room, where the only witness to such unacceptable weakness was my pillow.

But now, my iron-clad resolve felt more like a marshmallow fortress. Sam's claim that a submissive was hiding inside me brought every unacceptable weakness to light. I had to reach down deep and shore up my steel walls if I wanted to stay sane and strong.

As if sensing my retreat, Sam scowled, then lifted me off the table. His strong hand cupped the cheeks of my ass.

"What are you doing?"

"Taking you someplace private. You need some pampering."

Pressing his mouth to mine with an indulgent kiss, Sam carried me down the hall. His stiff arousal pressed against my folds, dismantling my attempt to rebuild my walls. When we reached his private room, Sam eased me to my feet. With trembling legs, I watched him unlock the door. Inside, the covers on the bed still lay in a tangled heap. Memories of the ecstasy we'd shared last night poured over me, reigniting the lingering lust he'd conjured in the dungeon.

As he moved in behind me, the heat of his body and heady masculine scent made me want to turn and crawl into his arms. Instead, I summoned patience, waiting to see what he intended next. Anticipation hummed through me, increasing when Sam raked his knuckles down the length of my arms. Settling his fingertips on the pulse points on my wrists, he trailed indiscriminate patterns on my skin while leisurely lifting my arms above my head. His moist breath wafted over the side of my neck before he pressed a soft kiss there, sending shocks of pleasure to zap through me. In silent invitation, I tilted my head to the side. Sam accepted my offer by scraping his teeth down the sensitive column before laving the same path with his tongue.

"I want you…want your surrender," he whispered in a husky, hungry drawl. "But most of all, I want you."

"You already have me, Sam," I moaned. Thrusting my hips back, I savored his hardness burrowed between my butt cheeks.

"Not all the pieces I crave, but I will…one day. One day soon."

Leaving his words to hang in the air, Sam plucked the hem of my shirt up and over my head. With his body pressed in close against my back, he couldn't see the sexy bra I'd worn to seduce him. But then clearly, I wasn't the one in charge—and probably never would be.

Gripping both my wrists in one hand, Sam kept my arms suspended as he nipped my neck, then wiped away the prickles of pain with his skillful tongue. Using his other hand, he reached around my body and captured one taut nipple, then the next, rolling and plucking my aching peaks between his finger and thumb. Arching my back as the sublime burn engulfed my breasts, I ached to feel the sweet sting once more. My psyche reminded me that pain wasn't supposed to feel good, and a ripple of confusion slid through me. Parting my lips to drag a protest off my tongue, I whimpered instead when Sam eased down the zipper of my skirt. He shoved it off my hips and sent it puddling around my ankles.

"Your skin tastes as sweet as cotton candy. And you smell like fields of lavender after a summer storm," he murmured against my flesh.

A strange, enticing sensation surrounded me. I felt small. Fragile. As if the slightest bump would shatter me like fine bone china. Yet, wrapped in the security of Sam's benevolent adoration, I couldn't help but remember his analogy of the baby bird. I suddenly realized that *I* was that baby bird. Sam had me cradled in the palm of his hand, and while I knew how effortlessly he could destroy me, I knew in my heart that he wouldn't. I'd given him that sliver of trust he'd asked for. And every touch, every stroke, every mind-bending caress he bestowed held a promise of protection. Safety. Sanctuary.

I closed my eyes, savoring each sensation he granted.

Only semi-aware as Sam eased from behind me, I lifted my heavy eyelids and found him standing in front of me. A hungry, feral expression lined his face as he stared at the skimpy bra barely covering my breasts. Lowering my gaze, I, too, stared at my caramel-colored nipples, swollen and drawn tight, framed by delicate red lace.

Sam sucked in a ragged breath. "Jesus," he exhaled as he reached up and stroked his thumb over each erect peak.

The adoration and approval swimming in his eyes was all but blinding. And for the briefest of moments, I wondered if Sam loved me...loved me as much as I did him. I didn't want to think the only thread holding us together was this blistering filament of lust.

"Keep your arms where they are, Allisinda." His gravelly command sent more wetness to slide from my core.

Sam removed his hand from my wrist. The void of his control seemed somehow unsettling. Missing his dominant touch sent a rush of alarm to zip up my spine. I was a split second from lowering my arms to regain my power when Sam reached behind my back and unclasped my bra. As he brushed the lace away, the cool air caused my nipples to crinkle tighter. Cupping each breast in the palms of his hands, Sam stared at the orbs. A subtle tremor quaked his body.

Silent seconds ticked by. Anticipation crested higher as I waited for him to open his mouth and draw my aching nubs into his heated slickness. Instead, Sam clenched his jaw and eased onto his knees in front of me.

His submissive posture stunned me. I stood mutely watching as he cradled my calf in his palm before lifting my leg to slide off one stiletto, then the other. Using strong, capable fingers and the perfect amount of pressure, Sam massaged the toes, instep, and ankle of each foot. I was lost in each luxurious squeeze and sensual rub, and a moan of appreciation slid off my lips. He flashed me a mischievous grin, then bent and placed a tender kiss on top of my feet.

Threading my fingers through his hair while he kneaded at the tiny bones, I rubbed his scalp while I purred in pleasure. Sam rendered me boneless in a matter of seconds. I'd have no trouble at all becoming addicted to this kind of pampering.

Without a word, he stood, then lifted me into his arms before striding across the room. After lowering me onto the bed, he raked a hungry stare over my naked body while he tugged the shirttails from his pants. After working the buttons free, he shucked off the garment, sending it fluttering to the floor. I lay watching, mesmerized at the sight of his glowing white skin and his muscles as they rippled and bunched. The light overhead caught the splattering of hair on his chest and cast a golden hue over his sculpted flesh. I couldn't keep from gazing at the shimmering trail that disappeared beneath his trousers. My stare stalled and fixed on the tented fabric hiding his straining erection. And when I unconsciously licked my lips, Sam let out a low, rumbling chuckle.

"Don't invite trouble, sweetheart. It's taking more control than you know to keep from seizing your supple body and fucking you into oblivion."

"So what's stopping you?" I asked coyly.

"You." He arched his brows, released his zipper, and kicked off his pants.

Gripping his cock, Sam fisted his swollen, dripping erection. My mouth watered as a new bead of pre-come blossomed atop his wide crest. I ached to crawl to the edge of the bed, cup his sac, and suck him to the back of my throat.

"I'm not stopping you. You're just being mean...standing there looking all good and shit. You haven't even touched me, you big tease." I moaned with a playful smirk.

"And you're not just as big a tease?" he asked, quirking a brow.

"I wasn't the one enticing you with a little striptease, mister," I quipped with a saucy grin.

"I simply removed my clothes," he explained in the same clinical tone he used at work.

"Oh? So you weren't trying to seduce me, Dr. Brooks?" I taunted.

"For a girl who claims she wants nothing to do with the lifestyle, you're all but begging for a spanking. You know that, right?"

"I-I... No," I stammered. My body tensed. My cheeks grew hot.

Shaking his head, Sam slid onto the bed beside me. "Relax, my frightened little sparrow. No spankings, no sex, just you...in my arms, right here."

No sex? What the hell? Why not?

Tucking me under his arm, Sam drew me in against his side. I curled one arm over him and tangled my leg up with his, then rested my head on his chest. Scraping my nails over the coarse hair covering his pecs, I listened to the steady beat of his heart. Sam wordlessly massaged the back of my neck. His methodical kneading at the tendrils of stress that knotted my muscles worked better than any drug on the market. My eyes grew heavy, and I exhaled a kitten-like moan as he began scratching my scalp.

"I've got you, Allisinda. I'll never let you fall," he murmured as he kissed me softly.

His reassurance suffused me in safety, as did the heat of his body. I issued a soft hum in response, then drifted off to sleep.

Waking to Sam's soft snores and a bladder screaming for relief, I carefully inched out from beneath the arm banded around my waist. After climbing off the bed, I crept toward the bathroom.

"Where do you think you're going?" Sam asked in a voice thick with sleep.

"The bathroom."

"Mmm, I'll allow it," he mumbled, peeking at me with one eye open.

I snorted. "I wasn't asking permission."

"Not yet."

"Oh, good god," I drawled sarcastically. Rolling my eyes, I closed the door behind me.

If the man thought I was going to ask his permission to go pee, he was buckets full of crazy.

Hearing his laughter beyond the door, I scowled. The butthead was messing with me. Well, two could play that game and paybacks were hell. After washing my hands, I paraded back into the room. Flashing him a shy smile, I dropped my gaze to the floor, then lowered myself to my knees.

The air in his lungs exploded in a whoosh. "Holy fuck," he growled. Launching off the bed, Sam skidded to a halt in front of me.

Staring at his long, perfectly sculpted toes, I watched his cock jerk and grow hard in my peripheral vision. If I were a real submissive, pulling a prank like this would probably get me a bright red ass, but since I wasn't one, I knew I had nothing to fear.

"Cin," Sam exhaled on a reverent whisper. "You look... Christ, girl. You look fucking gorgeous."

Jerking my head up, I flashed him a triumphant grin. "Gotcha back."

Giggling, I hopped up to my feet. A desolate look replaced his pride. His nostrils flared and Sam clenched his jaw.

I stopped laughing.

"Yes. You got me good," he replied in a detached and icy tone. "Get dressed. I'll take you to get something to eat."

Without waiting for my reply, Sam turned and gathered his clothes from the floor. Guilt pummeled me as my heart sank to the pit of my stomach. The tension in the room was as crisp and cold as Alaska in December.

"Sam, I'm sorry," I began. "I didn't mean to hurt your feelings.

I was just playing."

Spinning around, he glared at me. "I don't *play* at Dominance and submission."

His low, controlled tone sent a wintry blast of dread up my spine. My little prank had royally backfired. Before I could open my mouth and offer up another apology, I found myself facedown over Sam's knees. He wrapped his arm firmly around my waist. Shock and indignation tore through me at the realization of what he was about to do.

"Okay, you've proven your point. Let me up."

"Your safe word is red," he whispered an instant before landing a brutal open-handed slap to my bare ass cheeks.

"My what?" I screamed. "Stop. That hurts."

"I aimed it to." He softly chuckled. "Safe word. Red. Use it if you can't take anymore."

"Any more? One was enough. Let me up," I hissed.

"Not on your life. If you're brave enough to poke the lion, you're brave enough to feel the lion's wrath."

Sam aligned another wicked slap. I let out a long, mournful howl. Flopping on his lap like a fish out of water, I struggled to break free of his grasp. But he was too strong. I didn't want to find pleasure as my nipples scrubbed against the coarse hair on his thighs. Or delight in the shards of heat gathering in my core. And I certainly didn't want to derive pleasure from the burning sensation enveloping my ass...the liquid heat that sank deep into my tissue and throbbed in time with my clit. My body belied the embarrassment and rage that seethed in my brain.

Another swat sent tears spilling from my lashes.

"Stop," I cried.

"Wrong word, sweetheart," Sam replied in a low, hungry drawl before bestowing yet another blow to my stinging flesh.

As I cried out once more, a feeling of helplessness settled deep. But it was more than a bizarre sensation of being at Sam's mercy; I felt an undeniable sense of peace. As if that wasn't astounding enough, I realized that I wasn't afraid or mortified anymore.

The scorching pain should have crushed me, but it didn't. It only added to the indescribable hunger growing inside me. Suddenly Sam slid his fingers between my folds. As he gathered the moisture spilling from inside me, I couldn't deny how aroused his spanking made me.

"Sam. Please," I whimpered, needing something but unsure what it might be.

"Sir. You will address me as Sir in this room from now on, girl," he instructed on a feral roar.

When he shoved his fingers inside my pussy again, I moaned and rocked against his probing digits.

"That's it, sweet slut," he snarled. "Show me how desperate you are for my control. Prove you need all I plan to give you."

Slut? Sweet slut? His phrase clashed inside my head. Demeaning yet steeped in pride, filled with lust and desire. I felt as if he was praising me, but I couldn't foster the level of logic to interpret why such foul words elicited joy. My brain was occupied with other questions, like where had the soft-spoken, reassuring doctor with the compassionate bedside manner gone? This wasn't the Sam I knew. This man was overbearing, ruthless, and rigid. It was almost as if he possessed dual personalities...a modern-day Jekyll and Hyde. I didn't know whether to fear this dark side of him or feel grateful that he cared enough to share his alter ego with me. But the most perplexing question that plagued me was why did I enjoy his kinky cravings?

His nimble fingers delved deeper, dragging over my g-spot, stilling my internal musings to focus on the bliss Sam bestowed. My cunt sucked at his digits. His hot breath skimmed over my shoulder as he pressed a gentle kiss there. All the tension melted from my body, and I dissolved like spun sugar, falling limp and lax on his lap.

"That's my girl. Give yourself over to me, baby. Let me have it all," he whispered, accentuating his words by scraping his thumb over my clit.

Back and forth, he batted my distended nub. Sinking further and further into the depths of demand, I moaned in delight.

"Your pretty little cunt is all wet and ready for me. You're perfect, Allisinda...perfect for me in every way."

His voice was steeped in awe, laced in pride, and wrapped around me like a blanket of bliss. Perfect? He thought me perfect? No one had ever regarded me as such before. Not my friends, not Darnell, and certainly not my parents. I'd grown up wearing the expectations of others like a weight around my neck. I'd longed for recognition of my accomplishments, but the bar of success had been set so high, achieving anything close to perfection had been nothing but a pipe dream. Yet, with Sam, I'd not only reached that elusive pinnacle but surpassed it as well.

His unconditional approval filled me with triumph, so much so that I couldn't contain my emotions. Sobs of redemption slid off my lips while the accolades he bestowed warmed the cold, empty corners of my soul.

Sliding his fingers from inside me, Sam repositioned me astride his thighs. With my legs stretched out alongside his hips, his thick, rigid cock rested against my belly. Using the pads of his thumbs, he gently wiped the tears from my cheeks.

"What is it, my little sparrow? Why are you crying?"

"You think I'm perfect." I sniffed, wishing I could wipe away the doubt in my voice.

"I don't think it...I *know* it." Sam softly smiled before slanting his lips to mine.

My stomach chose that exact moment to issue a loud growl. He chuckled against my lips.

"I think I need to feed you, girl. Sounds like you skipped breakfast this morning." He arched his brows in a look of censure.

"Last night's dinner, too," I replied with a nonchalant sweep of my hand.

"Let me make one thing perfectly clear—if you skip any meals again, I'll take you over my lap, only next time you won't like it." His intimidating tone resonated in my ears.

I rolled my eyes. "Honestly, I'm not a child, Sam."

"It's Sir in here, remember?"

Ignoring his reminder, I continued. "You won't be dishing out any more punishments."

"I will if you don't take better care of yourself."

Sucking in a deep breath, I raised my chin. "So are we going to stay here and fight, or are we going to get something to eat?"

A glint of challenge flickered in his eyes while his lips thinned in disapproval.

My shoulders slumped. "I don't want to fight with you."

When he didn't respond, merely arched his brows inviting me to continue, I sucked in a deep breath.

"Okay, so the spanking wasn't horrible. I'll grant you a pass this one time. I basically earned it by messing with you, but trust me. There won't be a repeat performance."

With a stoic expression, Sam lifted me off his lap and eased me onto the mattress beside him before standing to gather his clothes.

When he slid back into his pants, I wanted to groan in protest as he carefully tucked his steely erection beneath the zipper.

"Then I suggest you walk a straight and narrow path from now on, girl," he stated pointedly. "Get dressed, my sassy little wench."

Challenging his Dominance was pointless. It would be like telling him not to breathe. So instead of inciting any more arguments, I merely grunted and started putting on my clothes. As I sat on the edge of the bed, slipping on my shoes, I glanced up at Sam. He had buttoned up his shirt and was stuffing the tails inside his trousers.

"Are we going to the restaurant with the decadent lasagna you mentioned earlier?"

Sam pondered my question as he fastened the buttons on his cuffs. "We'll save that for another date. Why don't we take Mika up on his dinner invitation? You're not uncomfortable with that, are you?"

The taunting twinkle in his eyes told me Sam was going to do everything in his power to keep me from finding my footing. That was fine; I'd play his game…as long as I could. Quirking up one corner of my mouth with a wry grin, I cocked my head. "It all depends. Will we be eating in a dungeon?"

"No. But I could arrange to feed you while you're cuffed to a cross if you'd like," he countered. The wicked grin that speared his lips told me not only would he do it, but he'd probably enjoy the hell out of it, too.

Rat bastard.

"I'd prefer eating at a table. But not a bondage table, thank you very much."

Sam tossed back his head and laughed. His rich timbre vibrated all the way to my bones.

"How 'bout I tie *you* down to a bondage table and devour you for dinner?" I countered.

"Oh?" He arched his brows. "You think I'd submit to you?"

"Sure. Why not? You can't tell me you wouldn't enjoy me wrapping my mouth around your cock before I crawled on top of you and—"

"Stop, sweetheart." Sam held up his hand. "That will *never* happen. From here on out, any time I want your mouth on me, you'll be on your pretty little knees."

The visual that exploded in my brain set my girl parts churning, yearning to feel him thrusting in and out of my mouth. No way was I going to agree to his condition. Instead, I flashed him a plastic smile, then hooked my finger beneath his chin.

"Looks like you're in for a long oral dry spell then."

Sam snatched my wrist before drawing my fingers to his mouth. As he nibbled the tip of my index finger, an evil smile curled over his lips. "We'll see about that. But first I need to feed you. See, you're going to expend a lot of energy…begging before I let you fall to your knees."

My mouth went dry. Heat rushed between my legs. Dammit, I wasn't supposed to be turned on by his caveman cravings. But I was, and it worried the hell out of me.

"Never going to happen," I chided, rolling my eyes.

"Let's go before I keep you here to prove you wrong."

Pressing his palm at the small of my back, Sam led me out of the room, down the hall, and out the back door. The cloudless sky bathed the buildings in bright yellow. Once inside his car, he fired off a text to Mika, then started the engine. As we headed north out of the city, Sam threaded his fingers through mine.

"You know, you can try deluding yourself all you want. But

there's a part of you that aches to break free from the social niceties and expectations that have been drummed into you all your life."

I shook my head, but before I could refute his claims, he squeezed my hand. "I know what that's like. I lived it, too. But there comes a point when you have to follow your desires and stop trying to conform to others' persona of you."

I flashed him an incredulous look. "You expect me to conform to your desires. How's that any different from my parents?"

"Because deep down, you want to conform to those same desires. I've seen you respond to my Dominance time and again. You can refute it all you'd like, but I know the truth. It's breaking the chains in here..." He lightly tapped a finger to my head. "That's the only thing stopping you."

I nibbled my bottom lip, gnawing on his words. He made accepting the BDSM lifestyle sound so easy. Yes, I wanted a bigger taste of surrender, but my inner control freak refused to let go of the reins.

Sam let the discussion of Dominance and submission die, opting instead to talk about work as we made our way along Lake Shore Drive. The change of topic was a welcome reprieve. So were the placid blue waters of Lake Michigan. Both did wonders to soothe my frazzled nerves.

When Sam pulled the car up a long driveway, I studied the massive mansion situated on the lake. A feeling of déjà vu slammed me. I'd grown up in the same type of ostentatious surroundings. Mika certainly hadn't struck me as the aristocratic type. But then again, I really didn't know the man.

As we made our way up the walk, toward the front door, I glanced up at Sam. "I had no idea owning a BDSM club could be so lucrative."

"Mika's family is well off, like yours, my little debutante," Sam said with a chuckle.

"Smartass," I groused as we reached the door. Just as Sam reached for the bell, I grabbed his arm. "Wait. What do I call her?"

"Who?"

"Emerald...err, I mean Julianna. Which name do I use outside the club?"

A wide grin lit up Sam's face as he pressed the doorbell. "You can call her Julianna."

The vivacious redhead opened the door wearing a broad smile, a pair of jeans, and a teal T-shirt. She looked like a normal woman and not the corset-bound submissive I'd met the night before.

"I'm so glad you decided to join us. Come on in," Julianna exclaimed, opening the door wider. "Everyone's out back on the deck, except Mika. Our little get-together has grown...um, I guess I invited too many friends. Anyway, Mika's gone to fetch the food."

Sam bent and kissed her on the cheek. "Thank you for letting us crash your dinner, girl."

"Yes, thank you, Julianna. I hope we're not intruding."

"What? Oh, heavens, no. Not at all," she replied with a wave of her hand. "Follow me." She grinned as she ushered us through the marble entryway.

Light from the huge crystal chandelier shimmered over several exquisite paintings and gilded mirrors adorning the walls. Childhood memories sprang to life at the familiar lavishness their home afforded. Reminding myself this wasn't the same sterile environment that sucked the life out of me growing up didn't stop my skin from crawling as Julianna led us toward the back of the mansion.

After passing an über-masculine, oak-paneled study and entering a more casual-looking family room, where toddler toys lay scattered over the floor, I finally began to relax.

"Your home is beautiful."

Julianna turned to me and snorted. "My old house was a three-bedroom ranch, about an eighth the size of this monstrosity. I'm still not sure if I've been in all the rooms here yet or not. But thank you."

Her lack of pretentiousness was a welcome relief and made me grin.

When we stepped out onto the deck, I blinked in surprise at the number of people relaxing around several large tables, drinking beer, laughing, and talking.

"Hey. Cindy and Sam are here," Liz cried as she leapt out of her chair and waved.

The sight of my bestie did wonders in calming my fears. I grinned as she scampered toward Sam and me. Both Ian and James were right behind her, wearing matching smiles.

Gathering me in her arms, Liz gave me a tight hug as she pressed her lips to my ear. "Yeah, you look real sick, you faker." Then her tone turned serious. "You freaked out like I did in the beginning, didn't you?"

"Something like that," I confessed.

"Just remember to breathe, but more importantly...lean on Sam. He's a good Dom. He'll help you sort the lifestyle out. And as always, I'm here for you too sister."

"Thank you." Unwilling to let go of the strength and determination Liz offered, I clung to her for several long seconds. "What's going to happen here? I mean, who's going to get beaten?"

"No one," Liz chortled. "Nothing is going to happen except good food and friendly conversations. This is very informal, nothing close to the protocol of the club. I highly doubt anyone is even going to get naked.

"Thank god," I murmured. "I was worried Sam was going to feed me to the wolves."

Liz pulled back and blinked. "Oh, honey. He'd never do that. It's his job to lead you down your path and protect you."

"I'm still not sure I want to walk that path," I confessed on a shaky whisper.

"What are you two talking about?" Sam asked with a mock scowl.

"Nothing, Sir," Liz replied, batting her eyes and slapping on an innocent smile.

"Oh, girl," Ian groaned. "Don't quit your day job, because you'll quickly go broke as an actress."

Liz stuck out her bottom lip in a pathetic pout while the guys around us laughed. Even I couldn't help but grin.

A few minutes later, Sam whisked me away and introduced me to his other friends. Suddenly a beer was shoved in my hand. Looking up, Drake towered above me wearing a wide grin as he blocked the sun from my face.

"It's good to see you again, Cindy. I had a sneaking suspicion you were a sub," he stated before jabbing his elbow into Sam's ribs. "Good going, Doc."

"Oh, I'm—"

"Cin still needs a bit of convincing in that area, but I'm working on it," Sam quietly informed Drake.

After taking a long pull on my beer, I redirected the conversation. "Is Trevor here?"

"Sure is. He's right over there." Drake turned and pointed across the deck.

In the corner, Trevor sat with a chubby, bronze-skinned toddler perched on his lap, reading the little tike a story.

"Go on over and say hello," he encouraged. "I know he'll be happy to see you."

Darting a questioning look up at Sam, I immediately frowned. What possessed me to seek his permission?

A wide, knowing grin lit up his face. "You may," he replied, biting back a laugh.

I sent him an angry glare, then lifted my chin and marched off toward Trevor.

"Holy... How did you manage to get her to do that?" Liz asked Sam from behind me.

Biting back an unladylike growl and the urge to flip her off, I painted on a smile before easing onto the vacant chair next to Trevor. He was oblivious to everything except the boy on his lap and the book in his hand. I sat quietly and listened as Trevor read the words in funny, animated voices. The little boy, who I assumed was Mika and Julianna's son, giggled and gazed up at Trevor as if he'd hung the moon. The palpable aura of love enveloping the two brought an honest smile to my lips.

"You boys seem to be having the most fun at this party," I said with a chuckle. Trevor jerked his head in my direction. His eyes grew wide in surprise, like saucers. I giggled.

"Cindy. Oh, wow. What are you doing... I'm sorry, that's way rude. It's so good to see you," Trevor sputtered. Leaning over he gave me an awkward hug.

"It's good to see you again, too. You look amazing. I'm here with Sam."

"Oh, really?" Trevor exclaimed dramatically. "So you and Sam, huh? Well that certainly gives a whole new meaning to playing doctor."

Even as the heat climbed up my cheeks, I couldn't help but

laugh.

"Weed, Unk Twebber," the beautiful toddler begged in a precious but demanding tone. "Weed. Me."

"Unk Twebber will weed you, Tristan. Just give me a second to say hello to my friend, Cindy, little man." With a huff, the toddler pouted. Trevor tapped his finger on the little man's lip and shook his head. "You'd better tuck that in before a bird comes along and poops on your lip."

"Ewww. I'own wike burd pooh, Twebber." Tristan wrinkled his nose and buried his face in Trevor's chest. Milliseconds later, the little boy raised his head and grinned. "I wike cake. Weed. Weed. Weeeeed."

Julianna swooped in and plucked Tristan off Trevor's lap. "Let Uncle Trevor visit with his friends for a bit, baby." She pressed a kiss to the toddler's chubby cheek. "He can read to you later on. I swear. You're as demanding as your father."

"Oh, sister. If Mika hears you, you're going to be in so much trouble," Trevor warned.

"If you don't nark me out, he'll never know." Julianna smirked.

Trevor gasped in feigned shock. "I'd never do anything like that to you...as long as you slip me a couple of twenties."

"Have you decided to start a career in extortion now?" She laughed.

"Maybe. I'll never tell." Trevor grinned before leaning up to blow a raspberry on Tristan's cheek. The little man kicked and squealed with laughter.

"Woman. Where the hell are you?" Mika's demanding call rose above the crowd. "I'm back with the food, and we've got a horde of hungry guests waiting to be fed."

Julianna rolled her eyes. "Here, take him again for me, please?"

she asked as she settled Tristan back on Trevor's lap. "I'll be right back, sweetheart. Daddy's bellowing for mommy, again."

"Dadada bellwoah 'gin?" Tristan asked, confusion wrinkling his chubby face.

Trevor blinked at the little boy, then laughed. "I won't nark you out. Your son will do that for me."

Her eyes grew wide. "Oh, good go—"

"Julianna?" Mika roared again.

"Coming, my love," she answered on a singsong sigh, then hurried away.

"Weed?" Tristan asked hopefully.

"Oh, all right," Trevor replied, pretending to be put out by the boy's request.

"Yay," Tristan yelled, kicking his feet. Obviously the little guy wasn't buying Unk Twebber's act for a second.

"In a second, little man," Trevor said with a laugh. "You're as impatient as your daddy."

I grinned, wondering how long it would be before Tristan repeated those words to Mika.

"You know, I never did get a chance to thank you for being so supportive during Liz's ordeal," I began, as Trevor's expression grew solemn. "You kept me from losing my mind. Thank you."

"You don't need to thank me," Trevor mumbled. "I don't think I ever thanked you for…"

He paused as if unable to let the words roll past his lips.

"Hey, I was just doing my job," I replied with a wave of my hand. "That was a terrible night, but look at you now. You've bounced back and—"

"No. Not really," he confessed.

Sadness clouded his face. Without another word, he picked up the book and began reading once again. A palpable awkwardness hung in the air. I wanted to kick my own ass for bringing up the horrific memory of his beating.

Allowing him to redirect his focus on Tristan, I patted Trevor's hand and issued a weak smile. "I'll let you two get back to your story. We can catch up later."

Trevor simply forced a tight smile and nodded. There was so much more I wanted to say, but knew my sympathies would pale in comparison to the demons he was obviously still battling. Instead, I kept my mouth shut and stood and wandered off to find Sam.

He wasn't hard to miss, as the setting sun reflected in his golden hair as he leaned up against the wooden railing of the deck, drinking a beer and talking with Tony, Ian, and James. I didn't want to interrupt their conversation, so I scanned the crowd, looking for Liz. She and another woman were chatting near the sliding glass door.

My nerves began to twitch. I took a swig of my beer, reminding myself that I was a big girl. I didn't need Sam or Liz to hold my hand among these strangers. And just because I was a lifestyle virgin, that didn't mean they planned to sacrifice me to the gods in lieu of dessert. Another gulp of beer and my pep talk finally succeeded in taking the edge off. And just when I thought I was safe treading these shark-infested waters, the hair on the back of my neck suddenly stood on end.

Flitting a gaze over the crowd, I found the reason for my discomfort. Tony Delvaggio who was sitting next to his pretty blonde wife, held me with a gaze of shooting daggers. He leaned over and whispered something in her ear before he stood and began walking toward me.

"Hello, Cindy." He smiled tightly. "It's good to see you again."

"Doctor," I nodded, returning an equally rigid smile while the tension in the air grew stronger.

"Please don't take this the wrong way, and I apologize for bringing this up here at the party, but I wanted to be sure that Sam has spoken to you about the club rules."

Ah, so the sexy shrink was afraid I'd divulge his secret. He was obviously as worried about me ratting him out as I was in regard to Freddy and Jeb.

"As a matter of fact, he did. Trust me. I know what's at stake. Your secret, along with everyone else here, is perfectly safe with me."

His wide grin reflected his relief. "Excellent. Thank you for guarding our anonymity, and welcome to the family."

Instead of wasting my breath to explain I was more like a distant cousin, twelve times removed—not even really related to the kinky clan—I simply smiled and thanked the man.

Liz sidled up next to me and looped her arm through mine. "Some of us are going to help Julianna in the kitchen. Want to join us?"

"Yes. I'd love to." Anything to keep from having my psyche sliced open by Tony was a welcome change. Turning to the man, I nodded. "If you'll please excuse me?"

"Of course, pet. I'll send Leagh along to help as well."

After a few short minutes of working alongside the other women, I started to relax. Their laughter and one-liners proved they were a close-knit group. They had me laughing so hard I had to hold my side. It was strange, but I had to keep reminding myself they were submissives—women who willingly handed their independence over to Dominant men. And I realized that Sam had been right, they were staunchly self-assured and funny as hell.

"How long have you been in the lifestyle?" a beautiful, delicate-boned African-American woman named Ebony asked.

"Cindy's just started dipping her toes into the water," Liz answered. I sent her a grateful smile for having my back.

"Oh, that reminds me," Julianna began. "Mika wanted me to be sure and let you know about the submissive classes we have at the club. They're every Saturday morning from nine to noon. We'd love to have you join us. It's really a lot of fun."

"It is," the women answered in collective agreement.

"I really miss those meetings," Savannah, a dark-haired beauty with big brown eyes, pouted. "But Trevor needs me more than you all do right now."

"You two will be back with us soon. How's his karate lessons going?" Mellie—who I'd learned moments earlier was Savannah's sister—asked with a note of concern.

A sad smile tugged the woman's lips. "He's a fast learner, but sometimes he crawls inside himself. I can feel the anxiety rolling off him. Thankfully, he's still seeing Tony on a regular basis. I'm sure he'll eventually work Trevor past the aftermath of his attack. It just breaks my heart though. I love him so much. It kills me to see him so…haunted."

A tear slid down her cheek. The others murmured in sympathy. The memory arose of Trevor being wheeled into the ER the night he was beaten. My heart ached for the sweet young man then as it did now. On the outside, he seemed perfectly fine—happy, in fact, as he read and giggled with Tristan. But then looks could be deceiving, a fact driven home by the group of strong-willed women surrounding me.

"Ixnay onyay evortray," Julianna warned in pig Latin. It took me a minute to decipher she was really saying to stop talking about Trevor. "I think he's coming inside to help."

"Speaking of which, what can I do?" I asked.

"Grab those potholders," Julianna instructed nodding toward the stove. "And start hauling trays of lasagna out to the dining room table for me, please. I'll throw the salad into a big bowl."

The sliding glass door opened and Trevor sauntered in. "Tristan is ready for cake," he announced with a laugh.

"When isn't he?" Julianna asked dryly.

"Give me something to do, sister," Trevor pleaded. "Something that will keep me from breaking down and giving that little heart-melter an entire cake for dinner."

"You do and I'll have Drake tie you to the bar naked for a month," Julianna warned, waving a wooden spoon his way. Trevor's eyes grew wide in horror. "You can check the tableware in the other room. Make sure we have enough for everyone, and keep Tristan far away from the dessert."

"On it." Trevor grinned, darting toward the dining room.

"Mellie, Savannah, would you please grab the salad dressings out of the fridge and set them on the table? Ebony, can you light the sterno cans beneath the chafing dishes so we can keep the lasagna and cheesy garlic bread hot? Leagh…um… Oh, hell, just stand there looking gorgeous as usual, doll. Everything else is covered." Julianna laughed, giving Tony's beautiful wife a tight hug.

"Is that all I'm good for…eye candy?" Leagh teased with a mock scowl.

"From what I hear, you're better at sucking the chrome off a Harley, but I don't know that for fact," Trevor called from across the room.

"Oh, yeah?" Leagh laughed. "From what I hear, so are you."

"Damn straight. Daddy loves it, too," Trevor preened.

And that's all it took for another round of verbal zingers to ignite and volley through the air. Tears of laughter slid down our cheeks when Mika burst into the room wearing a quizzical expression.

"What are you wild ones doing in here? Are we going to eat or laugh all night?"

"Where's Tristan?" Julianna gasped, trying to peer around Mika's muscular shoulders. "What did you do with our son?"

"I sold him to the gypsies," Mika drawled as he rolled his eyes. "Relax, pet. Drake has him. He's fine."

"Don't tease me like that. Dammit, you scared me," Julianna scolded.

"Watch your tone with me, my little wench, or I'll fire up your backside here and now," Mika warned. Marching toward her, he pulled back his hand, level with her butt.

Undaunted, Julianna thrust her backside out and wiggled it at him. "Please do, Master."

Narrowing his eyes, Mika shot her a glare that filled me with fear. "I'm going to edge you all night long. That should take the sass out of you," he threatened.

I leaned in close to Liz's ear. "What's edging?"

She grinned and murmured back, "When your Dom takes you to the point of release over and over again but doesn't let you come. It's wickedly awful."

Julianna groaned and shot him a pleading gaze. "No. Please. I'll behave. I'm sorry."

"Too late, pet." He shrugged. "If dinner is ready, I'll start sending the guests inside."

"Yes, Sir, it's ready." Julianna pouted. It was plain to see which parent Tristan plucked that ploy from.

"Good girl," Mika praised. Drawing his hand back once again, he landed a loud, hard smack to her ass.

The blow would have reduced me to tears, but Julianna simply purred, then wrapped her arms around Mika's neck. She flashed him a needy look, then drew him in close for a long, passionate kiss. Mika turned and strutted back out to the deck, wearing a proud, contented smile.

"Let's eat," Julianna announced, her voice giddy and breathless.

CHAPTER SEVEN

Sam and I sat at one of the big tables with Liz, Ian, James, Tony, and Leagh. We laughed and talked as we stuffed ourselves on gooey, lasagna and chased it down with rich red wine. Outside the walls of Genesis, everyone seemed…well, normal. Though the various topics of conversation left no doubt in my mind this definitely wasn't an Amway party. No, I'd let Sam drag me in behind enemy lines, and I was now deeply entrenched with the Kink Squadron. And as long as I kept from fixating on that fact, I relaxed and had a fun time. I felt like a fraud, though no one seemed to care I knew virtually nothing about the lifestyle. They were warm, friendly, and welcoming.

"Oh, you little twit. That's a bold-faced lie. Oh, my god, I can't believe you… Savannah, you are such a brat," cried a blushing Mellie from the table beside us.

Her sister didn't seem the least concerned about Mellie's scorn. Savannah simply cackled with those around her.

"Sirs, I respectfully request you beat Sanna's ass red tonight,"

Mellie demanded of the swarthy Native American Master named Nick, and Dylan, a buff blond with a charming dimple.

Suddenly, Joshua—Mellie's Master—sobered and lifted a sandy-blond brow. "Surely you're not giving instructions to Sanna's Masters, are you, precious?"

"No, Sir." The pretty dark-haired woman paled. "It was... I...I was only suggesting, Master." Even I could tell Mellie was blatantly backpedaling to keep her own butt out of trouble.

"Of course not," Joshua replied wryly. "So tell me, what was this clandestine shopping trip Sanna just ratted you out all about?"

"I didn't rat—"

"Pet," Nick interrupted with a scowl and a tone that brooked no argument.

Savannah sent her sister a pleading stare before mouthing, "Sorry."

"It's a surprise...or rather, it was supposed to *be* a surprise," Mellie explained while her shoulders sagged dejectedly.

"For me?" Joshua's eyes flashed with delight like a little boy at Christmas.

"No, for the mailman," Mellie drawled sarcastically. "Of course for you, Master. Do you honestly think I'd be buying gifts for some other man?"

Joshua let out a mighty roar, then gripped Mellie's hair before yanking her head back and planting a long, soulful kiss over her mouth.

A ripple of longing fluttered through me. Memories of Sam's fist in my hair and the tingles his touch ignited over my scalp made my pussy clutch.

"You may keep your surprise a secret, my mouthy girl," Joshua apprised after ending the kiss. "But your lily-white ass will be blazing and beautifully marked for me later on tonight."

"Thank you, Master." Mellie swooned as if happy to receive his pain. With a victorious and haughty expression, she flashed Savannah an evil grin, then stuck out her tongue.

Another burst of laughter resounded from their table. I, too, couldn't keep from grinning at the sisters' playful antics. But I wondered why the formality between Dom and sub—that I'd witnessed at the club—had all but vanished. It gave me hope that there might actually be such thing as part-time submission. Not that it mattered. After all, *I* wasn't a sub.

"Cin? Would you be up for something like that?" Liz asked, yanking me out of my pondering.

"I'm sorry, I didn't hear your question. I was listening to the banter at the other table. Guess that serves me right for being nosey."

"It's okay. Savannah and Mellie are hilarious when they get on a roll." Liz grinned. "Ian Sir asked if you and Master Sam would like to observe a session between the three of us."

Watch them? "Why?" The question flew off my tongue abruptly.

Surely she wasn't serious. I'd rather have a root canal, without Novocain, than watch my best friend strip down and get her ass beat.

Liz's cheeks turned crimson, and she flashed a nervous glance at her two Doms.

"Because we wanted to give Sam an opportunity to explain the dynamics of what we do in a more private setting, pet," Ian explained. Though his tone wasn't exactly a command, it certainly felt like one.

"Ah, sure. I guess that would be all right." I shrugged quickly, darting a glance at Sam. His gentle smile told me he approved of my answer.

Great. And wouldn't sitting there watching Liz be as awkward as hell.

At my blatant lack of enthusiasm, James sent me a sympathetic smile. "It won't be awful. More like a low-key, informal demo, Cin."

Since I had no clue what a demo entailed, I simply smiled and nodded. Still, if at any time during this *informal demo* he or Ian whipped out their dick, I would be outta there. No part of me wanted to watch my best friend get it on with her men.

Butterflies returned with a vengeance, dipping and swooping in my belly. I downed my glass of wine to the amusement of everyone at the table. I wanted to crawl under the damn thing and hide. Sam slid his broad hand over my thigh and gave me a reassuring squeeze.

"We'll set it up, soon," he agreed.

I swallowed tightly hoping soon might mean a couple of centuries from now.

"Any word on how our resident douchebag is doing?" Joshua leaned back in his chair at the other table and pointedly asked Sam.

"Dammit, man," Ian groused. "Why'd you have to spoil a wonderful evening by bringing that prick up?"

"Sorry, man. I didn't mean to curdle your dinner. I'm simply holding out hope he comes down with a nasty staph infection or something else fatal," Joshua stated contemptuously.

"I doubt we could be that lucky," Tony added cynically.

"You know, Sam," Dylan began. "I respect your Hippocratic oath and all, but none of us would have blamed you if you'd let him bleed out."

"Master," Savannah gasped as she stared, slack-jawed, at the chuckling men.

"What? Do you have a secret crush on Kerr or something?" Dylan's taunting grin caused his dimple to sink deep into his cheek.

"Gross. No. But that's a terrible thing to say," she chided.

"No, it's not," Mellie stated matter-of-factly. "It would save a lot of heartache for other subs."

Joshua exhaled a heavy sigh, then pulled her against his chest. "I'm sorry, love. I wasn't trying to pick the scab off old wounds."

Evidently Mellie had a history with Kerr. It would certainly explain the animosity shared by those around us. I made a mental note to get the whole story from Sam or Liz soon.

Mellie shook her head, then pressed her lips to the back of Joshua's hand. "You didn't, Master. I stopped wasting brain cells on that chicken-s—poop, a long time ago. Besides, you're who I want to focus all my attention on now."

The love in her voice brought a smile to Joshua's lips. "And I adore your attention, girl." He slanted his lips over hers and kissed her hard. "I intend to have you focused on all kinds of delicious things, later tonight."

Mellie shot him a shy smile, then slowly licked her lips.

"I said later tonight, minx." Joshua laughed.

"Well, Kerr might have survived surgery, but I can guarantee he won't be making an appearance back at the club for a while," Sam assured.

"Good. That gives us more time to warn the new subs who come to Genesis to stay away from him," Leagh stated with a hint of gratitude.

"Are you talking about the training classes?" I asked.

Leagh nodded. Sam's face lit up in approval.

"Hey, we're both off on Saturday," Liz reminded with a scheming glimmer in her eyes. "Why don't I pick you up at eight thirty and we'll—"

"Easy, my eager girl," Ian warned. "Let Cindy decide if she

wants to attend the sub classes first."

"But she has to," Liz countered before turning her focus on me. "You have to come. At least to one, just to see what it's like."

"I-I'll think about it," I stammered, wishing like hell I hadn't opened my big mouth in the first place.

"I think it's a wonderful idea. You should go, sweetheart," Sam encouraged.

With a tight smile and a curt nod, I somehow managed to keep my mouth shut and not argue with him…for once.

Thankfully, Julianna sauntered up to the table holding a sleepy-looking Tristan on her hip. "There's a ton of food still inside. Help yourselves, but save room for dessert."

The little boy jerked his head off her shoulder. "Cake? I wike Cake."

"Yes, my love, I know you do. But there's no cake tonight." Julianna smiled shaking her head. "I'm going to put this little bundle to bed, but Mika has set out the tiramisu. Go on in and get some when you're ready. I'll be right back."

"Yum, tiramisu. Master?" Leagh moaned.

"You may." Tony said with a grin. "And yes, I'd like some, too."

"With your sweet tooth? That's a given, Master." She grinned.

I automatically placed my palm to my stomach and shook my head. "I don't think I could eat another bite."

Suddenly all the submissives stood and headed indoors. Liz tugged my arm. "Come on. Let's get some dessert."

"I'm too full."

"Not for you, for Sam," she whispered loudly.

"Oh." I shot him a quizzical gaze, wondering why he didn't go inside and get his own, but then it slowly dawned on me. I was supposed to serve him, like the other subs. There was a fine line between stubborn and bitch, and if I refused to bring him dessert, it would only embarrass us both. Forcing my backside out of the chair, I followed my bestie into the house.

All the subs were clustered around the big table, laughing and talking as they plucked plates of dessert off the table. None seemed the least bit put out having to fetch food for their able-bodied Doms. I hadn't thought much about it earlier when none of the Doms were in the dining room loading up their own plates. Well, none except Ian, James, Nick, and Dylan. Since Liz and Savannah only had two hands, it made sense they had plated their own food.

For a lifestyle that seemed riddled with rules, I found the lines being constantly redrawn. How were the submissives to know what to, or what not to, do without more structure?

Lost and confused, I plucked up a plate, then hurried back to the table. When I all but tossed the dessert in front of him, Sam lifted his head and studied me for several long seconds.

"Thank you, sweetheart." He smiled as he clasped my hand and urged me back to the chair beside him. Sliding his fork into the decadent dessert, Sam slivered off a small piece, then turned and extended it toward my mouth. "Open."

Shaking my head, I placed my palm to my stomach. "I'm honestly too full."

"One bite," he insisted. "Open."

The other subs returned as I pondered Sam's command. A hush fell over the table, making me feel as if I were on stage beneath a spotlight. My pulse sped up, my mouth went dry, and my palms started to sweat. Maybe I was making a mountain out of a molehill. One bite didn't necessarily imply that I'd tossed my torch of liberation into the abyss and proclaimed myself a submissive. Still, the idea of bending to his command chafed.

Feeling every inch a well-trained Rottweiler, I opened my mouth and closed my eyes, desperate to ignore the compulsion of proving myself worthy to Sam and his kinky friends. The bittersweet cocoa, burst of tart espresso, and sweet, creamy custard battled for supremacy over my taste buds. A soft, appreciative moan vibrated from my chest as I savored the sinful dessert.

"I love it when you make that sexy sound," Sam growled low in my ear. Flashing my eyes open, I saw a lurid smile play on his lips. "We'll have to say our goodbyes soon, because I'm suddenly craving a different kind of dessert."

"Ice cream?" I smirked.

He simply shook his head at my smartassed reply. "Oh, I want cream all right…but it's not cold. I want your hot, silky cream coating my cock."

"Eat fast," I whispered, swallowing the sudden ball of lust lodged in my throat.

Keeping true to his word, after we'd said good-bye to both our hosts and other guests, I was sitting next to Sam in his car as we headed toward my apartment.

"Tell me the truth, Cin," Sam began without taking his eyes off the road. "When Liz coerced you into bringing me dessert, were you angry at her, me, or yourself?"

"I wasn't angry, more like confused and frustrated. It makes me uncomfortable not knowing the rules, or rather, what's expected of me. It makes me feel like I'm inside a carnival fun house. You know, the ones with those weird mirrors. It's like I see this lifestyle one way, but when I turn, it's all morphed into something unrecognizable, and I have to adjust my way of thinking all over again. I can't figure out which reflection is the real Cin or if any of them are me while the floor pitches and rolls beneath my feet. I feel like I'm going to be knocked on my ass any second."

"What if all of the reflections *are* the real you?"

"They can't be."

"Why not? You're not a one-dimensional woman. Not by a long shot."

"No, I'm not. But I'm not the squatty, rippling, twisted kind of woman you think I am, either."

"This has nothing to do with what I think you are, but what I hope you'll eventually see inside yourself. But until you're willing to strip away your perception of propriety, you'll only see yourself as you want others to view you."

I snorted, then frowned. "And how am I supposed to break free? I'm comfortable acting like a lady. That's the mold that suits me."

Sam grinned. "What makes you think finding your submission isn't ladylike? All I'm saying is, you're a grown woman. The only person you have to please is yourself."

"I know, and I do," I replied defensively.

"Then allow yourself to experience something other than what's expected."

"Do you have any idea how my parents would react if they—"

"Your parents? What do they have to do with this? Unless you plan to tell them you're a sub."

"Of course not. Are you insane?"

"Not according to Tony." Sam chuckled.

"Wait. You're a patient of Tony's?"

"No," Sam laughed. "Though I'm sure you think I should be. He and I are involved with a group of physicians who donate time to help out at a couple of inner-city clinics. It gives the overworked staff some much-needed time off. I've been picking up a couple extra shifts over the past few weeks for some of the doctors who've been unable to help out."

"I wasn't suggesting you seeing Tony was a negative thing. So, you've been helping inner-city patients and not dissing me for Destiny these past few weeks?"

"So that's what you thought I was doing. Oh, Cin," he tsked.

"Well...yes. I mean, it seemed like you were trying to work me in, and I...I thought it was because of her."

"We really need to work on our communication skills, sweetheart. Why didn't you talk to me about your feelings?"

"I didn't think I had to."

"Of course you do. I can't very well read your mind, can I?" Sam's exasperated tone filled me with guilt. I'd judged him unfairly.

"No, you can't. But why didn't you tell me you were doing charity work and that we'd get together whenever you were free?"

His face fell. "I didn't realize I needed to. I thought there was a deeper bond of trust between us. These past few days have shown me that I was wrong."

I felt as if he'd kicked me in the gut.

"I didn't say that to make you feel bad, Cin. Don't run off behind your walls now and undo all the progress we've made these past two days."

"What progress? I'm still on the fence about all this BDSM stuff."

"Progress in being truthful. I don't have to hide who I am from you anymore, and you've shared your secrets with me, too. I get why trust is so damn hard and why you're so damn determined to strive for success and perfection. I've learned more about you in a couple of days than I have in the past three months. But one thing I've learned for certain is that I was right...there *is* a submissive hiding inside you. And I aim to set her free."

I rolled my eyes and shook my head, still unwilling to buy his claim.

"Like I told you before...you can deny it all you want, but we both know it's the truth. And every time you try and deny the truth, I'm going to remind you of the bondage table." A flicker of delight danced across his face.

"Hold on. Don't go putting the cart before the horse. You may think I'm a submissive, but I'm not even sure I'm all that curious about the lifestyle."

"Oh, but you are. In fact, you're more than curious. You're dying to gain an understanding as to why Liz, Leagh, Mellie, Savannah, Julianna, and all the rest of the subs hand their power over to their Masters."

"Okay, but being curious about how it works for them doesn't mean I want it for myself."

"Semantics, Cin." He flashed me a wicked grin. "Do you want to sit out here and blow smoke up your ass that you're not a sub, or are you going to invite me inside for some sweet, kinky dessert?"

"How kinky?" I asked, nibbling my bottom lip.

"Kinky enough for you to handle, but not so kinky that I'll freak you out."

"Are you going to put me over your knees again and spank my ass?"

"Maybe. Depends on if you need it, or want it. If you stay sweet, you can beg me nice and pretty. If you're sassy...well, you'll be begging...begging me to stop."

"So, you're giving me the choice?"

His brows slashed. "Sweetheart. Like I've been telling you from the start...everything about the lifestyle is for *you* to choose."

"What if I decided no spankings at all?"

Sam leaned in and caressed a finger over my cheek. "Then I'll settle for you begging me to fuck you like an animal instead."

That was a game I wanted to play.

Before Sam could even unbuckle his seat belt, I was out of the car and sprinting toward my apartment. His deep, rich laughter echoed in the night air and chased after me, heating my blood with a surge of demand.

As I fumbled with the lock, Sam slipped in behind me and gripped one hand on my hip. With the other, he brushed my hair off the back of my neck. The warmth of his rugged frame enveloped me long before the hotness of his breath fluttered over my nape. And when he pressed his soft lips against me there, tiny explosions tingled down my spine. I closed my eyes and basked in the sensations erupting through me.

Gripping both my hips, Sam rocked his rigid erection between the cheeks of my ass. My fingers shook, and I inwardly cursed the obstinate key. "Sam," I whimpered in frustration.

"Hmm?" he answered, tracing delicate circles with his tongue on the sensitive spot behind my ear. And with each sensual slide, my body sang while my knees dissolved.

"I want to go inside, but this stupid key. God. I can't wait. I'm two seconds from stripping you naked right here and raping you in front of my neighbors."

A silent chuckle shook his body. I felt him grinning against my flesh. Undaunted by my threat and in no apparent hurry, Sam nibbled and laved up and down my neck. I loved every second of his decadent torment, but I was beyond desperate to get him inside my apartment and deep inside me.

Squirming, I turned to face him, then cupped his face. Pressing my lips to his in a sultry, urgent kiss, I snaked my fingers around his neck and scraped my nails over his nape. Parting my lips, I sucked his slick tongue inside my mouth, showing him exactly what I wanted to do to his cock.

"Get me inside, Sam," I begged breathlessly. "Take me to bed and make me scream until I can't scream anymore."

A low growl rumbled from deep in his chest. He tucked me against his side and urgently shoved the key into the lock. When the door finally opened, he scooped me up into his arms. Sam carried me over the threshold, then kicked the door closed. I clearly saw the desperation in his face before he fused his lips to mine in a fiery kiss.

Thank god, I wasn't the only one hanging by a suffering thread.

The heated friction of his mouth served to heighten the sweet ache between my legs. Only when he'd carried me into my room did Sam break the kiss. I wanted to weep in relief when he set me on my feet and furiously started stripping off my clothes. And as Sam skimmed his lips over every inch of skin he revealed, I closed my eyes and savored the thrill shooting through me. Anticipation spiked. My pussy wept. After he'd peeled off every stitch of my clothing, I opened my eyes. Sam stared at me with a heavy-lidded gaze, drinking in my coffee-colored flesh with a sinful caress. I reached out to unbutton his pants, but Sam gripped my wrists.

"I want you on your knees, taking me into your mouth, and sucking me down your sinful throat, gorgeous." His voice was hoarse and brimmed in need.

As he unfastened his belt and kicked out of his pants, I stared at his ready cock as he fisted himself. The fiery tongue of demand licked up my spine. I couldn't wait to feel his powerful shaft sliding in and out of my mouth and down my throat, to wrap my tongue around his throbbing veins.

Stepping closer, I started to kneel on the floor, but Sam reached out and clasped my arm, keeping me from completing my mission.

"Beg me, Allisinda. Beg me to let you kneel before me and suck my cock, girl."

My heart sputtered, but the blazing inferno coalescing deep in my womb overrode all refusal of his command.

Still watching him stroke his angry shaft, I swallowed tightly before slowly skimming my gaze up his magnificent body. Licking my lips nervously, I opened my mouth.

"Please, Sir…may I suck your glorious cock?"

Though my voice was but a shy whisper, Sam's nostrils flared. His chest expanded and his shaft jerked in his hand. Unguarded pride, awe, and reassurance shimmered in his brilliant blue eyes and nearly stole the breath from my lungs. His response shifted inside me as if the sudden yaw and pitch of tectonic plates slid through me. I'd relinquished my control. Handed him the pieces of my soul no other human had ever possessed. While I expected that realization to obliterate every ounce of desire in me, it didn't. Instead, an overwhelming sense of satisfaction and empowerment lifted my hunger even higher. The chains of conformity snapped and fell away while the want to bring Sam all the pleasure he could endure pumped through my veins.

"On your knees, girl," Sam thundered in a commanding tenor that shook me to the bone.

That was where Sam needed me to be so I could immerse his cock in my mouth. Bathe his sex with the all the emotions I held in my heart and soul for him. To give him all the passion, desire, and love I'd kept trapped inside me.

It was in that one pivotal moment that I realized the need to hand over my surrender far outweighed the need to placate my useless pride.

Gliding to the floor, I positioned myself on my knees. Tilting my head back, I stared up at Sam. He released his cock and cupped my cheek. His touch filled me with an inner silence. The world suddenly felt miniscule, like I'd been drawn into a vortex of perfection, where the only thing that held meaning in my life was Sam.

He stared down at me with a look of unequivocal rapture. Adoration reflected in his crystal-blue eyes, and a sense of peace settled in deep.

"How does it feel to bend to my will, little one?" he asked as he lightly brushed his thumb over my bottom lip. "Do you feel small? Centered?"

"Yes," I whispered, amazed that he could pluck the emotion from me so succinctly. I nuzzled my cheek against his palm.

"Is there an indescribable yearning to please me fluttering madly inside you right now, my beautiful temptress?"

There was, and he knew it before I'd even taken the time to analyze it. "Yes. How did you—"

"Let the desires expanding inside you blossom, girl. I've got you now, and I won't let go."

He bent forward and kissed me with a tenderness that made my heart ache. Then, without a word, he stood and guided his erection to my mouth. I reached up and wrapped my hand around his shaft. A wispy sigh slid from my lips as the heat and throbbing pulse surged over my palm, calling to the primal woman within me.

Parting my lips, I extended my tongue, snaking it over his velvety crest. Sam hissed as my taste buds exploded at his familiar tart flavor. With the tip of his cock, I painted my lips with his clear glossy need, keeping my gaze locked with his. Sam's hungry, heavy-lidded stare sliced me open while the empowerment of bringing him such pleasure melded me together again.

Opening wide, I wrapped my lips around the crown and flicked the tip of my tongue over his most sensitive spot. Sam's stomach muscles rippled. His legs trembled. And when he moaned in approval, cinching a fist in my hair, slivers of pain mixed with pleasure danced over my scalp, meshing with the sweet hum of arousal singing through me. His tangy, musky flavor and the silky texture of his tightly drawn flesh made my universe narrow to nothing but the feel and taste of him on my tongue.

"That's it, my little sparrow, suck me deep...wrap that wicked hot mouth around me and pull me in deeper." He voice was raspy and ragged yet still held a tone of command. It was erotic as hell.

My lips thinned and stretched. The corners of my mouth burned as I worked to devour his invading girth. Sam hissed and gripped my hair tighter before rocking in deeper, helping me imbibe inch after glorious inch. When his flaxen hair tickled my nose, I swirled my tongue over his distended veins, breathing in his virile scent. It was stronger now, and I burrowed in close, growing dizzy on his potent musk.

"Suck me, Allisinda...I need more," Sam growled, impatiently.

Unwilling to wait for me to cede to his demand, he plowed his other hand in my hair and took control. Sam guided my mouth up and down his rigid shaft, setting both the depth and tempo he desired. Wet heat seeped from my folds and my clit pulsed in need. Urged on by the low rumbles of pleasure vibrating in his chest, I doubled my efforts, sucking and licking as he directed my willing mouth over his shaft.

With a harsh roar, Sam pulled away. His reddened cock, swollen, pulsating, and glistening in my saliva, stood poised at my lips. I mourned the loss of his hot length on my tongue. But even more, I missed the overwhelming sense of completeness pleasing him had stirred inside me.

Holding tight to my hair, Sam sucked in several quick and shaky breaths. Then with a barely discernable curse, he jerked my head back and plunged himself back inside my mouth in savage claim. I clasped on to his thighs to steady myself, feeling his muscles flex and bunch with each demanding thrust he pressed past my lips.

Strong.

Virile.

Exacting.

My Sam.

Tossed in the tempest of passion, I greedily sucked and swallowed at his ruthless stabs. Each time he prodded the back of my throat with his blunt crest, I swallowed around him. Sam's hisses and curses sent a naughty thrill to sizzle my blood. I slid my palm up his leg, then flattened my hand over the sculpted planes of his abdomen. The muscles there rippled and quaked, reassuring me that the sexual fury uncoiling inside me was consuming him as well.

"You're so fucking... Dammit, love... I want..." His incoherent words scattered through the air as he pulled from my mouth with an audible pop.

Dragging me to my feet by my hair, Sam cut my yelp of surprise with a potent, soul-stealing kiss. The burn slowly receded from my scalp as he pressed me backward and onto the bed. Parting my thighs with a forceful shove of his knees, Sam tore his mouth from mine and stood. His eyes drank in every curve and line of my body, and a feral smile spread over his lips. He looked wild. Savage. Beastly. And all I wanted was for him to ravish me in every deviant way he desired.

Spreading my legs wider, I sent him a provocative smirk. A ferocious roar pealed from his throat as he flung himself over me. Supporting himself with his arms, Sam caged me in. Tilting his hips, he aligned his cock at my folds as his brows slashed and his face contorted to a look of raw, savage need.

"Tell me what you want, Allisinda…beg me for it. Beg me to fuck you long, hard, and deep." His demand pierced like a knife.

Oh, I would beg him, all right. Beg until the end of time to see him…feel him so uninhibited, abandoned, and free.

"Yes. Oh, god. Yes. Please. Fuck me."

"How bad do you want me? Need and crave the pleasure I want to give you?"

"More than air," I whimpered. "Please, Sam. Just fuck me already."

An evil smile spread over his lips. Dipping his head, he dragged his tongue down my throat, leaving a searing trail of saliva all the way to my nipple. "I can keep you here all night, wet, throbbing, aching for relief. And I can sit right here on the edge of the bed and jack off while you watch."

My eyes grew wide. I sucked in a gasp and shook my head.

"No. I don't want that, either, little one. What *I* want is for you to be a good girl. Convince me that if you don't have my fat cock stretching and filling that tight little pussy of yours in the next ten seconds, you'll lose your mind."

The only response I could muster was a pitiful whimper.

"Give it to me, Allisinda, and I'll soar you to the heavens."

Dipping lower, he opened his mouth and sucked in my tight, crinkled nipple. The air left my lungs in a whoosh as he laved his tongue over my areola before pulling on the peak with spine-bending suction.

"Please. Oh, god, Sam. Please. Please. I need you inside me...fuck me."

"How do you want me to fuck you, baby?" he murmured, holding my nipple clasped between his teeth.

"Fast. Hard. I don't care. Take me any way you want me. Just please... I need you to put out this fire. I can't take it anymore." My voice cracked, and tears of frustration blurred my vision.

With a gasp-inducing tug of my nipple, Sam raised his head and smiled at me. "That's a good girl, indeed. All that sweet desperation I hear in your suffering plea. I know now that if I don't drive inside you this second, you might fall apart on me. Isn't that right?"

I nodded and blinked, wondering what had happened to my sweet, generous Sam. Not that I was complaining. This version of Dr. Samuel Brooks was unbridled. Erotic. And fucking hot as hell.

"Answer me. With your voice," he demanded.

"I will. I swear I will. Help me, Sam. Please."

He released an animalistic roar as he slammed his cock fully inside me. He bent and covered my mouth with his, swallowing down my cries of pleasure-pain as he stretched and packed himself deep inside my tight, wet passage. A sublime burn consumed me as my cunt clutched and sucked, desperate to accept him. But it seemed the more I tried to relax, the worse the pain became. Twisting from his mouth, I screamed a curse and tried to inch back and escape his invasion.

"Easy, baby. Breathe," Sam whispered, as he pulled free from my passage.

Sliding his thumb over my clit, he circled the aching nub. And as he began threading himself back inside me, my thick, slick juices seeped around him and anointed his fat cock. I issued a blissful moan. With a slow, torturous glide Sam finally seated himself inside me, then moved his hips with long, deliberate strokes while my pussy gripped and sucked at his shaft.

Sam cursed as he pressed past my quivering tissues, working himself back and forth until he was driving in and out of me with reckless, raw abandon.

Needful whimpers rolled off my lips.

"That's it, sweetheart. Let me make it all better for you."

As if the flames he'd kindled weren't hot enough, his whiskey-smooth whisper nearly had me coming undone.

"Grab hold of the bars of the headboard. Don't let go," Sam panted. "Bind yourself for me, Allisinda."

It took a moment for his command to fracture the sexual fog coating my brain. Sam wasn't going to pin my arms above my head like he usually did. No, this time he wanted *me* to symbolically tie myself to the bed for him. A shudder of excitement and dread rippled through me. The mental rope he wanted to bind me with felt almost as frightening as actual knots.

Sam held my gaze, waiting…watching. He knew the level of turmoil pinging inside me.

"Grab hold of the brass bars, Allisinda. Don't try to analyze it, just do what feels right…for me, baby."

Punched with an overwhelming need to please him, I still couldn't find the courage to bind myself. When I hesitated, Sam pinched my clit between his finger and thumb. Crying out, I bucked beneath him.

"I can keep you here all night…just like this. Suspended in need."

Yes. He could, and would, too.

As if to further prove that point, Sam gripped my legs, then looped my knees over his forearms and lifted my ass off the bed.

Driving his cock in deeper, his blunt crest dragged over my g-spot. Demand surged in a blast of white light. With our gazes locked, I felt him dissecting me as he withdrew himself to the outer folds of my cunt.

"Give me more of your surrender, baby," he whispered before plowing deep and fast.

Sam made it clear he intended to claim and own the breath in my lungs, the blood in my veins, and the very essence of my soul.

The friction increased with each feral stab, as did my demand to unravel. But I wasn't naïve enough to think he'd let me escape that easily. I knew my release would be hard-won, and even more arduous if I didn't yield to him once more.

Fully seated inside me, Sam suddenly froze. The lines in his forehead softened as he leaned forward and feathered his warm, satiny lips over mine. With a gentle sweep, he stroked his tongue along the seam of my mouth. I could almost taste his bittersweet appeal.

"Trust me, sweetheart," he fervently whispered before sliding from inside me and climbing off the bed.

"No. Wait. Where are you—"

Sam turned and pressed a finger to his lips, then made his way toward my dresser.

His cock glistened, and it was then I realized that he had taken me bareback, once again. There was some deeper significance in that fact than simply forgetting, but as he reached up and snagged the maroon scarf off my mirror, panic consumed all semblance of logic.

Returning to the bed, Sam skimmed the cold silk up my belly. A placid smile lifted the corners of his mouth as he danced the soft fabric over my breasts. "Raise your arms, my little sparrow."

"I-I can't," I stuttered.

"Your safe word is still red." Compassion was written all over his face.

Though he offered me a lifeline, a way out if I couldn't hang, I needed to regain that all-encompassing drive to please him. Needed to wrap myself in that surety and regain a sense of empowerment once again.

Squeezing my eyes shut, I slowly raised my arms and gripped the cold spindles of the brass headboard. Holding my breath, I lay as stiff as a corpse while I waited for Sam to tie me up. Instead, he simply draped the fabric over my wrists. I expelled a sigh of relief and relaxed as he dragged his fingertips down my arms, over the hollow of my throat, and farther down, stopping at my aching pussy.

"Are you still with me, sweetheart?" he whispered.

"Yes."

"Yes, what?"

"Yes, Sir," I murmured.

"Very nice."

Without another word, he positioned himself between my thighs once more and lifted my legs over his arms before inching back inside me. I tried to focus on his slow, driving rhythm, but my mind kept drifting to the band of silk decorating my wrists. Turning my head, I glanced up at the blood-red fabric wishing he'd actually bound me to the brass bars. The notion stunned me. I closed my eyes and shoved the thought from my mind.

"There's no rush, sweetheart. For now, all I want you to focus on is the soft silk wrapped around your wrists. Feel how the heat of your body bleeds into the fabric. That's exactly how your submission will flow into you. It will simply start to melt into your heart, mind, body, and soul, until it consumes every single cell in your body."

I wanted to call him a liar. Protest that his claims were nothing more than fantasy. But I'd already tasted his esoteric Dominance. Felt the intrigue of the silk scarf on my flesh. I could no longer hide in fear of his command, not when it conjured such thrilling sensations inside me.

Like a butterfly crawling out of my chrysalis, I let my wings unfurl and allowed myself to sip the freedom Sam promised awaited in this new world.

CHAPTER EIGHT

Sam seesawed into me, dragging his wide crest over my eager nerve endings as if he were trying to steal my soul. I gripped the headboard tighter, searching for an anchor of self-control. But it was useless. He swept my will away...exactly how he'd aimed to.

"Your cunt feels like heaven...like pure liquid silk. So fucking tight, hot, and slick. I could stay inside you like this forever," he panted.

The strain on his face and the rivulets of sweat trickling down his forehead proved I wasn't the only one struggling to stave off the inevitable. As my keening cries filled the room, Sam sucked in a sharp breath.

I prayed he'd command me to come, because either way, I was going to explode in a matter of seconds.

"Are you suffering for me, Allisinda?" He whispered my name like a prayer.

"Yes. Oh, god. I can't... I'm going to—"

"Sail, Allisinda. Come hard. Come. Now," he panted with a

choppy growl.

Slammed beneath his annihilating splendor, my body bowed. My limbs grew rigid. The muscles of my tunnel contracted, clasping at his cock as a flurry of sturdy pulses rippled through me. Every bone in my body turned to white-hot liquid as waves of convulsions tore through me.

"Mine," Sam roared. Slamming into me one last time, he stilled and gripped my thighs.

Tossing back his head, he cried out my name as his hot seed jettisoned deep in my womb.

Long minutes later, when our ragged breathing settled and the twitching aftershocks subsided, Sam released my thighs, then slowly eased from inside me. My legs, heavy and boneless, landed together on the mattress like felled sequoias. With a chuckle, he wrapped an arm around me and flopped onto the bed, dragging me with him. We lay spooning with his steely arm banded around my waist while I snuggled against his hot, sweaty body, sated and purring.

"I know that's right," Sam murmured in a low, satisfied tone. "I don't think I'll ever get my fill of you."

"That's good, because I don't want the magic we make to ever end."

"Magic, huh?"

"Oh, yeah…and then some."

"Careful. You might make my overinflated doctor ego grow even bigger," he teased.

"Smartass."

"Smartass?" Sam's voice rose in feigned offense. Without warning, he flipped me onto my back and straddled me. "I'll give you a red ass, little one, if you don't watch your mouth."

I rolled my eyes. "Seriously? You've never been offended by

my gutter mouth before."

"I have," he quickly assured. "I simply haven't scolded you for it...until now."

"What?" I gasped. Before I could blink, he hoisted me over his lap with my ass poised in the air. "Wait. You're going to spank me because I said smartass?"

"Yes. And you're going to get an extra one for saying it a second time."

"Oh, no, you're not." I struggled and squirmed and twisted until I could see his face. A flicker of laughter danced in his eyes. "You're just messing with me, aren't you?"

Sam didn't answer, simply drew back his hand and slapped my ass.

"Goddammit. Stop," I screamed.

"Keep cursing, sparrow. I can mete out as many of these as you need."

"Okay. Okay," I screamed, still trying to process exactly how saying one word got me into this embarrassing and erotic position. "I get the point. I'll watch my mouth."

"Pity," he stated in remorse. "I enjoy turning your pretty ass red, sweetheart."

"You might, but I don't," I groused as he lifted his arm. I kneeled up and shot him a scowl.

"Oh, don't give me that look. You like it. You just won't relax and enjoy the sweet burn, that's all."

I knew he suspected that I enjoyed some of the kinky things he did to me, but he didn't have to be so smug. Of course, if I challenged him about it, he'd probably unleash something I wouldn't find fun at all. I kept my lips zipped.

"Though I do enjoy watching that inner struggle, you wrestle flash through your eyes. It's really quite beautiful."

I pinned him with a gaze meant to flash-fry him, but Sam merely laughed.

"I'm glad you find my battle so amusing," I drawled, flashing him a humorless smirk.

His expression turned somber as he hauled me up and into his arms. "I know this is all new and scary for you, and I'm not trying to make light of your turmoil. I'm just happy that you're willing to look past the confines of protocol and realize that a good Dom/sub relationship is filled with fun and laughter, too."

"But I'm not a s—"

"Yes, you are. The term, or rather your interpretation of it, is what's got you spooked."

When I opened my mouth, Sam settled his lips over mine. He had plans for my tongue other than the rebuttal poised on its tip. Like, tangling with mine to surge in the hot slickness. Rolling his thumbs and fingers over the peaks of my nipples, Sam swallowed my moans as he set fire to the insatiable blaze he so easily ignited inside me.

"Tell me you want me to spend the night," he murmured as he left a tingling trail down my neck with his tongue.

"I want you to spend the night," I moaned, while he inched lower still and sucked my aching nipple between his lips.

~

Sam's cock was still inside me, soft and slick, when my alarm went off. Sliding free from me, he groaned as I silenced the annoying buzzer.

"What time is it?" he asked in a raspy voice thick with sleep.

"Five fifteen," I groaned.

"Wanna call in sick and play hooky again today?" A wicked grin tugged his lips.

"I can't. I'll have to have a doctor's note to give to HR if I'm out two days in a row."

Sam chuckled. "Oh, baby. I'd be more than happy to write a note for you."

"Uh-huh," I scoffed. "And just what medical reason would you give for my absence?"

"That's easy. You're suffering from docnotdone syndrome."

"What in the world is docnotdone syndrome?" I asked as he looped his arm around my waist to drag me back against his hard body.

"It means this doc's not done ravishing your sexy body." He grinned. I couldn't help but laugh. Sam's tone took on a more clinical edge as he continued. "The most common symptoms are a growing ache, accompanied with a throbbing sensation, right here."

He circled my wrist and drew my hand to his thick erection.

"Oh, my. Yes. I can actually feel your suffering from the same syndrome, Doctor." I peered up at him, sliding on my most professional expression. "I must say; your symptoms are quite impressive, indeed."

"Why, thank you, Nurse Noland. But I must warn you that docnotdone syndrome is highly contagious." Reaching down, Sam parted my folds, coating his fingers in my slick cream before shaking his head grimly. "Just as I suspected. You've contracted it, too. I'll need to take a better look so I can see how advanced your syndrome has become."

I quivered as his warm breath wafted over my wet cunt. "With all your worldly knowledge and medical expertise, you've discovered a cure, right?" I gasped as he spread my legs wider and flicked his tongue over my clit.

"Yes. I have. It requires a special instrument in order to cure this disease. Lucky for you, I happen to carry that unique implement with me at all times." Fisting his cock, Sam shot me a mischievous grin. "Don't let the size of my cure scare you, sweetheart."

I giggled, then quickly sobered, skimming my gaze down his naked body as he slowly stroked his fist up and down his cock. As a clear bead blossomed on his wide crest, my backup alarm on my phone began to chime. Biting back a curse, I stretched my arm to the nightstand and silenced the device.

"You're going to make me late for work if I don't get moving." I sighed regretfully.

"Surely, being a medical professional, you know you can't leave. If I don't cure you right now, Miss Noland, why, you might spread this disease to everyone. We don't want that, do we?"

Flashing him a sly smile, I sat up. "Can you use your special instrument on me in the shower, Doc?"

He pondered my question for a couple of seconds, then nodded. "Yes, but you'll need multiple doses of the cure…say, at my place again tonight after work?"

I licked my lips. "Are you planning on feeding me, too?"

A lusty fire danced in his eyes. "I'll fill you up with every fucking inch," he growled.

My nipples tightened further as a rush of need sang up my spine. "Deal."

"Let's hurry and get you into the shower, so I can administer your first treatment."

With a laugh, I jumped off the bed and scurried into the bathroom. Sam was right behind me. Once inside the shower, he pinned me up against the wall and stole my breath with a sultry kiss.

"Turn around and place your hands on the tile, Miss Noland. I'll be as gentle as I can," Sam assured.

When I burst out laughing, he shot me a quizzical look. "I'm sorry. I don't mean to laugh at you, Doctor, but that's quite an oxymoron considering you're a damn Dom and like inflicting pain."

A wry smile tugged his lips as he turned me to face the tiled wall. "No. I like pushing a sub's limits," he amended before landing a stinging wet slap across my ass.

"Ouch," I yelped, rising up on my toes.

Sam moved in close behind me. "Spread your legs for me, Allisinda. I'm done playing games," he whispered against my ear in a feral tone.

Though I was being pelted with hot water, an even more encompassing heat blossomed beneath my skin when Sam inched himself into my core. Our grunts and whimpers melded with the sound of wet, slapping flesh as Sam took me to paradise.

Forty minutes later, we were dressed and heading out the door. Sam walked me to my car, kissed me good-bye, and promised to drop in on me during my shift. As I weaved my way through traffic, I realized I still hadn't questioned his recent lack of condoms.

"Is it any wonder? Each time he touches you, he steals the thoughts from your brain," I mumbled out loud with a snort.

Arriving at the hospital, I hurried through the double doors. As I studied the patient load on the dry erase board, Metcalf sauntered by.

"Good morning, Doctor," I stated with a chipper voice as I glanced at the watch on my wrist. Okay, so it was an infantile poke, but I wanted to be sure the little twit noticed I was twenty minutes early for my shift.

"Noland," he replied in a crisp, clipped tone.

Great. His cantankerous mood had returned. It wasn't going to be a rainbow-and-unicorn day in the ER, but then it never really was.

Liz strolled in a couple minutes before seven, looking unusually haggard. "Morning," she stated tiredly.

"What happened to you?" I asked, handing her the cup of coffee I'd just poured. She obviously needed it worse than I did.

"Thank you." She took a long gulp and moaned. "It was a long night."

"Aw, you poor baby," I ribbed with a chuckle.

"No, not that kind of long night."

"What happened?"

"Mika called around midnight and asked if we could come stay with Tristan so he and Julianna could go over and help Drake with Trevor. We didn't end up getting back home and to bed until three thirty this morning."

"What's wrong with Trevor?"

Liz's shoulders sagged. "He's not doing well…mentally. They called Tony, too, and between the four of them, they got Trevor settled down, but it wasn't easy this time."

The news broke my heart. I remembered how happy he'd seemed yesterday, especially while sitting on the deck reading to Tristan.

"If anyone can help him, Tony can," I assured her with a sympathetic smile.

"That's just it. Tony's worried, too. And Drake…well, Drake's sick and tired of pumping antidepressants down Trevor's throat and still waking up two or three times a night because of the nightmares." Liz's eyes filled with tears. "I'm scared to death that they're going to have to commit Trevor to a psychiatric facility if they can't help him work past this."

"Oh, honey. No." I plucked the Styrofoam cup from her hand, set it on the counter, and wrapped her in a tight hug. "They'll find a way to reach him. My god, so many people think the world of Trevor. With all the love and support that man has in his corner, he'll find his way out of the darkness. He has to."

"I hope so." Liz sniffed as she pulled back and wiped the tears from her cheeks.

"Honey, you need to go back home and get some sleep. I can call in a cover nurse for you."

"No, I can't." She shook her head. "Ian and James just dropped me off. They're headed across town to meet with a new client. I'm stuck here for the duration."

"Pile up on the sixty-four and Kennedy Expressway. We've got incoming," Dixie, a fellow trauma nurse, announced as she rushed from the communications office. "ETA, ten minutes and counting."

"Let the games begin," Liz drawled before downing the entire cup of coffee.

With the trauma rooms filled to capacity, the morning flew by in a blur. Though she still looked like hell, Liz kept pace with the rest of us as we raced around like Walmart shoppers on Black Friday.

By the time the patients from the multicar accident had been divvied up between surgery, ICU, and rooms upstairs, my feet were screaming and my stomach was growling. Snagging Liz, I hauled her down to the cafeteria with me so we could grab some lunch. I wanted to make sure she ate a good meal and spent some time off her feet.

The cafeteria was practically deserted, which afforded us some privacy to talk. But when Liz slumped against the seat of the booth and closed her eyes, I didn't have the heart to bring up the lifestyle. I tucked my questions away for another time.

"Are you sure you don't want me to drive you home before you fall asleep right there?"

"No," she answered sleepily. "I can hang for the rest of my shift, but if Ian and James think they're getting lucky tonight, they're going to get a big surprise."

I chuckled. "They'll probably be snoring before your head hits the pillow."

"Mmm. Tonight? I sure hope so," she mumbled before sitting up and scrubbing a hand over her face.

Staring at my bowl of soup, I wrinkled my nose.

"What's wrong? Aren't you hungry?"

"I was until now," I replied. "Maybe I really do have a touch of the flu. I thought it was just nerves that made me sick yesterday."

"Maybe you're pregnant," Liz teased before taking a bite of her sandwich.

My eyes flashed open wide. "Shut your mouth. I am *not* pregnant."

"The pill doesn't always work, you know," she teased.

"Mine does," I vowed, flashing her a scowl. I didn't find her the least bit amusing.

"What? You don't like kids?"

"I love them, as long as they're someone else's."

"Aw, come on. You and Sam would make beautiful babies," she said with a giggle.

"I'm going to cram that sandwich down your throat if you don't shut up," I growled.

"Sounds like a waste of a good sandwich to me." Sam chuckled, appearing seemingly out of nowhere. "Why are you threatening Liz, sweetheart?"

"Because I was teasing her about being pregnant," she blurted.

Sam paled before darting a look of absolute horror my way. "You're—"

"No." I shook my head. "Liz is trying to be funny, but she's not."

"Oh," Sam replied, visibly relieved. "Well, then. How are you two doing today?"

"Fine," Liz and I replied in unison.

Sam sidled in beside me, then plucked up my spoon and began to stir my soup. "I peeked in on you earlier, but you and Metcalf were holding some dude's spleen together. I figured it wasn't the best time to chat."

"Yeah, we tucked it back inside him before rushing him up to surgery."

As Sam extended a spoon of tomato-based broth and mixed vegetables toward my mouth, my stomach swirled. I inched back, pinched my lips together, and shook my head. "No. I'm okay."

"But you haven't even taken a bite yet, have you?" Sam slid the spoon back into the bowl, then raised his hand to my forehead. "No fever."

"She's pregnant," Liz repeated in a conspiratorial whisper.

"Stop saying that," I hissed.

Sam pinned me with a concerned stare. "You haven't missed any of your birth control pills, have you?"

"No," I replied in exasperation while Liz grinned mischievously. "She's pulling my chain and causing trouble. Maybe I need to give Ian and James a call and tell them to keep her up all night, spanking her ass."

The twinkle in her eyes vanished. Liz held up her hands. "No. Don't. I'll stop. I swear."

It was my turn to laugh. "Oh, this is going to be fun. Every time you give me shit, I'll just threaten to tattle on you. That will keep you in line."

"Two can play that game, you brat," Liz quipped arching her brows at Sam.

"Truce," I offered.

"You bet." Liz laughed.

Sam chortled. "Look, I need to run. Isaac wants me in his office in a couple minutes. We're still on after work, right?"

A sly smile curled my lips, as I was anxious for Sam to administer his special "treatment" again. "You bet. I can't wait to be cured," I teased.

"Actually, it takes years before you're fully cured, little one." He winked, brushed a kiss on my lips, then stood. "I'll meet you by your locker at seven."

As he turned to walk away, anticipation skittered up my spine.

"Do I even want to know what kind of treatment Sam's going to give you?" Liz smirked before downing the last of her soda.

"If I'm lucky, the full kind." I grinned.

"Good thing you're off work tomorrow. By the look in Sam's eyes, you might not be able to crawl out of bed, let alone walk."

"God, I hope so," I said with a laugh.

After dumping our food trays, Liz and I ambled toward the ER, poking fun at each other's sex lives, or rather, the irony that we both actually *had* sex lives now. Rounding the corner, I bumped chest-first into the hospital's executive director, Dr. Isaac. Yelping in surprise, I stumbled back as he grabbed my arm. Darting a look to the man next to Isaac, my heart all but stopped. Fear swarmed me from all sides, and black dots trailed behind my eyes.

Darnell? What the fuck was that son of a bitch doing in Chicago? In my hospital?

"Ah, Nurse Noland. I'd like to introduce you to our new head of neurology. Dr. Darnell—"

"Darnell Willingham Edmonton the third," I finished in a haughty, pretentious tone.

Liz sucked in an audible gasp.

Isaac blinked. "You two know each other?"

"Unfortunately, yes," I replied with a sickeningly sweet smile.

Darnell chuckled as if he found my reply amusing. "Now, now, Allisinda."

Hearing him say my given name felt as if I'd been sliced open with a knife and doused in alcohol.

"Such a curt tone isn't becoming for a lady of your breeding. I suggest we keep the past where it belongs, shall we?" Darnell offered with an oily smile.

Breeding? He acted as if I were nothing but a piece of livestock. Of course, to him, that's all I probably was.

"It's good to see you again," he lied. "Your parents miss you." Another lie.

Darnell leaned in as if to kiss my cheek. I took a step back and narrowed my eyes in warning as I raised an open hand. "What are you doing here? Why aren't you in New York?"

A flicker of anger flashed through his eyes before he quickly banked it and slid a plastic smile into place. "I wanted a change. New York is…well, you know."

No, I didn't. But the line he was trying to feed me smelled a lot like bullshit. He was covering his ass. Something had happened in New York. Something bad enough he needed to reestablish himself. But why Chicago, of all places? The only person who could give me the skinny was the last person I wanted to call…my father.

"So, I put some feelers out and viola." Darnell grinned as he tossed open his hands. "The offer from Highland Park was, well, it was far too tempting to resist."

My gut churned and my knees began to tremble.

"You mean you're relocated here...to Chicago?" I asked, nearly choking on the bile rising in the back of my throat.

"Well, I have an apartment until I'm able to find a suitable house for my family."

Family? I wondered which one of his whores he'd knocked up and had to finally marry.

"Unfortunately, my wife, Sha-Sha and newborn daughter, Shanté, won't be able to join me for several months."

"Sha-Sha?" I asked, arching a brow.

"Yes, Shaqueffa, my beautiful wife," Darnell preened.

Shaqueffa? Oh, dear lord, what parent named their child after a vaginal fart? I struggled to fight back a snort.

"They stayed in New York until the sale of our house is final. I expect them to be joining me here soon." A calculated smile spread over his face. "We should get together then. Go out and get dinner, catch up on old times. I'm anxious to meet your husband."

My husband? Oh, what a fucking bastard. He was pushing buttons, trying to rile a reaction from me. I didn't take the bait. Well, I didn't think I had.

"Oh, my. I can tell by the look on your face I've accidently hit a nerve. My apologies to you, dear. I shouldn't have assumed that you'd moved on with your life and had found a suitable husband by now."

The mock sympathy slathering his words made me want to kick him in the balls. A hot, violent rage seethed inside me. The air around us was choked with tension. Poor Isaac's head volleyed from side to side as if watching a tennis match, while his eyes grew exceedingly wider with each barb Darnell and I exchanged.

Suddenly, Liz issued a caustic laugh as she leveled Darnell with an acrid grin. "You obviously don't know Cin as well as you think, Dr. Edmonton. If she accepted the proposal of every man who's asked her to marry, she'd have dozens of husbands. Thankfully, she isn't a low-life, lying maggot capable of adultery. Besides, only a real man could capture such a vibrant and sensual treasure as Cin. Little boys who hoard their toys don't stand a chance in hell. I'm shocked you didn't learn…err, I mean recognize that about Cin, since you two are such good friends and all."

Well done, Liz. I wanted to plant a kiss on my bestie's cheek.

Darting a glance at Dr. Isaac, I noticed the man looked more than shell-shocked. His brows furrowed in concern as he blinked at the saccharine-sweet smile still plastered over Liz's lips. Yet he didn't say a word about the drama unfolding before him. I simply smirked as I watched a combination of fury and embarrassment roll over Darnell's face.

A soft chuckle slid past my lips. And I couldn't help adding a bit more fuel to my ex's internal fire. "Indeed. A woman should never waste her time kissing toads. Not when there are so many fine princes waiting in line for her." The superior tone—one I hadn't used in years—rolled off my tongue with a hauntingly familiar dismissive flare. Christ, I sounded just like my mother.

Darnell struggled to slide a passive expression in place but failed woefully. I softly shook my head at the pitiful excuse of a man, then looped my arm through Liz's.

"Please don't think us rude, Dr. Isaac," I began, looking his way with a placid, well-rehearsed smile. "Liz and I must get back to the unit."

Isaac blinked and nodded as if coming out of some drug-induced coma. "Of course. I didn't mean to keep you ladies so long. I'll bring Dr. Edmonton through the ER shortly so he can meet Dr. Metcalf and the rest of the staff."

"Can't wait," I lied. I inwardly wondered if the unit was big enough to hold both Darnell's and Metcalf's egos at the same time or if Isaac needed to requisition a special wing in order to accommodate them both.

"I look forward to getting the chance to see you working in your *nursing* environment."

As Darnell landed another jab, Liz reached for my hand and gave it a little squeeze before pulling me past the two men and down the hall. Bile rose in the back of my throat again and as the ladies' room came into view, I tore from Liz's hand, pushed past the portal, and raced into the first stall.

"Shit," Liz mumbled, standing behind me.

Pressing my palms on the cool metal dividers, I bent at the waist and began to dry heave. Tears of anger and embarrassment streamed down my face as my stomach continued to spasm.

"Oh, Cin," Liz cooed as she smoothed the hair back from my face. "Don't let that pretentious piece of shit do this to you."

"It's not him. Fuck him," I assured, spitting the bitter taste out of my mouth. "My stomach's been off for a couple days."

"Then maybe *you* should go home, in case you do have a flu bug," she suggested.

"No way. I don't have a fever, and I will be present and accounted for on the unit when Darnell comes through the ER. I refuse to let him think he got the best of me."

"Pride get in your way much?" Liz drawled, arching her brows.

"Only when it comes to that asshat, because my pride is all I have left when it comes to him."

"Bullshit," Liz challenged as she wet a paper towel in cold water and handed it to me. "You have way more than that idiot will ever have. Like a heart, for starters."

After I pulled myself together, Liz and I rushed back to the unit. As we made our way through the double doors, I spied Sam talking to Monica, the hospital social worker. Slowing down, I paused as Sam began to speak.

"Mrs. Wiggins is finally ready to file abuse charges against her husband. She's here again because she told him she was pregnant again. Like the sorry sack of… Like he didn't have anything to do with it." Sam shook his head. Anger marred his features. "The police are en route, but I'd like for both of us to be with her when they get here."

Monica tsked. "That poor woman. Of course I will. You never need to ask, Dr. Brooks. I'll go sit with her now, in fact."

My heart ached for Sam's patient. We shared the silent understanding that part of our time together tonight would be spent helping Sam purge the anger he had to keep bottled up inside him right now. It was one of the ways we complemented each other…let off steam, and processed the stress. I sent him a reassuring wink before I started to step around him. Monica darted off the other way while Sam snagged my arm.

"I need to talk to you about something," he stated in a somber tone.

"I'll be right back. I just need to clock in from lunch," I replied.

As I hurried toward the locker room, Liz came breezing toward me from the opposite direction. "You need to tell Sam that Darnell is being hired here."

"I know. I'll tell him tonight."

"Good." She nodded, then leaned in close with a sassy smirk.

"We don't want you getting a spanking, now do we?"

"Brat," I scoffed as she scurried away.

After locking up my purse, I hit the time clock, then spun toward the door. Sam leaned against the frame, assuming the posture he'd worn two nights ago. A hint of remorse flickered in his eyes. My blood began to chill and my pulse quickened. Something was definitely wrong.

"Are you here to break our date tonight, Doctor?" I forced levity that I didn't feel into my tone.

"No." He shook his head. "But I do have to tell you something that you won't want to hear."

I swallowed tightly and nodded. "Go on."

Willing back the tears that stung my eyes, I began steeling myself for heartbreak. My guts roiled, threatening to purge once more. My head told me Sam had come to realize he needed a true submissive and this was the end.

As he pushed off the doorjamb and made his way toward me, my chin quivered. I clenched my teeth together and tried to keep from falling apart. His eyes searched mine as a frown lined his face.

"What's wrong?"

"I—I'm sorry. I know you think I didn't try, but…maybe I really didn't… I don't know. I thought I might be able to be what you wanted, but—"

Confusion wrinkled his brow. "Stop. What in the hell are you talking about?"

"You're breaking up with me because I'm not submissive, right?"

Thunderclouds rolled across his face as his lips thinned in a tight line. Scowling, he gripped my shoulders and pressed my back up against the wall, holding me in place with his wide chest.

"No," he barked. "Dammit, Cin. When are you going to get it through your thick skull that I'm never letting you go? Why is it you automatically rush to the worst-case scenario? Just because I have something serious to talk to you about doesn't mean I'm giving up on you. Do I make myself clear, girl?"

His commanding Dominant tone set me on fire. His imposing timbre nearly took me out at the knees.

"Yes."

"Yes, what?" he pressed.

"Yes, Sir," I whispered.

"Good girl."

The pride suffused in those two words kindled a sense of success within me. I felt as if I'd achieved something monumental. Goosebumps skipped over my flesh, and I couldn't keep from smiling.

"You're one hell of a complicated little sparrow, you know that?" Sam smirked, then quickly sobered. Scanning the room to ensure we were truly alone, he pressed a hungry kiss to my lips.

I whimpered and wiggled out of his grasp enough to throw my arms around his neck and give back the same passionate kiss as he gave.

"Oh, lord. Don't tell me you've lowered your standards to such a level that you're banging all the interns now, Allisinda."

Darnell's condescending tone showered me in a blast of ice water. I jerked from Sam's lips. My face blazed in anger and embarrassment as I peered over his shoulder. Both Darnell and Isaac stood in the portal, my ex wearing a smarmy smile, the hospital director staring in shock with his mouth agape.

Every muscle in Sam's body turned to marble. His nostrils flared and his jaw ticked in anger. Slowly, he turned, and I watched as he stormed across the room and clutched Darnell's shirt and part of his suit jacket in one beefy fist.

"As you can plainly see, I'm not an intern, Edmonton. I'm Allisinda's lover, protector, companion, and friend. You have nothing, and I mean absolutely nothing, to say to her ever again. You gave up the right to concern yourself with any part of her life a long, long time ago."

Darnell's eyes blazed in hatred.

"Dr. Brooks, you need to take your hands off Dr. Edmonton this instant," Isaac demanded.

"No," Sam replied in an arctic tone. "You need to do your homework on this low-life piece of shit, Isaac."

"Shut the fuck up," Darnell erupted.

"Oh?" Sam taunted. "What's wrong, Edmonton? Afraid you'll be found out before the ink's dried on your contract here?"

"What are you insinuating, Brooks?" Isaac countered.

"I called the renowned neurosurgeon Nathan Noland. Father of our esteemed ER head nurse, Allisinda Noland, and personal friend of old Darnell here."

I sucked in a gasp as the room began to spin. Sam had spoken to my father…about Darnell? My knees turned to rubber, and I plopped down on the wooden bench by my locker.

"You just had to stick your nose in someplace it didn't belong, didn't you?" Darnell spat.

"I think we need to take this conversation somewhere private," Isaac suggested. "Like my office."

"No," I blurted out as I stood. "I need to know what's going on. If this concerns my father, I have the right to know."

Sam released Darnell with a little shove, then turned and smiled at me. "I'll fill you in on all the details soon, sweetheart. You go on back to the unit. They need you there far more than this sack of shit will ever need you."

"Come on, Edmonton. I think we need to have a more in-depth discussion."

"You prick," Darnell spat at Sam. As he turned his venomous gaze on me, his lips curled in a feral snarl. "I'll take care of your big mouth soon, Allisinda."

Sam let out a roar as he gripped Darnell by the neck. "You so much as breathe another word to her? And I'll hunt you down, make you wish you'd never been born."

"Gentlemen. Gentlemen. Please," Isaac intervened, prying Sam's hands off Darnell. "My office. Now."

The man barked out the order like a Dominant. I almost laughed. Instead, I sat staring at the three men in stunned silence as they turned and stormed out of the room.

I took a couple deep breaths and pulled myself together, then hurried back to the unit. Liz's eyes were as big as saucers. "What the hell is going on? I just saw Sam and—"

"I don't know. But Sam... Shit, he called my dad."

"He what? Why? Wait...did you tell him about..."

"Yes, I did."

"Whoa, damn. That's huge for you, Cin." Liz smiled.

"Sam means a lot to me, and I guess I mean a lot to him, too. I think that's why he called Dad, so he could find out why Darnell isn't working in New York anymore."

"So did you get an answer to that yet?"

"No." I sighed exasperatedly. "They were talking all cryptically and shit. Like they both knew the truth but didn't spill the beans. Whatever Darnell is trying to hide, it must be big."

"Oh, girl. When you find out, you'd better let me know ASAP, 'cause I have a feeling this is one juicy story," Liz predicted with a giggle.

"I think you're right. Maybe he slipped and his dick landed in a patient." I snorted.

Liz let out a loud belly laugh just as Jeb and Freddy burst through the doors pushing a man on a gurney, covered in blood.

"Well, hell," Liz mumbled. "I was hoping we could sneak up to Isaac's office and listen through the door."

"You're a mess," I laughed. "Come on. Let's see what meals on wheels brought us now."

And let's just hope they don't blow our little BDSM secret to the rest of the staff.

CHAPTER NINE

As I approached the pair of EMTs, my knees trembled. Still, I held my head high, projecting self-assurance. Neither Jeb nor Freddy let on that our paths had crossed at Genesis. They acted as they always did—cordial and professional. I exhaled an inward sigh of relief.

Focused on the patient, I watched Liz begin taking vitals while Metcalf surveyed the young man's injuries. I keyed information Jeb read from the run sheet into my tablet. A rival gang had shot the seventeen-year-old male in the street, like a dog. Four bullet wounds riddled the boy's body, but by some miracle, his numbers were strong. Metcalf barked out orders, like he always did, and in a matter of minutes, the patient was wheeled up to surgery.

With another crisis under control, I sipped a cup of coffee and stared at the door, as if I could will Sam's return. When two uniformed officers entered the unit, I directed them to Sam's patient, the beaten, pregnant woman in trauma three. I started to pull out my cell and send Sam a text when he sailed through the double doors.

His expression was grim, but he shot me a quick wink as he strode by. My head knew he needed to be with the frightened woman, but my patience was running thin. I was tired of being in the dark in regard to Darnell. I wanted answers...starting with why Sam had phoned my father, of all people. And wouldn't I have loved being a fly on the wall during *that* conversation. Had he told my father that we were dating? Probably not. My mother would have been burning up my cell phone. She'd either want to praise me for snagging a successful surgeon or chastise me for some unrelated and unacceptable failing.

Ugh. I didn't want to participate in any conversation with her. With a heavy sigh, I made my way to the nurses' station to start updating charts. My mind was heavy with questions, and I struggled to focus on my task. When a mother brought in her screaming toddler—with a high fever and wicked ear infection—I was almost relieved. At least I had something to focus on other than the myriad of questions clouding my brain.

After dropping off the toddler's discharge papers, I caught sight of Sam's familiar gait, his broad shoulders, and blond hair as he raced from the unit. As I sprinted toward the double doors, I saw the officers and Monica, who had her arm draped around a visibly battered woman, leaving the trauma room. Rushing out to find Sam, I spotted him waiting by the elevator.

"Sam! Wait up."

"I'm sorry, Cin," he began as the doors opened. He held up his hand, preempting the barrage of questions perched on the tip of my tongue. "I have an emergency surgery. I'll fill you in on the other topic tonight. I promise."

Before I could respond, the doors closed, and Sam was gone. "No. It's not all right, dammit," I grumbled at my reflection in the shiny metal. "Shit."

As I turned to head back to the unit, the phone in my pocket buzzed.

Yanking the device from my scrubs without checking the caller ID, I pressed the phone to my ear. "Yeah, you'd better not fucking leave me hanging like that, mister…or you'll have a tiger on your ass tonight," I spat.

"Have you lost your mind, Allisinda? Your vulgar language is wholly unacceptable, young lady. Where in god's name is your pride?" My mother's incensed and arrogant tone made me cringe.

Shit.

Shit.

Shit.

"My deepest apologies, Mother. I thought you were someone else," I explained, wishing I'd taken the time to see who was calling.

"Which makes your tawdry, uncouth verbiage even more inappropriate. What kind of gutter-snipe trash are you associating with that makes such repugnant words suitable?"

Hookers, pimps, and drug lords, of course. I pinched my lips together to keep from spewing that reply. "Did you need something, Mother?"

My question was met with several long seconds of silence and finally an angry huff.

"Is extending a pleasant tone to your own mother too difficult for you, Allisinda?"

I knew where this conversation was headed, and it wasn't good. "I'm sorry, Mother, but I can't talk right now. I'm at work. If you'd like to call me later tonight, we can discuss my offensive phone etiquette or whatever else you'd like."

"Allisinda," she snapped. "What is your—"

"Sorry. EMTs are coming through the door with a patient. I have to go. Bye."

Disconnecting the call, I shoved my phone back in my pocket with a bitter sigh. I could have eventually wheedled the information I wanted about my ex from Mother. But I didn't have the stomach to endure her crippling litany of my ineptness before arriving at the topic of Darnell. Just one of the many reasons I refused to be anything like my mother.

When my shift was over, I clocked out, grabbed my purse, and waited an extra ten minutes for Sam to show. When he didn't, I trudged to the parking garage assuming he was still working the earlier emergency.

Looking forward to the next two days off, I planned to sleep in and tangle the sheets with Sam as often as possible. Making a mental note to shave my legs when I got home, I reached inside my purse and plucked out my keys. When I looked up, Darnell was standing directly in front of me wearing a confrontational expression. Startled, I sucked in a sharp breath and skidded to a halt.

"What are you doing here?" I loudly demanded. Though I hadn't seen another soul in the garage, I prayed someone might be within earshot.

"I'm looking for your boyfriend," Darnell replied with a malicious smile. "Where is he?"

A blast of icy fear slithered down my spine. Darnell's polished veneer hadn't only cracked before my eyes but had completely splintered.

I lifted my chin defiantly while inside I quaked with fear. "I have no idea. Now if you'll excuse me, I'm going home."

"No. There is no excuse for you, bitch," he spat. "You set him up to do your dirty work, didn't you? After you called your fucking father...that egotistical prick turned his back on me when I refused to marry his precious little daughter," Darnell snarled. "I should have told him what a fucking ice queen you were, but then I'm sure he's used to humping that iceberg you call Mother."

Acting on reflex, I slapped him across the face with the same hand that held my keys. He issued a thunderous roar and gripped my wrist. Long, bloody scratches appeared on his face as his lips curled in a feral snarl.

"That's going to cost you, whore," he hissed between clenched teeth.

His expression was savage. Demented. Shoving my free hand inside my purse, I found my container of pepper spray. Gripping it tightly, I waited to see what Darnell planned to do next. Memories of Liz being drugged and kidnapped by her ex-boyfriend, Ryan, spooled through my head. No way was I going to leave this parking garage with Darnell. I'd fight him with every breath in my body before I'd let him take me away.

"I don't give a shit what kind of trouble you're in. You're nothing but a bad memory to me. And for your information, I haven't talked to my father in months. Whatever you did in New York is on you. Not me." My heart drummed against my ribs as I tried to pry my wrist from his hand. "Let go of me this instant," I demanded.

"Not until I get some fucking answers. You and your lily-*white* boyfriend just couldn't leave well enough alone, could you?"

I didn't remember Darnell ever having a prejudiced side, but then he'd fully unmasked himself. God only knew what other personality flaws he intended to reveal.

Once again, I tried to jerk free, but he held on even tighter. My fingers went numb as he pinched muscle to bone.

"I had nothing to do with whatever happened between you, Isaac, and Brooks."

"Maybe not, but that white boy you're fucking certainly did. How many white men have you let crawl inside you since me?"

"That's none of your fucking business," I spat. "How many whores are you subsidizing these days?"

"More than you'll ever know." He laughed in a chilling, maniacal tone.

His demeanor frightened me beyond words. I didn't know what to do aside from keeping him talking in hopes someone—preferably a big, strapping linebacker—appeared in the garage to scare Darnell away.

Darting a furtive glance at the security camera over Darnell's shoulder, I began to struggle harder, hoping to alert whomever was manning the security feed.

"Yes, fight me, bitch. I like it when you struggle. I bet that white boy doesn't satisfy you like I used to. Does he?" Darnell pinned me with a smarmy smile, then leaned in and licked the side of my face. "You may have been an iceberg, but I rocked your world. I can do it again."

Images of him slamming me over the hood of my car and raping me flashed through my brain. *Over my dead body*, I inwardly yelled. Flipping the safety lever on the container of pepper spray, I pulled the vial from my purse as I thrust my knee directly into Darnell's balls. As he began to crumple to the ground, I hit him in the face with a steady stream of pepper spray. He landed on the ground coughing and screaming. I pressed the fob to unlock my doors as I sprinted to my car. Yanking the door open, I jumped into the driver's seat and locked myself in before starting the ignition. I jerked a glance over my shoulder to see Darnell on his knees, hands pressed to his eyes. I could hear his screams and curses seeping through the rolled-up windows.

I didn't wait for him to rise to his feet. Instead, I threw my vehicle into reverse and slammed my foot on the accelerator. With the squeal of tires and a cloud of burning rubber, I flew out of the parking garage, trembling like a palm tree in a hurricane.

Racing toward my apartment, I sucked in several deep breaths to calm the fear thundering through me. Though I knew it was unlikely he'd recovered enough to follow me, I kept checking my rearview mirror, like a scared rabbit. Wiggling my cell phone from my pocket, I quickly scrolled through my contacts and pressed Liz's number.

"You made it home fast," she answered with a light laugh.

"I-I'm not there yet. I… Can you talk to me until I get home?" I begged as my voice cracked with fear.

"What's wrong?" A tone of worry slathered her words.

"Darnell…he just…attacked me in the parking garage."

"Oh, shit. Are you okay? Did he hurt you? Where are you now?" she asked, her voice rising in terror.

"No, I'm fine, just a bruise," I replied, looking at the rising purple patches on my wrist. "I pepper-sprayed him and kicked him in the balls, then left him where he fell. Right now I'm in my car…on Deerfield Avenue…just past Highway Forty-One."

"Cin's ex-fiancé just attacked her in the hospital parking garage." Liz relayed my plight, to probably to her lovers, I wasn't sure. "Take a deep breath. You're almost home, baby. Me and the guys will meet you at your complex. Try to stay calm and don't get in a wreck. I'll be here with you…I'm not hanging up. Tell me what happened."

The reassuring tone of her voice did wonders to settle the panic consuming me. As I told Liz the events, I heard one of her men talking in the background. Relief that they planned to meet me at my apartment further soothed my jagged nerves. The less frightened I became, the more foolish I felt for letting Darnell unhinge me to such a degree.

"Where are you now, Cin?" Liz asked.

"I'm pulling into the parking lot of my complex."

"Good. We're maybe thirty seconds behind you. Stay in your car. We're on Deer River Run."

"You don't need to walk me in or anything. I'm here. I'm safe. You guys go on home."

"Nope. We're pulling in now," she stated as the headlights from James' gas-guzzling truck blinded me in my rearview mirror.

When he pulled in next to me, Liz nearly climbed over Ian as she scrambled out and raced toward me. Wrenching my car door open, she all but yanked me from my seat, then wrapped me in her arms as she trembled.

"All I could think about was what Ryan did to me. Oh, god. I'd die if I lost you," Liz sobbed as she clutched me tight.

The horror rushed back, unbridled, as we stood holding on to each other, crying for several minutes while James and Ian tried to soothe us both with reassuring words. The sound of tires squealing on pavement had me jerking from Liz's arms. A blast of fear flashed through me. But when I saw the familiar red Audi careen into the parking lot, fear bled from my veins.

After bolting from his car, Sam slammed the door, then marched toward me. Without a word, he wrapped me in his arms, stealing the air from my lungs, and pulled me off the ground. He pressed his face against my neck, breathed in my scent, and held me tight as his entire body shook.

"I called the cops and told them to check the security footage at the hospital. I'm sure they'll have him picked up soon," Sam assured. "I'm sorry I got held up longer than I expected and wasn't with you."

"Oh, Sam. It's not your fault. You were dealing with your emergency. Neither one of us could have predicted what Darnell was going to do. He wasn't initially waiting for me, anyway...he was waiting for you."

"For me?"

"Yes. He thinks you, or rather, the two of us are to blame for what happened in Isaac's office. Of course, I still don't know what the hell happened."

"Come on, let's all go inside and have a stiff drink," Ian suggested as he slung his arm around Liz's shoulder and snuggled her close beside him. "I think you've earned a few, Cindy."

"You got that right," Sam agreed on a powerful exhale. "Then you're going to pack up your things because you're moving in with me for a while."

"I'm what?" I blinked. "No way, Sam. I'm not—"

"No argument. That's exactly what you're going to do." His tone was harsh...ten times stricter than his most ominous Dom voice.

It was just as I'd feared. I'd given the man an inch of submission and he wanted to take a mile. I had no intention of following his command like a spineless, helpless little girl. Darnell might have scared me, but I'd taken that asshat to the ground all on my own. The last thing I needed was for Sam to don his Superman cape and swoop in to save the day after the fact.

"Fine. Then I won't argue, but my answer is still no," I bit out angrily.

Setting me on my feet once more, Sam gripped my shoulders

and pinned me with a glare. "Goddamnit, Cin. That fucker could have done anything to you...taken you, raped you, or worse, killed you."

"But he didn't," I barked. "I handled it. I kicked him in the balls and pepper-sprayed him. Then I got the hell out of there. I'm fine. Now leave it alone."

"The hell I will!" Sam yelled. "Why the fuck didn't you call me? You didn't think twice about calling Liz, so why not me?"

"Because you were busy."

"Bullshit. I'm never too busy for you."

"Come on, guys," James interjected, glancing at the people now popping out on their patios and craning their necks toward the scene Sam and I were making. "Let's take this inside and sort it out privately."

"No." I shook my head, and I wiggled free of Sam. "I'm fine. Everyone go home. Ian and James, thank you for driving out here to make sure I made it home safe and sound."

"Someone needs their ass reddened...fired up, proper," Ian mumbled under his breath.

"Don't I know it," Sam grumbled.

Ignoring them, I turned to Liz, whose eyes were wide with shock. "Thank you for talking me off the ledge. I had no business letting Darnell freak me out. I'm sorry."

"*You're* sorry? That asshole attacked you," Sam barked.

Like a rabid dog, I turned on him. "Enough." I wasn't trying to be a bitch, but Sam's overbearing attitude wasn't only suffocating me to death, it was pissing me off.

A flare of fury flashed in his eyes, followed by a cold, hard stare. His expression said everything far more effectively than words could. If I'd been a betting woman, I'd have wagered it all that a knockdown, drag-out was in our near future.

Sucking in a calming breath, I turned to Liz. "I'll call you tomorrow when I wake up. Thank you again for everything."

Liz nodded sympathetically. "If either of you need us, just call."

"Come on, pet," Ian drawled as he held open the truck door for her.

"Thanks guys," Sam called out. "I appreciate you calling me while you followed Cin home."

"No thanks needed," James called back with a wave before climbing in behind the wheel.

As Sam and I watched the trio drive away, a part of me wished I hadn't run them off. I had a feeling, before the night was through, I might need a referee or two.

"Want to come in for a drink?" I offered. A part of me prayed he'd say no, but I knew Sam was champing at the bit to get me alone so he could rip into me properly.

"I'd love one," he drawled derisively.

Oh, yeah, things were about to get ugly. Very ugly

Without another word, Sam followed me into my apartment. I'd no more shut the door than he scooped me into his arms and claimed my mouth with a wildly possessive kiss. His cock sprang to life, nudging against my belly, before he'd pushed his tongue past my lips.

"You scared the life out of me, girl," he murmured as he dragged his lips and teeth down my neck. "Don't ever do that to me again. Understood?"

Tears prickled the backs of my eyes. He wasn't angry with me. No, he was freaked out that Darnell had gotten to me so easily, and that Sam hadn't been there to protect me. If I hadn't been so damn defensive in the parking lot, I might have seen past my own anger and realized that Sam was acting out of panic. Guilt, hot and oily, slid over me like sludge.

"I'm sorry, Sam. I'm sorry I didn't call you first. I just—"

"If you ever need me, call! I'll drop everything to come help you. Don't you know that?"

"No. I mean, yes, I assumed you would, but I didn't want you to have to. I didn't call Liz with the intention of them coming to rescue me. I didn't need them to do that. I just wanted Liz to talk to me while I drove home. She has this knack of calming me down."

"And I don't?" he challenged.

"No. You do, too. It's just that…I knew you were—"

"Busy? So you've said." He narrowed his eyes on me. "Is that the only reason?"

"Of course. I didn't want to disturb you if you were up to your elbows in ovaries and fallopian tubes."

That made him smile. It was undoubtedly the most beautiful sight I'd seen all day.

"Silly girl," Sam chided. "It doesn't matter if I'm delivering sextuplets, if you're in danger and need me, you'd better damn well call."

Leading me to the couch, Sam pulled me down onto his lap as he sat. "Tell me what happened, sweetheart."

"Wait. First, what possessed you to call my father?"

"To find out what he knew about Darnell leaving New York," he replied.

"And?"

Sam frowned. "Let me start at the beginning. After I left you and Liz in the cafeteria, I went up to Isaac's office. You can imagine my surprise when he introduced me to the prick, but of course, I stayed—"

"Calm, cool, and in control...as always." I smirked.

"Pretty much." Sam shrugged. "Anyway, as the conversation in Isaac's office proceeded, there was something about Edmonton's demeanor that didn't sit right. At first, I thought he'd come to Chicago to try and rekindle things with you. But he mentioned something about a wife and daughter, so I nixed that assumption. And when Isaac started showering your ex with accolades, Darnell grew nervous and visibly uncomfortable. Nothing like I expected from such an egomaniac. Something was definitely off. So, when I returned to my office, I looked up your father's number and called him. I introduced myself as a friend and fellow colleague of yours, then bluntly asked him why Darnell was applying for a position at Highland Park. Your father was...less than happy to discover Darnell had come to the same city and hospital you work at."

"You didn't tell my father we were dating, did you?"

"Why, are you ashamed of me?" Sam smirked.

"No. Oh, god no. I was just curious. My mother called me earlier. It seemed too coincidental is all."

"No, sweetheart. What you tell your family is for you to decide."

"Thank you. But trust me, Sam. I'm not ashamed of you. It's just...well, you're the type of man my mother would love for me to marry." I slapped my hand over my mouth and groaned. "Oh, god. I didn't mean to blurt that out."

Sam laughed once again. "It's okay, Cin. After your father cooled off a bit, he told me that Darnell had resigned his position at Belleview Hospital. And that he's pretty much been blackballed in New York."

"Why? What did he do?"

"Well, your father didn't go into great detail, but told me the

Medical Board was preparing to bring Darnell up on charges of sexual assault, sexual misconduct, coercion, and attempted blackmail. He'd been caught having an affair with one of his patients. She was a young woman who suffered from manic depression and frequent migraines...thus the reason she sought out his neurological services in the first place."

"The man is a snake."

"Indeed. Anyway, Darnell resigned and skipped town before the board could strip him of his license."

"How did Isaac not know any of this and offer him a position?"

"I asked him that. He was rather embarrassed when he explained that he hadn't bothered to check Edmonton's references. That he'd simply let the man's reputation—or former reputation—color his decision."

"Idiot," I grumbled. "But why Chicago? Darnell could have gone to any city."

"No clue. Neither your father nor I could figure that out."

"Thank you for acting on your suspicions. I wouldn't have been able to work with that jerk." I shuddered at the thought.

Sam smoothed an errant strand of hair behind my ear and dragged his finger down my cheek. "I, too, would have serious issues with that. So, what happened in the parking garage?"

As I began retelling the events, Sam's expression remained unchanged, but I felt his body tighten, tensing in anger.

"Ice queen?" Sam choked in disbelief.

I felt my cheeks grow hot. I lowered my gaze. "He wasn't...he wasn't...Oh, hell. He only cared about getting himself off," I blurted.

Sam threw back his head and laughed.

"I'm sorry, sweetheart, but..." He stopped and chuckled some more. "Finding out the famous Darnell Edmonton, Esquire, the third or sixth or whatever, is an incompetent lover… That's poetic justice right there."

"He's pretty much a sixty-second wonder."

Sam howled. When he finally stopped laughing and dried his eyes, he cupped my face and settled a soul-stealing kiss on my lips.

"Well, that's one thing you'll never have to worry about with me."

"Why do you think I keep you around?"

Sam's brows shot up in surprise before he narrowed his eyes. "That's not the only reason you're keeping me around, is it?"

"Of course not." I shook my head, then added, "You have a very talented tongue, too."

"I'll show you just how talented after you pack your things and follow me back to my place."

Now it was my turn to tense. "Sam…"

"I already told you, sweetheart. No arguing with me about this. There's no way in hell I'm letting you stay here alone. I want you with me until Darnell leaves Chicago."

"Oh?" I challenged. "And what if he decides to stay here and get a job delivering pizzas or something?"

"Then I guess you won't have to worry about renewing the lease on your apartment," Sam countered with a mischievous smirk.

"You can't be serious. I'm supposed to let one altercation with Darnell throw me into such a tailspin that I toss my independence to the curb and move in so you can protect me? I don't need a bodyguard, Sam."

"What's wrong with me wanting to guard your body, sweetheart?" he murmured, skimming a kiss over my lips. "I didn't say anything about giving up your independence. That's all in here."

Sam touched the pad of his finger to my forehead.

Irked that I didn't have a snappy comeback, I clenched my teeth.

"You'll have every freedom at my place that you have here. You can spend an hour in the shower or, hell take a long bubble bath, cook in the kitchen if you'd like, and go out with your friends. My house is not a prison. You can come and go as you please, as long as I know where you are and that you're safe."

"Ah-ha! There's always a catch. How can I be independent if you're keeping tabs on me?"

Sam inhaled a deep breath as if searching for patience. "I'm going to keep tabs on you regardless. Darnell has shown he's decidedly unstable. God knows what he's capable of. I, for one, have no desire to find out."

"You think I do? But locking me up in your ivory tower isn't... I won't stand for it, Sam. I won't."

Sam smirked as I ranted. How the man found humor in any of this was beyond me. "What's so damn funny?" I hissed.

"If I tell you, it will likely piss you off even more." He grinned.

I narrowed my eyes and growled. Which he countered with more laughter.

"I can't help it, sweetheart. You're just so damn cute when you're all fired up, hissing and spitting."

"Oh, really? Well...fuck you, Sam. Just fuck you," I snapped as I tried to climb off his lap.

He pulled me back down, then stood and hoisted me over his shoulder like a sack of flour before heading toward my bedroom.

"And just what in the hell do you think you're doing?" I asked as he tossed me onto my bed.

"You said fuck you, so that's what I'm doing," he replied, loosening the buttons of his shirt and reaching for his belt.

Gasping, I sat up. With wide eyes, I stared at him as if he'd lost his mind. "You're nuts if you think I'm having sex with you."

"Oh, you will, sweetheart. Because the only time you stop trying to fight me is when I'm balls deep inside you," Sam insisted as he slowly released his zipper.

The minute his cock jutted free, my hormones silenced the rebellion in my head. Men taunted each another about being pussy whipped, but when it came to Sam, I was totally cock whipped. Still, if I lay back and spread my legs, I'd only be playing into his Dominant hands.

Ugh. Why were men so damn complicated?

As he stalked toward me, fisting his cock, I didn't know if I wanted to beg or yell at him.

"What's it going to be, Allisinda? Do you want me as your lover or sparring partner tonight?"

Dammit, I was putty in his hands, and he fucking knew it.

The sting of tears burned my eyes. I was coming unhinged but didn't know exactly why. An overload of worries, fears, and excitement clashed within, tossing me over the bow of my own emotional Titanic. I only knew I was sinking fast.

Staring at me with concern etched over his face, Sam released his cock and spread his arms open as he reached the edge of the bed. I dropped my head, swallowed back a sob, and crawled to him.

"I've got you, little one. You're safe. No one's going to hurt you now."

I closed my eyes and rested my head on his chest, feeling the fool for all the uncertainty pinging inside me. But the steady rhythm of Sam's heartbeat offered the salvation I needed most.

Security.

Slowly, Sam lifted me off the bed before peeling my clothes

away. All the while, his gentle hands caressed, soothed, and calmed me—so did his reassuring whispers. To think that only a few days ago, I was ready to throw him away.Shame crested, then slowly receded as he stripped me totally naked.

He pulled back the covers, then lifted me into his arms and laid me on the middle of the mattress. Sam climbed in beside me, pulled me against his chest once more, and silently brushed his fingers through my hair.

"Close your eyes and find that peaceful place inside you," Sam whispered. "Then I want you to sleep knowing I'm here with you all night long, keeping you safe and warm."

Obeying his edict, I let my eyelids drift shut…let the soothing touch of his fingers drag me beneath a blanket of shelter. Tumbled deeper and deeper to a place I knew Darnell would never find me.

"Thank you, Sam," I whispered as the darkness pulled me down further.

He didn't reply, simply pressed a tender kiss to my head and exhaled a contented sigh.

Sunlight streamed through my window when I woke the next morning. The bed was empty, and a pang of regret settled in my chest. Kicking the covers off, I padded into the bathroom, then slid on my robe and made my way to the kitchen.

A note lay on the kitchen table.

Cin,

I'm sorry I had to leave you alone this morning, but I have a full day of patients at the office. Text me if you go out. I'll come by late this afternoon. Have a bag packed and we'll grab some dinner before heading to my place.

See you soon,

Sam

Before I let my knee-jerk reaction or rather, anger rule me, I nibbled my bottom lip and pondered Sam's instructions. His note wasn't a request but a demand. Though I'd proven myself a worthy adversary, the feminist in me bristled. But Sam was only worried for my safety.

"It's too early to strain my brain like this. I need coffee," I grumbled.

After starting a pot of liquid caffeine, I headed down the hall to the bathroom and took a shower. Even if I didn't end up spending the night in Sam's bed, at least my legs were shaved. I dried my hair and pulled on a pair of yoga pants and a T-shirt, then trekked back to the kitchen.

As I lifted the mug of hot, steamy coffee to my lips, my cell phone began to ring. Sipping quickly, I picked up the device and checked the caller ID.

"Mother. Oh joy." I rolled my eyes.

"Hello," I answered as I took a seat at the kitchen table.

"Allisinda, darling. Please tell me you are all right. Your father just informed me that Darnell is working at Highland Park. You've not had to have any dealings with that…that heathen, have you?" she asked, her tone drenched in horror.

"Actually, Mother, he didn't get the job, but accosted me in the parking garage last night. I took care of him."

"You what?" Natia choked in dismay. "What do you mean, you took care of him?"

"I kicked him in the…groin and shot his face full of pepper spray."

"Oh, lord. Your father is going to have an apoplexy when I tell him this. You weren't harmed, were you, darling?"

"No, Mother. I'm perfectly fine."

"What is that animal doing in Chicago?"

"Well, from what I've heard, he was drummed out of New Yor—"

"Yes, well. I know all about his revolting behavior. I've got to say, Allisinda, it was a blessing he ran out at the wedding. I shudder to think what your life would be like. Why, it would be nothing short of catastrophic."

I pressed my lips together to keep from screaming. "Yes, it was the best thing that could have ever happened." Or so she wanted me to believe.

"I've tried not to pry, but have you put yourself back out there, dear… You know, taken a step back into the dating pool?"

Oh, boy, the one topic I didn't want to broach with the woman. "A little. Yes."

"I'm glad to hear it. You know a man…a decent man would make your life so much easier."

"My life is quite fine the way it is, Mother," I assured, striving to keep the animosity from my tone.

"But if you had a man to take care of you, I'm sure you could find time to return to school and get your—"

"Mother," I snapped. "My life is quite complete. I'm happy, even."

"Well, you don't sound happy. You sound hateful. What is your problem, Allisinda? We gave you a wonderful life. A safe and secure upbringing. You didn't want for a thing. Honestly, I think you're just one of those people who never seems to find an ounce of gratitude."

I ached to tell her that I was so deliriously ecstatic that I farted butterflies and daisies. But I swallowed my scathing retort. Such a comment would only prolong this conversation. "Truthfully, Mother. I couldn't be happier if I tried."

"Even with all this tawdry business surrounding Darnell? Surely you can't be serious."

"I don't give a whit about Darnell or his inappropriate actions. The man is scum, Mother. I don't wish to discuss him any further, now drop it."

"Watch your mouth with me, young lady. I'll excuse your caustic tongue this once because I believe he who won't be named again has obviously upset you more than you care to admit."

"No. I simply refuse to waste good air on bad rubbish, Mother. If you must know, I'm dating a well-regarded surgeon. I am happier than I've ever been in my life." Even as the words came pouring off my tongue I wanted to bite them back. I'd just given her fuel to add to the fire.

Dammit.

Dammit.

Dammit.

"A surgeon? How marvelous," she nearly squealed. "What's his specialty, dear?"

"Obstetrics and gynecology."

"Oh, my." The disdain in her voice was as loud and clear as if she'd yelled through a foghorn. "I...I see. Well, that is rather...unexpected."

CHAPTER TEN

As if angels from heaven had swooped down to save me, my phone beeped.

"I'm sorry, Mother. I have another call coming in that I have to take. Talk to you soon. Bye."

Without waiting for her reply, I checked the ID on my phone.

Sam.

"I am bathing your entire body in kisses tonight," I answered instead of hello.

"Excuse me?" Sam laughed. "I'd rather you...well, I can't say right now, but it involves kisses. It definitely involves your sinfully wicked mouth," he added in a whisper. "And what exactly did I do to achieve this level of indulgence you're willing to give?"

"I was on the other line with...my mother when you clicked in."

"Ah," Sam drawled in understanding. "In that case, you owe me far more than just your mouth."

"Anything. I'll gladly pay whatever you ask as long as I don't have to listen to... Oh, hell. I'm sorry. Good morning, Sam. How's your day going?"

"Morning, sweetheart." He chuckled again. "Quite well actually. I had my nurse rearrange my schedule, so I'll be over in about an hour to pick you up and get you settled into my place while I head back to the office. We'll head out for dinner as soon as I'm done for the day."

Cringing, I closed my eyes. I'd planned to decide whether or not I was going to move in with him later...not this second.

"I take it from your lack of enthusiasm, you're still not sold on the idea of moving in with me, hmm?"

"I-I was going to think about it this morning."

"What's there to ponder, Cin? I'm not going to slap a collar on your neck and chain you to a cross the minute you step through my door. I've never done that before, have I?"

"You don't have a cross at your house," I replied dryly.

"Oh, but I do. A whole dungeon, in fact."

"Why haven't I ever seen it?" I challenged, knowing he was simply pulling my chain.

"Because you weren't ready. But I think you are now, girl." His words took on an unmistakable Dominant edge. "So, what's your decision?"

The idea of *needing* a man for protection shredded every ounce of dignity I possessed. Weak women, like my mother, relied on men for...well, for everything. Despite her attempt to cast me in the same mold, I'd swung to the opposite side of the pendulum and refused to rely on a man for anything.

Stubbornness is not a virtue, Allisinda. In fact, most men find it absolutely repugnant. My mother's voice reverberated in my head.

Closing my eyes, I swallowed down a snarl. "Fine. You win. I'll pack a damn bag."

My terse outburst was met with silence. I glanced at my phone thinking the call had dropped. Finally, Sam spoke. "This isn't a contest. It's about ensuring your safety and, well…frankly, my sanity."

The disquiet in his tone confirmed Darnell's actions had impacted Sam far more than they had me. While I appreciated his fears, he refused to comprehend that I could protect myself.

"Your lack of faith in me is…disheartening. I refuse to allow myself to fall victim to Darnell or anyone else, and that's a promise."

"The world is a scary place, Cin. Don't make promises beyond your control."

"You like to control a lot of things, Sam, but even you can't control the crazies," I lobbed back at him.

"True, but having you in my house, I'm minimizing your exposure to one crazy in particular."

"That's because control is your middle name," I goaded.

"Actually it's Sullivan. And you love it when I push your buttons, especially one in particular. The one that gets you hot and flowing like chocolate syrup." His voice lowered to a whisper. "I wish I was there to slide my tongue over your hard little button right now."

My knees quivered. A hot current of desire sailed straight to my clit, and I found myself clutching the phone tighter.

"You're an evil, wicked man, Samuel Sullivan Brooks," I scolded.

"I've only given you a little taste of the wickedness prowling inside me."

A heated thrill shot through me. Everything Sam had introduced me to so far had felt amazing…a little scary, but incredible all the same. His titillating phrase left no doubt—I'd merely touched the tip of his Dominant mountain. Knowing there was more made me dizzy with curiosity, and arousal.

"Maybe, but what's been placed on my tongue has been delicious," I purred.

"Fuck," Sam hissed. "You've got my cock hard, girl. I'll have to sit here at my desk until I settle down to keep from embarrassing myself."

A mischievous grin spread across my mouth. "If I were there right now, I'd be hiding under your desk...on my knees...slowly unzipping your pants. I'd wrap my hand around your big, hard—"

"Enough, you little minx," Sam growled.

I giggled. "What's wrong? Am I making it *hard* for you to get your work done?"

"And then some, but don't worry. I'll take care of my inconvenient problem...and your tempting little tricks in an hour."

I issued a low, sensual moan. "I sure hope so."

Sam chuckled. "Don't get too excited. I didn't say you'd like it, did I, sweetheart?"

"What?" I choked, my eyes growing wide.

"Seems I've given you something to ponder while you pack, haven't I? Simmer for me, girl. I'll be there soon," Sam instructed, then hung up.

A chill slithered down my spine while my mind wondered what Sam had planned. Would he spank me? A quiver of excitement rippled through me. No, he knew all too well I enjoyed that. No, Sam had something else in mind...something I wouldn't like.

Forcing down the dread flittering through me, I dragged a couple suitcases out of my closet and began to pack my things. Unsure of how long Sam intended to keep me under his thumb, I packed nearly everything, just in case.

Snagging up my toiletries, my hands were overflowing when my phone rang again. I figured it was Sam telling me he was on his way.

"Yeah, yeah. I'm packed. Happy?" I greeted in a snarky voice.

"Why? Where are we going?" the unexpected voice of my brother, Matatino, asked with a laugh.

"Matti," I screeched in excitement. "Oh, my god. Where are you? Are you still in Bhutan?"

"I'm back home. After helping the Ministry of Health, I stayed a couple more months and traveled a bit. But when my craving for pastrami on rye grew to be too much, I caught a flight back to New York."

I laughed. "Your life is still ruled by your stomach, I see."

"For sure," he chuckled. "So what's this I hear about Darnell showing up in Chicago? Do you need me to come there and kick his ass for you, baby sis?"

"Ugh," I groaned. "No, Matti. What is it with you men, anyway? You're always wanting to save some damsel in distress."

"You're my only sister. I'll always kick the shit out of any prick who messes with you."

"Thanks," I replied dryly. "But I don't need your help. I've already got one caveman pounding his chest. I don't need two."

"Oh, right. The surgeon. Who is he?"

"Christ, is Mother a walking, talking tabloid these days?"

"When hasn't she been? So tell me about him."

"It's still early. There isn't much to tell," I lied.

"Uh-huh. If you say so. Oh, I almost forgot. According to mom's friends, the Haughty-Hotline, I guess Darnell knocked up one of his play toys before he skipped town."

"What? That lying sack of crap is telling everyone here that he's married and has a kid."

"Sounds like he needs to stop self-prescribing to me. Anyway, the woman he ditched is trying to get his medical license pulled. Evidently, she's claiming you've taken him back since he ran off to Chicago. I thought you should know."

"Eww." I wrinkled my nose. "He's the last man on the planet I want to see. But enough about him. Where are you off to next?"

"Funny you should ask." Matti chuckled. "Chicago."

"What? You're coming here?" I squealed. "When?"

"Um, I land in about an hour. Wanna pick me up at the airport?"

"Of course." I spied my luggage, and my heart sank. "Well…uh, that might be a problem."

"Why? Oh, right. You answered the phone saying something about being packed. Where are you headed off to?"

"Uh…I-I've decided to stay with a friend of mine for a few days. Just until…"

Until what? Until Darnell leaves the city? Or until I can't stomach being pinned to a board like a bug and studied under a microscope any longer and haul my luggage back home?

"What is it you're not telling me, Cin?" Matti asked suspiciously.

"Oh, hell."

Flopping down on the mattress, I proceeded to spill my guts about everything. Well, everything except Genesis and Sam leading me down the path of kinky debauchery. Though Matti had been my life-long confidant—the only member of my family who'd encouraged me to follow my dream and become an RN—he was still my brother. I wasn't going to discuss the strange and confusing world of power exchanges with him.

"I think I like this guy, Sam. And I definitely feel better that he's having you stay with him while Darnell's sniffing around."

"Of course you do. You're as overbearing and laden with testosterone as Sam is," I teased.

"Possibly, but I've never trusted Darnell…with good reason. I'm afraid for you, sis. I think the prick's lost touch with reality. I'll be glad when I land and can help look—"

"No way! I will not have you hovering over my every move. Sam's going to drive me crazy enough doing that. I don't need you suffocating me, too."

"Easy, girl. I was going to say that I'd look after your place if you don't mind me staying there. But if you feel like Sam's going to be suffocating you, maybe you shouldn't move in with him. Stay in your own apartment, with me, instead."

Matatino's suggestion was so brilliant I felt as if my heart might explode out of my chest.

"That's a wonderful idea," I replied breathlessly. "I'll pick you up in an hour. Text me your flight info. I'm on my way."

After ending the call with my brother, I exhaled a deep breath. Being able to stay in my own apartment filled me with relief. Of course, Sam would undoubtedly be disappointed, but surely he'd be satisfied knowing I had round-the-clock security now. Besides, I hadn't spent any amount of quality time with Matti since I'd moved to Chicago. I was looking forward to having him near.

I rang Sam's number, expecting the call to go to his voice mail. But when he picked up, a wave of dread settled through me.

"You're not on your way over, are you?"

"Indeed I am. Why? What's up?"

"Oh, well…you see. There's been a change of plans."

"What change?" Sam's tone was filled with suspicion.

"I just got a call from my brother. He's flying in today. In fact

I'm picking him up at the airport in a few minutes and...well, I explained the whole Darnell situation, and Matti—ah, that's my brother—he's decided to stay here with me for a while. So it solves the whole bodyguard issue."

The absolute silence on the other end of the line told me Sam didn't find the news joyous whatsoever. When he didn't say anything after several tense minutes, I closed my eyes and swallowed tightly.

"Obviously, I've upset you. I'm sorry, Sam. That wasn't my intention."

"No?" The tone of his question was caustic. "I'm definitely not doing somersaults and cartwheels, that's for damn sure. Tell me something. Is the arrival of your brother a convenient excuse for you to keep from moving in with me?"

"I wouldn't call it an excuse, but it alleviates me having to haul all my stuff to your place for a few short days."

"This isn't about your brother, Cin. This is about pride."

"You're wrong, Sam. And what's so wrong with having a little pride? I've relied on it for years, and it hasn't failed me yet."

"So have I, but I don't let it define who I am."

"Neither do I," I huffed, wishing he'd simply relent and give all this moving-in nonsense a rest.

"What if I hadn't intended you stay with me for a *few short days*? What if I was hoping you'd remain with me permanently?"

He wanted me to literally move in with him...forever? No. Did he really just say that? But the air freezing in my lungs, the skittering of my heart, and the dizzying wave that crested through me confirmed I had heard him correctly.

"But...why? Why didn't you at least talk to me about that? I...I... You can't just spring this on me, Sam. That's not fair."

"No. Having the chance to live with you ripped out from under me isn't fair. I've done everything in my power to prove myself to you. Show you that you can trust me. That I'm not just some prick who keeps you around to fuck when I get the urge. I opened my soul to you so you can see how invested I am in our relationship. But you keep shutting me out. Keep closing doors in my face. How many more do I have to kick in before you'll finally believe that I truly care about you?" Sam growled, then sucked in a ragged breath.

Tears stung my eyes. My throat constricted. And my heart felt as if it were breaking apart.

"I'm—"

"Yes. I know. You're sorry. So am I," he replied dolefully. "I'm going to head back to the office. I'll have to take a rain check on dinner tonight. I need a couple days to think."

"Sam," I cried out on a sob. "Wait."

"No. Give me a couple of days. You enjoy your time with your brother. But keep an eye out for Darnell. I have a feeling he hasn't accomplished whatever it is he set out to do. But I want you to stay safe. I'll talk to you soon."

Without saying good-bye, Sam hung up.

"No. No. No," I screamed.

Tears rushed down my face as a penetrating numbness swallowed me whole. Sam had thrown in the towel. He'd jumped through hoops for me, over and over again. But I'd been too stupid to see what was right in front of me. I'd been so focused on protecting my pride, my stupid independence, and my fragile self-confidence. But from what? The only thing I'd managed to keep from seeping inside my walls was the chance for true happiness.

Bullshit, my inner voice scoffed. *You were ready to toss him to the curb a few days ago. You didn't trust him. You still don't...not fully, or you'd have jumped at the chance to move in with him. You're still waiting for Sam to do something vile and humiliating, like Darnell. Remember what Liz said: "Sam isn't Darnell." You know it, too. Hell, they're not even in the same ballpark. Same planet. Yet he's still paying the price for Darnell's deceit. Well, are you happy now? You're all alone—again, but you've got your fucking stubborn pride to keep you warm. Priceless.*

The ring of my cell phone pulled me from the come-to-jesus meeting my psyche had called.

I palmed my tears, sending up a silent prayer that Sam had changed his mind. But all my hopes sailed out the window when I glanced at the caller ID.

Quickly pulling myself together, I sucked in a shaky breath, sniffed, then answered. "Have you landed already, Matti?" I asked in a forced cheerful tone.

"Not yet, but things have gone crazy…crazy fantastic but… Dammit. I'm sorry Cin, as soon as we land, I need to grab the next available flight to San Francisco."

"What? No," I sniffed. "Why?"

The universe was playing some kind of cosmic joke on me.

"One of my premiere clients is ready to update his group's entire neuroradiology departments. We're talking twenty-seven hospitals." I couldn't miss the excitement in his voice. A wan smile tugged my lips. "So, I guess you'll be bunking over at Sam's after all. I'm sure you're heartbroken about that," he teased with a chuckle. "I'll plan a layover on my way back to New York when this job's done, okay? Oops. We're getting ready to land. Love you, baby sis. Talk to you soon."

"Love you too, Matti," I replied, then hung up.

Turning off my phone, I curled up on the bed as tears spilled from my eyes. Matti was wrong. My heart *was* breaking. Breaking because I'd been a fool, fooling no one but myself. I feared there was no way to repair my failures with Sam. Why would he purposely lay his heart out for me once more when all I'd done, all along, was step on it? Over and over again. At least he'd been kind. He hadn't ended it all with a wicked, ugly fight. So why did this way seem even worse? Because he still cared—at least for my physical well-being.

"Oh, god. I always worried that Sam would end up hurting me, like Darnell had. But neither of them can hold a candle to the pain I self-inflicted," I sobbed.

When I'd cried all the tears I could, I crawled out of bed and washed my face. The numbness had returned. I felt as if I were a walking zombie with a massive hole in my chest. Gone was my heart. Ripped out by my own hands because of my inability to trust and ineffectual martyrdom. Standing at the sink, I studied my reflection in the mirror. No longer cloaked behind a false bravado of self-assurance and confidence, was the real Allisinda. The mask that had hidden the insecure, scared little girl who'd spent her whole life craving unconditional love and approval had fallen away.

You mean the kind that Sam offered...the kind you refused to accept?

Covered in a dark cloud of depression, I spent the rest of the day in bed. Sleeping was the only way I could find respite for my shattered soul. But a body could only sleep so much. And at three in the morning, I was wide-awake, unable to escape the pain stabbing my heart. As I lay in bed, staring at the ceiling, I wondered what Sam was doing. Was he sleeping, content with his decision? Or was his gut churning and heart breaking, like mine?

I rolled over and picked my phone off the nightstand, then

stared at his number. I spent an hour fighting the urge to ring him up, to hear his raspy voice settle over me and relieve the burning emptiness that consumed me. But I couldn't bring myself to disregard his wishes. He wanted time to think, or so he'd said. Maybe that was just his compassionate way of letting me down easily. Maybe he'd already made up his mind. Had he finally realized that I was too damaged beyond repair? Too broken and fractured for even his masterful hands to suture back together?

When I finally decided to leave my bed, my body felt as if it weighed a ton. Wandering aimlessly through my apartment, I could feel the veil of sadness settle deeper, feel the emptiness inside me expand. This wasn't anything like I'd envisioned when I'd been the one deciding to end things. Yet I knew in my heart it would have hurt exactly this same way I'd simply been too naïve to realize that fact. Somehow I'd convinced myself that if I were the one in control, losing Sam wouldn't affect me to such a degree. This was more than embarrassment or humiliation under the scrutiny of my disconnected parents and artificial friends. This was pain on a level I'd never known existed.

I wondered if I could weather this storm. Would I come out on the other side with my sails intact? I had no clue. A saying by Haruki Murakami suddenly swirled in my mind: *When you come out of the storm, you won't be the same person who walked in. That's what the storm's all about.*

Everything I projected myself to be had been a lie. A lie I'd told myself each and every day, thinking that was the only way I could survive. I'd built walls around me to mask weakness. But now those walls had been destroyed. The thought of having to reconstruct those barriers all over again was far too daunting, as was the idea of reinventing myself to keep from becoming a clone of my mother. I

felt more naked and exposed than ever before in my life.
Who was the real Allisinda Dayea Noland?
Did I possess the courage to find out?
Where did I even begin?
Why was I so terrified of what I might find?
The woman inside me was nothing but a stranger.
Curling up on the couch, I cried myself back to sleep.

~

I spent the next two days lost in surging waves of anger and pride, longing and sorrow, regret and guilt. The weight of so many emotions pulled me down with such force I feared I would be crushed to dust. Forced to peel back my emotions, I began to analyze all the feelings Sam conjured within me. Sadly, it was then I discovered I'd been to blame for most everything. The revelation only served to send me on a long, slow slide into a numb, despondent fugue. I forced myself to drink, but I couldn't eat a thing without retching it back up. I knew it wasn't healthy, and I needed to shake off the depression holding me in its grip. But prying the cold, bony fingers of despair away seemed impossible. All I seemed capable of was reliving every moment I'd spent with Sam, while every mistake I'd made pounded at my already shattered heart.

The man had been a saint. He'd put up with my defiance time and again, extending yet another level of patience I didn't deserve. I'd been too blind to see his love…too focused on the expectation of him saying the words when I should have heard them in all the things he did for me…to me. No apology seemed sufficient for him to forgive my reprehensible and childish behavior.

Suddenly a knock came from my front door. My heart drummed

in my chest as I rose from the couch and quietly padded across the room. Sam had said he needed a couple of days—dare I hope he'd returned to me?

Swallowing tightly, I pressed my eye to the peephole. My shoulders sagged and pain pierced me like a knife once again. Liz stood on the other side of the door, her face wrinkled in worry. Surprisingly, she was alone. I watched as she raised her hand and knocked once more. And I jumped at the loud reverberation against the wood.

"Come on, Cin. I know you're in there. It's me, Liz. I need to know you're all right. My calls keep going straight to your voicemail. I know what happened with you and Sam. Now open up. Matti? If you're in there, open the door, sugar. I'll take the beating Cin has no doubt threatened to give you."

Dropping my gaze to the floor, I turned and silently walked back to the couch.

Liz continued to drum on the door and call out to me. I didn't have the emotional strength to talk to her about anything at that moment.

"Dammit, Cin. Open this fucking door right now!"

Covering my ears, I curled into a ball and squeezed my eyes shut. The next thing I knew, Liz was pulling me into her arms as tears spilled down her face. In my fog of misery, I semi-remembered I'd given Liz a key to my place.

"Oh, baby...look at you. You're a mess," she whispered.

A whole new flood I didn't know was locked inside me burst free. I held onto her and cried like a newborn baby.

"Why didn't you call me?" Liz murmured as she brushed the hair from my face.

I couldn't even answer, only sob.

"Shhh, it's okay. It's all going to be okay," she whispered, rocking me back and forth with one arm while she pulled out her cell phone and made a call.

"D-don't call Sam," I begged, suddenly filled with panic.

"I'm not, sugar...I'm just calling Ian to let him know where I'm at. Where's your brother?"

"He...he didn't come. San Francisco." I sucked in a shallow breath and whimpered, "Don't call Sam. Please. Don't call Sam."

"I'm not. I swear." A minute later, she spoke into the phone. "I need help."

"No. I don't w-want anyone to see m-me like th-this," I choked.

Seconds later, Ian entered the room, his face lined in a tight frown and his eyes filled with pity.

"I don't want y-you here," I sobbed.

In two long strides, he was beside the couch. Bending, he cupped his palm to the back of my neck. He sat down on the couch, then pulled me up into his lap. "I don't care what you want, little one. I know what you need. Please shut the front door, pet, then make us some hot tea."

"Yes, Master," Liz replied before following his instruction.

Ian didn't say another word, simply held me against his chest until my tears dried up. He took a cup of tea from Liz as she sat down and stroked my hair.

"Here, I want you to take a of sip of this for me," Ian instructed. As I complied, he issued a tiny nod and a tight smile. "When was the last time you ate something, girl?"

He was in full-on Dom mode, which made the fact that I was in his arms somewhat less awkward. The kindness he extended was sweet. Ian always struck me as far stricter than James.

"I can't keep anything down," I confessed.

Ian nodded. "Okay, here's the deal. Do you have any soup?"

"Yes. Chicken noodle."

"Good. I'll have Liz heat up some of the broth. You eat that and keep it down and I won't call Sam."

I jerked my head up and pinned him with an incredulous stare.

"The choice is yours, girl. It's been yours from the very start."

I knew immediately Ian wasn't talking about soup but rather the horrible way I'd treated Sam. "All right," I whispered.

"Pet?"

"On it, Master."

"No offense, little one. But you could use a shower." Ian smiled.

"I'm sorry."

He softly chuckled. "Good girl. That's a start."

My body tensed. "Please don't call me that... Don't call me good girl. Sam..."

"Very well. I understand. What I don't understand is why you haven't reached out to any of us. Not Liz, Sam...no one. You're part of our family now, Cin."

"I-I needed to...to strip myself down. To see who I am beneath all the...bullshit."

"I see. But watch your language, little one. I know Sam would want you to refrain."

I shrugged. "It doesn't matter anymore. He doesn't want me."

"Oh?" Ian arched his brows. "He said that to you, did he?"

"He didn't have to. I shoved him away, again...like I always do. He was tired of trying to reach me...tired of fighting me."

"You know, Cin. Part of any relationship is good communication. But in the Dom/sub dynamic, it's a must. You mentioned stripping yourself down. What have you discovered along the way?"

"Nothing."

"Excuse me?"

"I'm nothing. I'm a fake…a phony. Someone who put on airs, just like my mother, but mine weren't meant to impress, they were meant to deflect."

"Well, I know without a shadow of a doubt you are far more than nothing. The feistiness inside you isn't all for protection. It's part of your personality…the part that Sam fell in love with. The part he still loves. Never lose that, Cin. It will help you discover what you truly want…what's deep inside your heart."

"All I want is Sam, but it's too late for that now. I've screwed things up past the point of no return."

Ian cocked his head and studied me for several long, silent minutes. "If you had the chance to fix things between you and Sam, how far would you be willing to go?"

"To the moon and back," I whispered.

"What if you didn't have to go quite that far?" He grinned.

"What are you suggesting?"

"Tell me your thoughts on submission, now that you've stripped away your armor."

My brows furrowed as I pondered his question. "All the things Sam did to me were…amazing. But I was too afraid to truly enjoy them. I guess I really didn't want to."

"So on some level, you enjoyed letting Sam control you. Is that what you're saying?"

"Yes." I was finally being honest not only with Ian but myself as well.

"Good. Then if you'd like another chance with Sam, here is what I suggest."

Ian laid out his plan. At first, I thought he was insane, but the more he explained, the more sense it made. Ian assured me that the friends I'd made at the club would help me. And when it came time for me to pass the ultimate test, he assured me I'd be more than ready. The only guarantee Ian couldn't give was that Sam would take me back.

It was a risk I was willing to take because I'd already lost what was most important, and desperately wanted Sam back.

When the soup was ready, Ian led me to the kitchen table. As I sipped the warm broth, he explained the plan to Liz, who simply grinned and nodded.

"You're going to be playing a vital role in all this, pet. James and I give you permission to do what's necessary to help Cin."

"Thank you, Master." She beamed.

"We'll work out a schedule. We'll meet here in the evenings, provided neither of you have had too taxing of a day, and work on what we can," Ian instructed. "When it's time to move onto more involved issues, we'll meet at our place."

I smiled for the first time in two days. It felt good. "Thank you, Sir."

Ian simply grinned. "I think you'll get on just fine, little one."

After he and Liz left, I took a long, hot shower, put on clean pajamas, and sat on the couch once again. Tomorrow I would be back at work and no doubt running into Sam, at least from time to time. I wasn't kidding myself—I didn't expect him to show up on the unit like he had before. And I wasn't entirely sure how I'd react to seeing him, or rather, so little of him. But I had something inside I hadn't for a very long time...hope. Hope that even if Ian's grand plan didn't work out, I would eventually find the real me. For some strange reason, that prospect no longer frightened me.

The next morning, I was a nervous wreck. Getting ready for

work, I spilled my coffee down the front of my scrubs and had to change before I even left the house. Arriving at the hospital without any other catastrophes, I locked up my purse, then turned to clock in. Sam was leaning against the doorjamb, arms crossed over his chest, like a dozen times before. His eyes were sunken in as if he hadn't slept for a week, and his lips were drawn tightly together. Tears stung the backs of my eyes, but I blinked them away as I fought the urge to run and leap into his arms.

"Good morning, Cin."

I swallowed down the ball of emotion lodged in my throat and nodded. "Morning, Sam."

"I just came down to see if you were all right."

I nodded as I fought the tears now blurring my vision.

He cleared his throat and stared at a spot on the wall behind me. "I know I told you I needed a couple days to think, but…"

Don't say it. Please, god. Don't let him say it.

"It's okay, Sam. I understand."

"Do you?"

"Yes. I wasn't ever honest with you…or fair. I know that now. I…I'm sorry."

"Yeah. Me, too." He paused as if gathering himself together. "See you around, Cin."

When he turned and left, my chin quivered and I bit my lips together, choking back a sob. But I wasn't going to give up. Not without a fight. Not without proving to Sam that I could be the woman of his dreams and more. Unfortunately, it was up to him. Would he be willing to risk his heart and take a chance with me again?

Time would tell.

Liz strolled in and gave me a hug. "I passed Sam in the hall.

You okay?"

With a sniff, I nodded, then sent her a watery smile. "I will be. I'll see you out on the floor."

"I'm right behind you."

I didn't see Sam again that day or the next. While it was difficult to remain positive, I wasn't going to allow myself to slide back into a dark chasm. Instead, I began to get comfortable in my own skin and started looking at myself through my own eyes. Not what I thought others should, or rather, wanted to see.

It was as if I'd knocked a giant chip off my shoulder.

And it felt really good.

CHAPTER ELEVEN

After running to the grocery store, dry cleaners, and post office, I grabbed some dinner, then climbed into a steaming-hot bubble bath, sipping wine. I should have taken a quick shower and gone to bed. The hour was late, but I didn't care. I needed this reprieve...this erstwhile ritual of indulgence. Most of my nights when I was single, I'd spoiled myself in this manner. And since I was single again, I found the wine and bubbles offered a unique and comforting symmetry once again.

After taking a sip of wine, I closed my eyes and rested the back of my head on the porcelain tub, when a loud banging came from my front door. Cursing, I set the glass down. I flipped the lever with my toe and began to drain the tub, then stood and quickly dried myself off. All the while, the pounding continued. Padding down the hall, I tied the sash of my robe, then tiptoed to the portal and peered through the peephole. The warmth the wine had provided instantly vanished as a cold chill shook my entire frame.

Darnell. The demented prick had tracked down my apartment.

Suddenly Sam's words flooded back to me. *If you ever need me, call! I'll drop everything to come help you.* Yes, I'd known he would, but that was before I'd fucked everything up and he'd walked away. I needed help, but I *wanted* it from Sam.

Easing away from the door and the incessant pounding, I prayed the wooden barrier was strong enough to keep Darnell out. Sprinting to my purse, I grabbed my cell and brought up Sam's number. My finger hovered over the call button as indecision claimed me.

"Wake up, baby. You're lover's home," Darnell called, his words slurred as if he were drunk.

Revulsion spiked.

I pressed the button to call Sam.

"Cin? Is everything all right?"

"I-I'm sorry to bother—"

"What's wrong?" he demanded.

"Darnell. He's outside my apartment. I think he's drunk."

Fighting the knee-jerk reaction to apologize to Sam, tell him I'd handle it, and hang up was a far more brutal battle than I'd expected.

The old Cin railed inside my head, scolding me for not simply calling the cops.

But the new me, the one no longer surrounded in a fortress of walls, needed Sam's strength, his control. Needed him to make the maniac outside my door go away and calm the fear within me, whether it proved me weak or not.

"Hang up and call 911. I'm on my way."

"Allisinda," Darnell called out in a demented singsong voice. "Open up, baby. I've got a big, hard present for you."

Bile rose in the back of my throat.

Following Sam's instructions, I called the police. While the emergency operator kept me on the line, I raced to the kitchen, grabbed a butcher knife, and retrieved my pepper spray. Standing in the middle of my living room, trembling, I wedged the phone between my shoulder and ear and waited for help to arrive.

Somewhere in the distance, a siren wailed. I didn't know if those particular officers were coming to help me or some other unfortunate soul. The operator assured me over and over that help was on the way, but it seemed an interminable amount of time had passed and still nothing.

Darnell was growing more impatient and angrier as the seconds ticked by.

"I'm afraid this idiot is going to break down my door," I confessed to the low-keyed woman on the other end of the line.

"Just a couple more minutes and the officers will be there," she assured. "Stay cool. Stay with me."

Outside my door, I heard shouts and a loud, dull thud.

"Allisinda, you bitch. You called the fucking cops?" Darnell yelled. "Get your black ass out here and get me out of this mess, you stupid whore."

"You have the right to remain silent."

The sound of another man's voice was music to my ears. "They're here. They've got him. Thank you."

"You're welcome. Good luck, Miss Noland," the operator replied, then hung up.

I closed my eyes and sucked in a shaky breath, then quickly put my weapons away before racing to the front door. Pressing my ear to the wood, I listened to the commotion unfolding on the other side.

"Cin. Goddammit, come out here and tell them to let me go. I didn't do a fucking thing to you. I only wanted to love you again."

Darnell continued screaming that I save him, and professing his love…well, when he wasn't maligning my character with insulting slurs. I was certain my neighbors were cursing me for the drama unfolding in our usually quiet complex.

"You! You cocksucker. This is all your fault," Darnell growled. "Arrest that motherfucker. He's the cracker who stole my woman."

"Get him out of here, and take him downtown," a man barked.

As Darnell's screams began to fade, I slowly opened the door and peered out. Sam was pulling his wallet out of his pocket, then handed his license over to one of the officers. When he glanced my way, relief lit his eyes.

"May I go inside with Miss Noland?" Sam asked the officer studying his ID.

"Would you like Dr. Brooks to join us, ma'am?" the cop asked.

"Yes. Please. Come inside." I swung the door open wide.

Sam followed the officers in, but instead of walking past me, he wrapped me in his arms and pulled me to his chest. His ragged breath spilled over my neck, hot and moist. His intoxicating scent filled my senses and made me lightheaded. The heat of his rugged body wrapped me in a blanket of safety and shelter. But of all the sensations rising inside, the sizzling current of desire burned brightest. The fiery conflagration Sam ignited spread from my toes and enveloped my body. Demand coursed through me, threatening to incinerate me from the inside out.

It was all I could do to keep from falling to my knees and begging him to forgive me…pleading that he'd give me a second chance.

"I'm glad you called me, Cin," Sam mumbled as he pressed his lips against the top of my head. "Come on. Let's sit down. The police need to ask you some questions, I'm sure."

As he released me, I nodded. "Thank you for coming. I appreciate it."

"Where's your brother? Why wasn't he here with you?" Sam asked.

I dropped my gaze to the floor and pressed my lips together. "He had an unexpected change of plans. Matti wasn't able to come and stay with me after all."

Sam's body grew tense. Thunder rolled across his face, and lightning flashed in his eyes. He clenched his jaw as his posture stiffened as hard and unyielding as marble.

Finally he inhaled a deep breath and nodded. "It looks like things are under control now. I'll leave you to give your statement to the police."

Wearing his calm, controlled Dominant mien like an expensive Italian suit, Sam walked out the door. I knew my list of atonements had grown exponentially longer, and my hopes of a second chance with the man were dwindling fast. Fighting back my tears, I closed the door behind him. The snick of the lock seemed to reverberate with a finality I fought to accept.

As I made my way to the couch to begin answering the officer's questions, I wondered if the scale of disappointment between Sam and me would ever level out. Something inside me said I hadn't even scratched the surface.

~

Toward the end of my shift the next day, Jeb and Freddy brought a woman—a very pregnant woman—to the ER. My heart drummed in my chest as I darted furtive glances toward the double doors…waiting for Sam to come striding through. I didn't have to wait long. And butterflies swooped and dipped the minute I saw him. Though his professional expression was all he allowed me to see, I still thought him the most gorgeous man on the planet.

As Sam talked to the woman in that familiar calm and reassuring tone, my heart ached, remembering all the times I'd gotten upset or freaked out. He always used that same tenor on me. My fingers trembled over the keypad of my tablet as Freddy recited from the run sheet.

"We're going to do all we can to keep junior in there cooking for a few more weeks," Sam reassured the worried mother.

I set the tablet down and smiled at the woman. Suddenly her face contorted, and she let out an ear-piercing scream. Sam quickly positioned himself between her legs and issued a curse. Glancing up at me, he rattled off the list of instruments he needed. Dashing around the room, I collected the items and set them on a tray, but as soon as I lifted it, the mother threw her arms up. The sterile instruments scattered all over the floor.

"Goddammit," Sam barked, shooting me an angry glare. "We don't have time for this."

Turning away, I prepared a second tray as I fought back tears. Never, in all the times I'd worked alongside Sam, had he ever lashed out so vehemently…at any nurse.

"Dr. Brooks?" the mother wailed. "Is my baby—"

"Forgive me, Gretchen." Sam's tone immediately softened. "I didn't mean to frighten you. But it looks like junior has decided he's ready to join this big ol' world. Everything is going to be fine, I promise. Try to relax. Take some deep breaths."

Relax. Take some deep breaths. Sam had spoken those same words to me in the past. I felt myself beginning to spiral into a wasteland of regret. But I sucked in a deep breath and delivered the tray of instruments to him. He barely raised his eyes at me, then gave me a curt nod.

"Nurse Noland, would you please call a neonatologist and his team to come down here?"

"Yes, Sir. Right away."

Sam jerked his head up and flashed me a look I couldn't quite put my finger on. Was it sorrow? Disappointment? I wasn't sure. But before I could try to analyze his strange expression, he looked away. My fingers were still trembling as I rang the neonatal unit.

The mother screamed again, and I watched as a tiny, purple-skinned, wet baby girl slid into Sam's waiting hands. He quickly tied and cut the umbilical cord before wrapping the limp infant in a cotton blanket. There was too much blood rushing from the mother. I knew that wasn't a good sign.

With a ringing telephone pressed to my ear, I stopped one of the nurses in the hallway and told her to gather reinforcements. Seconds later, the room was a flurry of activity. While Sam tried to stabilize the mom, I worked on clearing the baby's airway. Thankfully the neonatologist rushed into the room, and after handing off the infant, I moved in to help Sam. My body hummed being so close to him. His heat surrounded me and I drank it in, savoring the sensation. But it was the familiar scent of his cologne that sent a flash of bittersweet memories to spool through my brain. Shaking off the sorrow that filled me, I watched as Sam packed the mother's uterus with sterile towels. I knew he was preparing to take her to surgery.

"I'll call ahead and have the OR set up a room for you," I offered in a low voice.

"Tell them I need it stat," he whispered.

"Of course."

Sam placed his hand on the mother's knee. "Gretchen, you have an awful lot of bleeding happening here. What do you say you and I go up to surgery, and I'll get that taken care of?"

"Do I have a choice?" she asked, suddenly turning ashen.

Sam sent her a crooked smile, meant to put her at ease. But I could see the worry in his stunning blue eyes. "No, not really. But I'll be quick. I promise."

While I was on the phone with the surgery department, the little baby let out a loud, long cry. Sam and I shared a brief glance of relief, but it was far too short.

"What about my little girl? Can I hold her?" Gretchen gasped.

"Not yet. They're still cleaning her up. She's a tiny one, but she's got a good set of lungs." He smiled. "She'll be waiting for you up in Neonatal ICU when you get out of surgery. Don't worry, Momma, you're both in good hands."

As soon as the words were out of his mouth, the neonatal team placed the infant in an incubator and quickly wheeled her away.

I hung up the phone and turned to Sam. "They'll be ready for you in room six."

Together we loaded up the mother. Once again, the heat and scent of his body played havoc with my concentration. I wanted to thread my fingers through his soft hair, touch his lips, and press my mouth to his. Because I was lost in the fantasies that were once my reality, Sam had to remind me—twice—to release the lock on the bed. After flashing me a scowl, he wheeled the mother out the door.

Watching him go, my heart twisted.

Turning away, I blinked back my tears and began helping the others clean up the trauma unit. When another emergency came through the doors, I knew it was going to be a late night. Even Metcalf stayed to help, which was a rarity.

At a quarter to ten, I punched the time clock and retrieved my purse. Tired and ready to go home, I slogged through the unit, toward the double doors. But before I could reach them, Metcalf stopped me and asked for a minute of my time. Curious, I followed him into an empty trauma unit, or rather, one I *assumed* was empty. Stepping inside, I found Sam with his hands in his pockets, wearing a grim expression.

"Did Gretchen—"

"She's doing fine," he confirmed. "I asked to speak with you because I wanted to be the one who told you."

"Told me what?"

Sam scrubbed a hand through his hair and blew out an explosive sigh. "I've asked Doctor Metcalf to bar you from my team here in the ER."

Like machine-gun fire, shock ricocheted through me. My lungs seized and my heart tripped double time. A dizzying wave made the room spin, and I sent up a silent prayer that I wouldn't pass out. Placing my palm against the wall, I used the surface as an anchor to keep my knees from giving out. A look of guilt crawled briefly across Sam's face, and I knew I'd failed to mask my shock and anguish. But then again, why should I hide the proof of what he'd done to me? The old Cin certainly would have…would have kept a stony exterior in place, then laid into Sam like a banshee. Never, ever would the old me have allowed him to witness the devastation he'd just inflicted.

But then Sam didn't have a clue that I no longer was *that* woman.

Sucking in a deep breath, I looked him directly in the eyes. "I appreciate you informing me yourself, Dr. Brooks. I will refrain from assisting you in any capacity from here on out."

Sam blinked. Confusion was written all over his face.

"Well, that went better than expected," Metcalf drawled. "Good night, all."

As soon as the other doctor left the room, Sam cocked his head and studied me for several long seconds. "That's it?"

"I'm not sure what else you want me to say. I'm sorry you find my skills…lacking?"

"You know better than that," Sam bit back as his brows slashed in suspicion. "What's happened to you?"

"I'm sorry. I don't understand your—"

"Why aren't you trying to fight me?"

I shrugged. "Because you're the physician, Dr. Brooks. If you no longer want me on your team, that's your prerogative."

"You're an extremely competent nurse, but I think, given our…history, it's probably easier on both of us this way."

"I agree. If you have nothing further, I'd like to go home now, Doctor."

A glimmer of sadness skittered over his eyes as he nodded. "No. Nothing else. Have a good night, Nurse Noland."

"You, too."

As I walked to my car sadness spilled over me, but along with it, a strange combination of victory and defeat. Victory that I hadn't turned into a raving bitch and verbally ripped into him, like an escapee from the psych ward. Defeat that he no longer desired me to work alongside him. The realization only made me anxious for my appointment with Liz and her Doms tomorrow night. Placing all my eggs in one basket was a big risk, but I had nothing left to lose. I'd already lost him.

Hopefully, if this all worked out right, Sam would see that I wasn't the same woman I used to be. And maybe, just maybe, he'd change his mind, too, about everything.

~

The following day couldn't go by fast enough. My stomach felt as if a rabble of butterflies swirled and dipped. I was both nervous and anxious as to what the evening might hold. Sensing my giddiness, Liz teased me relentlessly.

"What am I supposed to wear tonight?" I asked.

"I've got that taken care of. Come by around eight, but make sure you eat dinner first. I'll have plenty of water. It will be fun."

"Fun?" I choked. "I'm just hoping I don't pass the hell out."

"You won't. I promise." She giggled, then added, "Not in the first five minutes, anyway."

"Ugh," I groaned. "Are you trying to scare me away?"

"Not on your life. You'd better show up, or I'll come drag your ass to our place myself."

I quickly sobered. "No. I'll be there. This might be the only way I can reach Sam now."

A look of sorrow settled over her face. "I know. I heard he pulled you off his team."

"Good god. News sure travels fast around here."

Liz grimaced. "No. Sam came by late last night to talk to Ian and James."

"What did he say?"

Her shoulders slumped. "You know I can't tell you."

"Why not? You all weren't inside the club, for shit's sake," I whispered. "You let Ian see me when I was…"

"That was totally different," she spat softly. "I was worried I'd have to haul your brokenhearted ass to this hospital."

"If you had tried, I would have…I don't know, changed my damn locks." I threw up my hands and smirked. "I'm glad you didn't, and I'm glad you love me so much that you've put up with me being such a bitch all these years."

"You'll always be my bestie, bitch or not." Liz giggled.

"I love you." I pulled her in for a quick, tight hug, then looked at the clock. "Only another thirty minutes. Yikes. I'm going to be climbing the walls by the time I get to your place."

Liz shook her head and laughed. "Relax. It's going to be fine."

~

Everything was, until I arrived at the trio's house and Liz took me back to her bedroom.

"You mean I'm actually supposed to go prancing out there, in front of both your Doms, wearing *this*?" I gasped, holding up a tiny red thong and elegant corset.

"Oh, relax." Liz chided. "All your private parts will be covered. Besides, Ian and James won't do anything sexual to you, and vice versa. These lessons are aimed to teach you the dynamics of the power exchange, not sex. You already know all about that."

"I can wear my yoga pants and a T-shirt to learn in. Why do I have to dress—"

"Because fetish wear," she began as she loosened the laces of the corset, "will help center you. Put your head in a more submissive place. Not to mention, make you feel incredibly feminine. At least for me they do."

When Liz had finished trussing me up, I stared at myself in the mirror. The hard boned stays covered in red satin, embellished with a wide band of black lace and beads, outlined the bust and hem. The corset hugged my body like a glove. The metal busk closures along the front held my breasts in place as they arced over the beading, like toffee-colored pillows. Liz was right. I did feel decisively more feminine.

I couldn't help but wonder what Sam would say if he could see me now. A bittersweet smile tugged my lips.

"Oh, I keep meaning to ask you." Liz smirked. "Are you still having morning sickness?"

My mouth fell open and my eyes grew wide. "Not funny. I told you before, I'm not pregnant. I'm fine. It was nothing but a bit of the flu."

"Damn." She frowned. "I was hoping for a little baby Brooks to cuddle and coo over."

"If you want a baby, don't hold your breath for me to pop one out. Get busy making your own."

"I would love to, but right now, we're just practicing." She grinned, then sobered. "Are you ready to begin?"

I sucked in as much breath as the corset allowed and gave her a nod. As I followed her back to the spacious living room, it felt as if ants were crawling under my skin. But when Ian and James saw us enter the room, the approval in their eyes settled some of my anxiety.

"You look lovely, girl," Ian praised as he extended his hand to me.

"Remove your robe," James instructed Liz.

I couldn't help but smile when I saw she was wearing a corset as well. Though hers was black with white iridescent beads, she looked simply stunning.

"You are a vision, precious." James beamed.

"Thank you, Master," Liz replied shyly.

Ian flashed a proud smile her way, then focused his attention on me. "Tonight, we will work on basic submissive postures and protocol. Protocol being the most important of the two, as far as I'm concerned, but each Dominant has their own preference."

I listened intently as he kept his eyes focused on mine.

"When I ask you a question, the proper response I expect to hear is yes, Sir. Or no, Sir. Understood?"

"Yes, Sir," I replied.

"Very good." Ian smiled. "Now I'd like you to kneel for me."

"Am I supposed to say yes, Sir again?" I blurted out.

He chuckled and shook his head. "No, that's not necessary. Only if I ask you a direct question."

With a nod, I lowered to my knees and sank into the thick, soft carpet. Out of the corner of my eye, I saw Liz do the same. A rush of confidence and gratitude, for her being here alongside me, blossomed.

"Very nice," Ian complimented. "Rest your butt cheeks on the tops of your heels. Keep your back nice and straight, like it is now, then drop your chin. Good. Good. Now cast your eyes toward the floor and don't move."

Relieved that his directions were concise and simple, I couldn't help but wonder how many submissives he'd trained this same way.

"You look simply beautiful in your submissive pose, girl," he praised.

Warmth washed over my skin.

"Place the backs of your hands on your thighs, palms up…and simply let them rest there." I did as he instructed and waited. "Good. Now I want you to remain in this position while you clear your mind. I don't want you to focus on anything other than the serenity flowing through you and the sound of my voice when I speak. Do you understand?"

"Yes, Sir."

At first, I found myself studying the fibers of the carpet and not doing as Ian had said. But slowly, a gentle calmness started to settle through me. It was nearly the same sensation I'd felt when Sam had me on the bondage table at the club.

I missed him. Missed his control and command. Missed his warm laugh and gentle smile. Missed his lips, his arms, and the incredible way he sailed me to the heavens. My body ached and craved all the things I couldn't have.

"I can feel your mind churning, girl," Ian barked unexpectedly. I jolted. "Clear the thoughts from your head. Now."

As I invited back the peace I'd experienced moments before, my breathing began to slow, as did my pulse. I felt encapsulated in a kind of snow globe. And as the indescribable tranquility sank deeper and deeper, time seemed to evaporate. Lost in my inner silence, I didn't hear a doorbell or knock, only James' voice instructing Liz to answer the door and pulling me out of my reverie.

"Hello Master Sam," she greeted nervously. "Um, won't you come in?"

Yanked away from the gossamer, peaceful place, I jerked my head up and began to twist around.

"I didn't instruct you to move, sub," Ian thundered as he covered the top of my head with his palm, keeping me from stealing a glance back at Sam.

My body trembled. My plans were thwarted. I'd been thoroughly busted.

"What in the hell is going on here, Ian?" Sam barked.

"Why don't you ask the girl?" Though I couldn't see his face, I could hear the smile in Ian's voice.

In the blink of an eye, Sam's shoes appeared in front of my knees. "Look up at me, Allisinda," he demanded. I raised my head and gazed into his eyes, blazing in fury. "What the fuck are you doing?"

"I'm beginning a submissive training class, Sir."

"You're what?" His eyes grew wide. He staggered back as if I'd slapped him. "Why?"

I swallowed tightly.

The words that tumbled from my lips next would no doubt seal my fate with Sam. Either he'd realize that I was determined to be the woman he desired or he'd turn and walk away, for the final time.

"Because I know now how much I want you...need you. Need you in my life more than the stupid walls I'd built. Walls I thought would keep me from ever being hurt. But being away from you has hurt more than any pain I've ever endured. I want you, Sam, because you make me feel complete and whole." His expression softened, but only slightly. "I'm learning the ways of submission because I know this lifestyle is a big part of who you are...what you need. I finally understand that your Dominance is what makes you complete and whole."

"And what exactly do you hope to gain from this training?"

A lump formed in my throat. "A second chance with you, Sir."

Jerking his head toward Ian, Sam pinned the man with an icy glare. "Did you offer her *your* protection?"

Sam's angry demand had Ian raising his palms in surrender. "No. Hell no. I wouldn't do that to you. Christ, man. I'm simply teaching her the basics."

"Well, you can stop right here and now. If anyone is going to teach her, it's going to be me!" Sam bellowed.

Though the fury rolling off Sam was all but incinerating, my heart leapt for joy. Hope exploded inside me, like the grand finale on the Fourth of July. Tears of joy slid down my cheeks, and I bit my lips together to keep from grinning like a loon.

"I, ah...I think it might be best if the three of us head to the club...spend the night there even," James suggested with a laugh as he slipped an arm around Liz's waist.

My bestie was grinning from ear to ear as she flashed me an encouraging wink.

"I'll get our girl a coat and meet you two out front after you bring the truck around," Ian called out to James. Turning back toward Sam, the man seemed suddenly edgy. "Feel free to make yourselves at home. The dungeon's unlocked, and there's plenty of food in the fridge."

As Ian turned to escape, Sam grabbed him by the arm. "You fucking set me up, didn't you?"

Ian cracked a guilty grin, then quickly sobered. "Look, a few days ago, neither of you was fit for anything besides straightjackets."

I gaped at Sam. Hearing that he had suffered too filled me with shameful relief. Guilt darted across his face, as if embarrassed by Ian's disclosure.

"We're leaving so you two can work your shit out. Now do it."

I could tell Sam didn't like taking orders from Ian, but instead of arguing with the man, he simply issued a curt nod. Clenching his jaw, Sam locked his gaze on something behind me as Ian grabbed a coat from the closet and headed out the door. Neither of us said a word until the sound of James' truck faded into the distance.

"Tell me, who are you learning the lifestyle for? You or me?" Sam asked softly, still staring off as if lost in his own head.

"Both of us, Sir."

Finally, he settled his gaze on me. "What does being under a Dom's protection mean to you?"

"That I am not a free sub for other Doms. And that I only follow the commands of one Dom."

"That's right. And the Dom who offers you protection should not only train you but push your limits as well. Do you know what limits are?"

My mind had been blown so completely the night he'd taken me to the club, I couldn't remember if he'd talked about limits or not. I remembered clearly the conversation about free subs and protection, because I was seething with jealousy at the time.

"Things a submissive won't allow?" My reply was nothing but a stab in the dark.

"Are you asking or telling me, girl?"

Sam readjusted his stance. Squaring his shoulders, he tucked his hands behind his back, then spread his legs ever so slightly. His posture screamed power, authority...Dominance. My pussy grew hot and wet. My heart began hammering in my chest.

Still, a foreign sense of isolation emanated off Sam, as if he'd drawn the shades and barred the windows to keep me from delving too deep into his soul. I felt off-kilter and nervous. Yet the fact that he remained standing in front of me was a thread of hope. I clung to it tightly.

"Asking, Sir. I don't know the answer for certain."

"Pretty good guess," he replied flatly, then narrowed his eyes.

"There are three cornerstones to a successful BDSM relationship," he continued. "Honesty, communication, and trust. We'll begin with honesty. Right now."

He bent and gripped a fist in my hair, then tugged. I rose to my feet, trying not to moan, as tingles of pleasure-pain careened over my scalp. The wetness between my legs increased as he led me across the room to the couch.

"Sit."

I'd never witnessed his Dominance so potent and intense, not even at the club. His strict, no-nonsense demeanor sent a naughty thrill to skitter through me.

I eased onto the edge of the cushion, spine straight, shoulders back, and head level. Though Ian hadn't had time to teach me a proper sitting posture, I remembered seeing some of the subs at Genesis comport themselves in such a way. I wanted to show Sam that I wasn't playing a game but, instead, intending to give this my all.

He dragged an ottoman from a nearby chair over in front of me. Straddling it, Sam sat down. He slowly skimmed his gaze up my body, like a sinful caress. His stare lingered at my breasts, plumped up in offering beneath the sexy corset. The heated glimmer in his eyes and growing bulge beneath his zipper told me he approved of my outfit. Even beneath his draconian veneer, he couldn't hide his hunger from me.

Folding his arms over his chest, Sam dragged his stare to my face. "When you discovered that Matti wasn't staying with you, why didn't you call me? You knew damn well I didn't want you to be alone."

"Because you were angry with me. You said you needed a couple of days to think. I assumed that was merely a benevolent way of saying we were through."

"You assumed," he drawled with a frown. "So instead of asking me directly, you turned off your phone, stopped eating, and crawled into a black hole of depression, correct?"

"Yes, Sir."

I wanted to curse Ian for ratting me out. But then again, if it weren't for him, Sam and I wouldn't be having this conversation.

A sympathetic sadness flickered in his eyes. "Embarrassing to confess, but I didn't fare much better myself. Is that when you and Ian concocted this submissive training idea to try and manipulate me?"

"It wasn't meant as a manipulation, Sir. Rather a declaration, but yes."

"And that's the same day Ian and Liz discovered Matti wasn't staying with you?"

I nodded softly.

"Use your words."

His feral growl made goose bumps erupt over my flesh. "Yes, Sir."

His nostrils flared.

"Funny," he began without a hint of humor. "I've been talking to Ian since you and I parted. He never mentioned you were alone and unprotected. But then again, I assume he's kept my secrets guarded like he'd done for you."

Clearly Sam felt betrayed by all of us.

"I'll be honest with you, Cin. I'm more than a little suspicious about your sudden interest in the lifestyle."

"I'll be equally honest with you, Sir. I spent those two horrible days soul-searching. I discovered I'd been doing everything in my power to keep from turning out like my mother."

"You have a lot of issues with your parents, especially your mother."

"Yes, I do. I still haven't worked them all out. Maybe I never will." I shrugged. "But I'm determined to stop letting my past rule my future. I want to unlock the submissive inside me, for you or for a Dom who desires to take me under his wing."

The scowl on his face told me he didn't like the idea of me being with any Dom but him. Good. I didn't want another man, only him.

Sam patiently listened as I explained how I'd unearthed the stranger inside me. He nodded, accepting my apology for constantly arguing with him at the drop of a hat. And studied me intently when I confessed that I was working on discovering the real Allisinda Noland.

"So you see...I have removed the doors you'd grown so weary of kicking in." I smiled weakly.

"I never asked you to stop being you. I simply wanted the opportunity to teach you how to bend."

"I don't know why you even wanted to. I was nothing but a bitch." Sam arched his brows at my colorful language but couldn't hide the tiny smirk that tugged his lips. "The thought of bending...of giving even so much as an inch was overwhelming. I'd convinced myself that compromise was weakness. Deep down, I wanted to bend but was terrified I would break. Then everyone, especially you, would see I wasn't the smart, strong, independent woman. Simply the epic failure I'd been brainwashed into believing. But in the end, I only served to fail myself along with you and pretty much everyone around me. I know it sounds insane, but in my mind, the only way I could keep from turning into someone I loathed was by being someone I wasn't."

My explanation sounded psychotic and totally irrational even to my own ears.

"Please don't call Tony and have me committed. I'm not crazy; I've just been horribly confused for a really long time."

A huge grin spread over Sam's lips. His eyes sparkled in amusement, and I felt as if the sun had burst through dark storm clouds above me. Warmth and light shined down over my skin and illuminated all the dark, empty corners of my soul.

"You're not crazy, girl. I've known for a long time how you use defiance to deflect your fears."

Blinking, I gaped at him. "I wish you would have told me that."

Sam let out a laugh. "What? And provoke World War Three? Not on your life."

I couldn't help but chuckle. "Yes, it was probably a good choice."

"Thankfully I didn't have to. You dissected your own issues. Some people never look inside themselves. It's easier and a lot less painful to simply turn a blind eye to the things we don't want to see, not only in ourselves but life in general. I'm very proud of you for not doing that."

I felt heat rise to my cheeks. "Thank you, Sir."

Sam sent me a tender smile. For the first time in days, I finally felt as if everything might truly work out.

"I need to know something." His smile vanished. "The few things I introduced to you in regard to the lifestyle…controlling your orgasms, the spankings. On a scale from one to ten, how much did you honestly enjoy them?"

"Nine," I blurted out.

This time it was Sam's eyes that grew wide and his mouth that fell open. "You're fucking kidding me, right?"

"No, Sir," I whispered. "I-I was afraid. Not that you were going to beat me or hurt me. But afraid that…well, of a lot of things, actually."

"List them for me. One by one," he instructed in that panty-melting Dominant tone.

I mentally aligned the fears that kept me from embracing the lifestyle. "You already knew I equated submission with weakness. You tried to tell me that wasn't the case, then I spent time with some of the subs at Mika and Julianna's, and I finally saw that for myself."

"I'm glad you kept your mind open enough to discern that, girl."

I nodded gently.

"Continue."

"After Jeb and Freddy showed up the night Kerr was shot, I worried that rumors would start circulating and that I'd lose my job and have to explain to my parents why. At the time, that was so ungodly overwhelming I wanted to steer clear of the club and everything it represented."

"And now?"

"A bit, but I've decided to pull up my big-girl panties, so to speak. How I choose to live my life is no one's business but my own...kinky proclivities and all. If I'm outed, I'll deal with those consequences, but I'm done borrowing trouble and automatically jumping to negative conclusions."

Sam's smile said he approved, but he cautioned, "I don't want you putting undue pressure on yourself, because breaking old habits is hard. Simply do your best. We'll establish a set of rules later that will help you accomplish what you want. Go on. I need to hear the rest."

"I don't want to do or say anything that will embarrass you in front of the other club members. I'm afraid—"

"Stop right there," Sam interrupted. "Every member of that club was new at one time or another. Most are well aware that you've had no formal training...yet. They're not as judgmental and unforgiving as you assume them to be."

"I'm not concerned with their opinion of me. Well, that's not entirely true. To some degree, I am, but I'm worried I won't exemplify your status, Sam...I mean, Sir."

A strange, quizzical expression settled over his face. "Did Ian talk to you about submissive responsibilities?"

"No, Sir." My heart fluttered. "Is there some kind of test I have to pass in order to get my...I don't know, submissive badge or something?"

He bit back a laugh and shook his head. "That's not a bad idea, girl. But no, we're not a kinky scout troop or anything."

"See?" I groaned. "That's what I'm talking about. I don't want to embarrass you in front of your friends with my ridiculous questions."

Sam reached out and cupped my cheek. A current of electricity zapped my senses. "There are no ridiculous questions. I thought you didn't care what other people thought anymore."

"I don't...not about me. But my ineptness is a reflection on you."

He smirked. "Trust me. If you cross the line, I'll take you straight over my knee."

Desire rippled down my spine. My nipples grew taut, and I bit back a moan.

A knowing grin spread over Sam's lips. "On second thought, I'll arrange another form of punishment. One you won't enjoy quite so much."

"As you wish, Sir."

"Now that's a sweet response I'll never grow tired of hearing, girl." With a wink, he released my face and silently waited for me to continue.

"I think what I feared most and what caused me to fight the lure of submission you awakened within me is that I would like it too much. I wouldn't be able to walk away if I needed to."

"From me or the lifestyle?"

"Both, Sir."

"Are you still worried about that?"

"No, Sir."

"Why not? What changed that for you?"

CHAPTER TWELVE

Instead of answering him, I slid from the couch and knelt at his feet. Casting my eyes to the floor as Ian had taught me. Sam hissed a curse and shoved the ottoman aside. I could practically feel the heat rising inside him. Uncertain if his fire was lust or anger, I inhaled a deep breath and readied myself to see either.

Lifting my head, I skimmed my gaze up his body, forcing myself to continue the trek past his enticing erection, and stared into his eyes.

Lust. Definitely lust.

Thank god.

"When I finally found the courage to strip myself bare, I realized that bringing you pleasure not only roused a sense of empowerment but also awakened a primitive and fundamental need deep within me. A need so visceral that all the dark, kinky eccentricities outweighed my fear of the unknown. When I was on the table in the dungeon, across your lap for that spanking, and again kneeling here tonight, a sense of absolute peace filled me. I want more of that, but only with you."

A slow smile crawled across his mouth. "I'd say the submissive within you has woken."

"Yes, Sir. I believe she has."

"And that doesn't frighten you any longer?"

"No, Sir. It makes me hunger for more."

"Let's see if we can fill you up, shall we?"

The idea set me ablaze. "I'd like that, Sir...very much. There's one more thing I'd like to say."

"Go ahead."

"The day I was supposed to stay with you," I began softly. "I'm truly sorry for disappointing you."

Sam stooped, settling on his haunches before tucking a finger beneath my chin and forcing my gaze. A look of pain etched his face. "You didn't disappoint me, Cin. You kicked me in the teeth. I was serious when I said that I hoped you would stay forever. I'm sorry, too. I lashed out at you in anger and slammed my own door in your face. Afterward, I questioned whether or not I'd done the right thing. My head and heart went to war. The battle was bloody and lasted for days. Like you, I couldn't eat, barely slept, and all the while, I tried to convince myself that letting you go was for the best."

The torment in his voice and the haunted lines in his face broke my heart. Sam's confession was costing him. That much was clear. The apology I'd rendered paled in comparison to the agony I'd inflicted. I made a silent vow to make it up to him...if he'd let me.

"Even after I'd succeeded...or rather, thought I'd succeeded, and set you free, the paralyzing numbness didn't go away." He closed his eyes and exhaled a heavy sigh before capturing my stare once more. "Last night, when we were working on Gretchen, I wanted to crawl the fuck out of my skin. Your scent, the gentle sway of your body... Fuck. All I could think about was grabbing you, slamming you up against the wall, and claiming your mouth, kissing you senseless. I wanted to drive myself inside you, brand my soul so deep to yours that you'd never forget me."

Tears trickled down my cheeks. "How could I ever forget you, Sam? You're so deep inside me...wild horses couldn't drag you away. That's why you removed me from your team, isn't it?"

"Yes. I was so distracted and unfocused that I had to fight to do right by my patient. It scared me, Cin. I knew that if I didn't pull my shit together, I'd eventually fuck up and hurt someone. I couldn't live with myself if I let that happen. I'm sorry. It wasn't fair to do to you, but I simply couldn't see any other way. Telling Metcalf to pull you nearly ripped my guts out."

"It's okay, Sam. I understand... I do." I sent him a watery smile.

"I never stopped wanting you."

"Take me home, Sam," I sniffed. "I want to pack my bags. That is...if you'll have me."

Fire smoldered in his eyes, and his nostrils flared as he cupped my cheeks and wiped my tears with the pads of his thumbs. Leaning forward, he tumbled onto his knees, then captured my lips in a spine-melting, earth-quaking kiss. I tasted his longing, his claim, his unbridled passion, but most of all...his love. Sliding my fingers against his scalp, I poured every particle of my soul into the kiss.

As I swallowed his moan of approval, Sam lifted me into his arms and laid me back on the couch. His lips never left mine as our tongues danced in a sweeping duel of passion. And when he tore his mouth from mine to devour my neck, and the lobe of my ear and to trace the line of my jaw with his lips, I issued a groan of bliss.

I arched up to him, wordlessly offering. Silently begging.

Yearning for him to consume me at will. And he did as I writhed beneath him, heated, wet, and ready.

This is where I belonged.

Suddenly, Sam pulled back and stared down at me. His lips were swollen and glistening, and in his eyes I saw my future. No longer hindered behind a worthless fortress of denial, I reached up and cradled his rugged face in my palms.

"I love you, Sam," I softly whispered.

As if I'd taken a hammer to granite, his fierce and hungry expression crumbled. Even the muscles straining his arms and shoulders softened, and a tender smile settled over his lips.

"I love you, too, sweetheart," he murmured, low and earnest.

"Kiss me. Please," I pleaded, unable to peel my gaze from the raw emotion shimmering in his eyes.

"Only because you beg so sweetly." He smirked before capturing my mouth beneath another devastating assault.

He cupped one hand around my breast. The heavy fabric and rigid bone stays made it impossible for me to feel the heat of his flesh, let alone the sublime slide of his thumb over my nipple. Yes, I felt the sensation, but it lacked the usual zing to my core.

"I need... Oh, god... I need..." I murmured as he bathed my neck in kisses.

"What, my gorgeous girl? Tell me, and I'll make all your needs come true."

He nipped the sensitive flesh at my pulse point and I groaned. "Your flesh."

With his lips still pressed to my throat, he chuckled. The vibration rumbled through me like wicked thunder.

"We need to leave, sweetheart. I want to properly undress you with my teeth, lick your sweet, milk-chocolate skin, and sip the spicy nectar as it pours from inside you."

Chills raced beneath my flesh. I nodded and issued a breathless, "Yes."

He chuckled, stood, and then helped me off the couch. I wobbled slightly, drunk on everything about the man.

"I'll go grab my clothes," I offered.

"No." His one-word answer stopped me dead in my tracks. "You no longer tell me what you're going to do, girl. But you may certainly ask my permission."

"Oh, right. Oops. Sorry, Sir. May I please get my clothes from Liz's bedroom?"

"No. You may not. I happen to enjoy looking at your sexy little body the way it is. We'll pick up your clothes and your car after work tomorrow before we stop by your place to pack your bags. Right now, you're coming home with me…just the way you are."

"Yes, Sir." I grinned.

Before leaving, Sam shot off a text to Ian, thanking him for the use of their home. And informed him that we would lock up and added a rather ominous postscript that the two of them would be having a long, serious discussion soon. When I asked Sam about the latter, he flashed me a brittle smile.

"He knowingly left my girl unprotected. Ian and I *will* have words."

That was one conversation I wanted no part of. "I don't want my selfish actions to come between you and your friend, Sir."

"Relax, girl. It won't escalate into an argument. Trust me."

I couldn't help but smile. "I do, Sir. Explicitly."

After sliding out of his suit coat, Sam draped it around my shoulders, then escorted me to his car. Seated in the soft, buttery leather seats once again, I closed my eyes and inhaled the familiar scent of leather and Sam. I felt as if I'd come home from a long, arduous journey. One I didn't want to repeat. And in many ways, I had.

We reached Sam's house in record time, and I followed him up the grand staircase and down the hall. Instead of turning into his bedroom, Sam gripped the knob—on what I'd always thought was a linen closet—and opened the door.

After flipping on the light, he pressed his hand to the small of my back and urged me inside an elegant dungeon. It was decorated in black and red, and the recessed lighting illuminated several pieces of glossy, polished wooden furniture. Floggers and whips and other toys I couldn't recall the names of hung on individual hooks along the wall, much like at Genesis. The pungent scent of leather filled my senses. A long padded table covered in smooth black hide captured my attention. It resembled the one Sam had coerced me into lying on at the club.

He moved in close behind me and settled his mouth close to my ear. "Tell me where you're at, sweetheart."

Turning my head, I frowned. "I'm in your house in your dungeon."

Silent laughter shook his body as he grinned. "Yes. Indeed you are." Unable to wipe the smile from his face, he kissed me quickly. "I meant, where are you in relation to anxiety or fear?"

"Oh, I'm fine, Sir. I'm not afraid at all. Anxious? Well, yes, I'm anxious to experience what you have in store for me, but I'm not afraid."

"Very good. We'll adopt the same phrases commonly used for safe words and stoplights. Green means you're totally fine. Happy. In a good place mentally and wish to continue. Yellow is, of course, caution. You've reached a point where you're not sure you want more. You need me to stop or at least slow down while we discuss the scene for a bit. And naturally, red stops everything. Use that word when I've hit an unknown trigger or you can no longer endure the sensations. Does all that make sense?"

"Yes, Sir."

"If you have any questions, ask. In light of your inner awakening, I think communication will be a much smoother road for us. However, we need to invest a lot more time and energy into conversation. If I can keep my mouth off you long enough to talk, that is." With a feral growl, he nibbled the ticklish spot behind my ear.

With a squeal, I started to giggle. My laughter quickly morphed into a low whimper when Sam slid his jacket from my shoulders and snaked a hand to my cunt. Sliding his fingers beneath the fabric of my thong, he swiped them along my saturated folds.

"Mmm," he moaned. "Hot and wet. Just the way I like you."

I closed my eyes as a blissful sigh tumbled off my tongue. Suddenly Sam stepped away, and I slowly dragged my heavy lids open.

"Your safe word is still red. Now up on the table, my little sparrow," he instructed, patting his hand on the thickly padded surface.

I sucked in an anxious breath and climbed onto the cool leather. It felt good against my heated skin. Sam extended his hand and I placed my fingers in his palm as he helped me recline. An icy chill rippled through me as my body slowly began to warm the chilly hide.

"Tell me where you're at now, girl." Sam smiled as he trailed his hand up and down my leg.

"Green, Sir. Totally green."

"Good girl."

Another quiver racked my body, this time from the pride infused in those two small yet powerful words.

"You won't be needing this any longer," he explained as he reached over and gripped my thong. After dragging it down my legs and off my body, Sam raised the scrap of silk to his nose. Sucking in a deep breath, he inhaled the scent of my arousal as if it were a rare, expensive wine.

"Christ, I've missed the smell of your tart and tangy spice, girl."

Everything about him screamed controlled savage. Arousal spiked. Anticipation, like a string of tiny explosions, fired in my cells. Sam was my own personal demolition team. And I thoroughly suspected that before this night was through, he would flatten me...all the way to my foundation.

"You look... I can't describe it. Words don't do justice. Having you spread out before me like a succulent smorgasbord of submission...well, you're even more beautiful than my fantasies. Oh, yes, little one, I fantasized about you gracing my dungeon, constantly."

My cheeks warmed and my heart melted. "I'm honored to be here, Sir. Hopefully I can make the dreams you've longed for come true."

"You already have, my love. You already have."

Bending, Sam softly kissed my lips, then stood and plucked up a bundle of white rope. My pulse quickened, and my mind sailed back to the silk scarf draped over my wrists. Holding the rope in his open palm, Sam studied my reaction with the pinpoint precision of a hawk.

"Still green, gorgeous?" he asked, arching his brows.

"Yes, Sir." I nodded.

"Good. Reach out and touch the rope for me, girl. Caress your fingers over the braided silk. I am going to bind your wrists tonight, Allisinda. But only your wrists," he explained as I stroked the soft twine. "If for any reason you get scared, I want you to use your words. My responsibility is to help push your submission to endless levels, but your responsibility is to communicate with me. Tell me if you feel that I'm pushing you too hard…too fast. Do you understand your job?"

"Yes, Sir." I sent him a confident nod.

"Very well. Relax and hand everything over to me. Let me be the guardian of your body, heart, mind, and soul."

Butterflies fluttered, dipping and swooping in my stomach. But I needed to press forward, for both of us.

Sam lifted the rope to my lips. "Kiss the cord that I bind you with."

"You want me to kiss the rope, Sir?"

"Yes. You worship my cock with your mouth to give me pleasure, correct?"

"Yes, Sir." I timidly placed my lips on the soft cord.

"I take tremendous pleasure using various implements during a session. They're like an extension of me, and I expect you to worship them as you would any other part of my body."

"I will, Sir."

"Good girl."

He bent once more and claimed my lips in a deep, soulful kiss. As he held my focus with his talented tongue, Sam lifted my arms up over my head. He held them there until I was dizzy with desire, then slowly lifted from my mouth.

Taking a step back, he admired me. His eyes twinkled in awe as if I were a goddess on a pillow of gold.

"What do you want, sweetheart?"

"To please you, Sir."

"Fuck. You already do, love. In many amazing ways."

Trailing his fingers up my arms, Sam stopped and unwound the rope. I arched my neck and watched, waiting for him to bind me, but he merely draped the soft fabric over my wrists, seesawing it back and forth. Anxiety and impatience galloped through my veins, neck in neck, like racehorses at the Preakness. I closed my eyes and inhaled a trembling breath, working hard to tamp down the edginess blossoming inside.

Sam wanted every uncompromising cell in my body, and for once, I was brave and secure enough to give him exactly what he craved, without reservation.

"Where are you, Allisinda?" Sam asked in a voice thick with emotion.

"I'm green, Sir. Greener than…grass and frogs."

Sam chuckled. "That's pretty green, girl. Is there something you want to ask me?"

"Yes… I mean…no, Sir."

"Which is it? Yes? Or no?" he asked, now taunting me by looping the rope around each wrist, then releasing it.

"I'm fighting the urge to demand," I confessed on a disgruntled groan.

"Demand what?"

"That you stop tormenting me and tie me up already," I blurted out.

Reaching beneath my corset, Sam pinched my nipple. I sucked in a startled breath as the sweet burn spread deep into my flesh. He smiled and leaned close to my ear. "I'm not trying to make you suffer, girl. Not yet, at least. All you have to do is ask…beg me to tie you up, Allisinda."

His smoky tone of voice spread over me like a blanket of velvet. Soft. Thick. Comforting.

"Please, Sir...will you bind me?"

I didn't have to beg twice. A deep rumble rolled from his chest as he gathered my wrists together and cinched the rope around them in a matter of seconds. I tried to lower my arms, but the rope held firm.

Strong.

Unyielding.

"Green?" Sam asked, arching his brows.

"Oh, yes, Sir. Green as a meadow in spring."

He chuckled again. "I like your analogies, sweetheart. But I like seeing you bound for my pleasure a hell of a lot more."

He drank me in beneath a heavy-lidded gaze. I could all but feel the caress of his fingers stroking my skin.

"It's time for this to go. It's in my way."

His fingers moved painstakingly slowly, releasing the bus, before he spread the edges of my corset open, like the pages of a book. A book he'd read a thousand times. Yet now, we were starting a new chapter...together.

"Stunning," he murmured, brushing a rapturous stare over my naked, bound body.

I couldn't feel his touch fast enough. Impatience spiked. And as if reading my mind, Sam placed his wide, warm hands upon flesh, caressing with such reverence I felt as if he were worshiping me. Tinges of confusion niggled my brain. Wasn't I supposed to worship him? He brushed his thumb in a feather-soft slide over my nipple. I closed my eyes and drifted away while a salacious ache invaded my body.

"The sweet scent of your cunt makes my balls churn," Sam growled. I opened my eyes and sent him a shy smirk. "Makes me want to spread you open...latch on to your pretty wet orchid to lick, suck, and tongue fuck you into oblivion."

His lurid words painted such vivid images in my head that I couldn't form syllables. With a whimper and a moan, I rolled my hips as slick nectar spilled down, coating the puckered opening of my ass.

"Not yet, my eager girl. I'm only beginning to warm you up."

Beginning? The flames he'd ignited inside were already consuming me. Obviously, he wanted me to burn even higher and brighter. I wasn't about to complain.

Sam cupped my breasts, kneading and squeezing the orbs, as he further tormented my hard, erect peaks with his thumbs. No, there would definitely be no complaining. Instead, I mewled as my muscles melted like putty in his hands.

"What an amazing gift you give me, Cin. Your power is heady and so fucking strong, but make no mistake, sweetheart. The things I'm doing to you, right here, right now, aren't about me but about you. About proving that you can toss away that refined, good-girl persona and be the naughty nymph clawing inside to be free." A carnal smile stretched his lips. "Trust me, baby. I'll make all your dark and dirty dreams come true."

His words seared my veins, stole my breath, and touched my psyche far deeper than his hands ever could. Sam intended to set me free.

Free to seek out who I always wanted to be...me.

That peaceful, floating sensation settled over me once again. The only tension I felt was the gentle reminder of the rope embellishing my wrists and emphasizing my need to please Sam.

Gripping my breasts in each hand, he forcefully squeezed the orbs, sending my nipples to jut toward the ceiling like chocolate candy kisses. He licked his lips, then opened his mouth and sucked one peak in, deep. I cried out as the slick, heated softness of his tongue and gentle suction sent a scorching coil of demand to unfurl low in my womb. Several sweet torturous minutes later, he released my nipple—glistening wet and hard as a pebble—before latching on to the other with the same sinful devotion.

My fingers twitched, and I tugged at the rope, longing to grip his hair and hold Sam to my breast while he bathed me with this captivating splendor. But my restraints held tight, keeping me bound to Sam, tethered to his soul, in idyllic and helpless surrender.

In that one pivotal moment, I handed him all of my control. I finally understood what it felt like to be truly loved, decidedly treasured, and wholly owned.

As if he sensed the shift within me, a subtle shudder rippled through Sam's body.

He raised his head and captured my stare. "Yes, my sweet slut. I'll nurture, protect, and love you while I mold you into all you've ever longed to be."

Sam bent and dragged his lips over mine. "Thank you, Sir...I love you, too," I murmured against his mouth.

He smiled and reached up before massaging my fingers and palms. A smirk tugged his lips. "How does it feel to be...my captured *slave*?"

My cheeks grew hot at the memory of how I'd rudely scolded Mika that first night at the club. While the term didn't evoke the same level of disgust, I wasn't ready to embrace the word wholeheartedly. Maybe someday...

"Don't fret, sweetheart. When it's time, I'll claim you as my slave, but not tonight."

Dragging his hands down my arms, Sam sent me a hungry smile. "Spread your legs for me, girl. Spread them wide."

Oh, yes. That Dominant tenor—the one that made me tingle from head to toe—had returned.

As I complied, his heated expression contorted to a raw and savage one. He looked almost beastly. It turned me on even more.

Inviting his pleasure, and mine, I let my knees fall open wider. When the cool air met my sweltering folds, I couldn't hold back a loud whimper. Sam's stare locked on my splayed-out pussy as a vicious snarl curled over his lips.

"Are you intending to tempt me, girl?"

"Most definitely, Sir," I replied in a sultry voice.

"Well, I did ask for honesty, now didn't I?" Sam chuckled and shook his head. "Then I suggest you stop right now. What you're doing is called Topping from the bottom. In other words, you're trying to control me, or rather, control what you want *from* me. Unfortunately, all you'll gain from such manipulation is a long session of edging."

I sucked in a startled gasp and shook my head. "No. I'll stop. I-I don't want *that*."

"You know what edging is? How?"

"At the party, Mika threatened Julianna. Liz had to explain to me what it was. I-I don't have any desire to experience that."

"It's not always used for punishment, sweetheart. Edging serves a duel purpose. Besides, there are other ways to obtain forgiveness."

Expounding on his promise, Sam picked up a whip. He slid a fist over the snake-like leather braid. Pivoting sideways, he raised his arm and arced the whip high in the air, then gave a gentle snap of his wrist. The concussion split the air so loudly that I jumped and yelped.

"I trust you'll behave properly?"

"Yes, Sir. I'll be an absolute angel." I nodded emphatically.

"We wouldn't want you to be too perfect, sweetheart. It takes away all the fun of keeping you in line."

I couldn't help but grin. "I'll remember that, Sir."

"I suspect you won't have any difficulty presenting me with challenge, girl." He winked, then quickly sobered. "Now where was I?"

"Is that a rhetorical question, Sir?" I smirked.

"You'll find out soon enough," he countered with a wicked grin.

His ominous warning only piqued my curiosity. As I watched him move to the foot of the table, I wondered if this piece of equipment was as *user friendly* as the one at Genesis. Preparing myself in case the bottom literally dropped out from under me, I wrapped my fingers around the taut rope and held on.

With a look of fierce concentration, Sam began disassembling and reassembling portions of the table. A few minutes later, he reached up and stroked my leg. With a reassuring smile, he lifted each ankle, then guided my feet onto the wide wooden flanges fixed to the outer edges of the table.

"Keep your feet where they are, or I'll tie them as well," Sam warned.

Reaching beneath the table, he pulled a metal bar free. The center section fell away, landing on the carpet with a thud. As he knelt between my legs, his own knees resting on the soft padding, I marveled at the ingenuity of the table's construction. Sam's broad hands slid up my thighs. His hot breath wafted over my sex, and the wonders of ergonomic furniture went right out the window.

Holding me with a hungry gaze, he scraped his fingers through my dewy curls. "Bronze, bound, and beautiful. Just exactly how I want you, my sweet slut."

The gratification sparkling in his eyes sent a satisfied thrill skipping through me. It made me want to give him more than just my physical body, the air in my lungs, or the blood in my veins. It made me ache to give him all the pieces of my soul.

Before my inner awakening, I'd focused on the orgasm awaiting me at the end of our hot and sweaty coupling. But now, I felt as if some potent and life-altering surprise would be set free long before any sexual release.

Brushing his lips against the insides of my thighs, Sam teased my flesh with his heated breath, the flick of his tongue, and the gentle scrape of his teeth.

"What a glorious creature you are, Allisinda. Helpless…tied to my mercy…my command, and all the darkness that prowls the corners of my mind," he drawled in a whiskey-smooth voice.

A sturdy shiver racked my body. My nipples drew impossibly tighter, and a rush of liquid fire spilled from inside me as Sam crawled deep inside my head.

Drawing the flat of his tongue up my folds in a languid sweep, he continued. "But you don't want to escape the pleasure I long to give you. Do you, sweetheart?"

"No, Sir."

"I'm going to make you beg for me, little one. Beg and scream, and oh, yes…cry. Make you spill tears of frustration, of agony and bliss…all for me. And I'm going to sip those precious tears between my lips…girl. Drink in the beautiful torture that flows from your soul."

"Sam," I cried in a mournful wail.

Without warning, he slapped his fingers over my pussy. I let out a scream as the sting merged with throbbing tissue.

"How do you address me, sub?"

"Sir. I mean, I'm sorry, Sir," I quickly amended as I sucked in a ragged breath.

"Much better, my sweet slut. You've earned yourself a reward."

Latching on to my cunt, Sam sucked and licked my clit as he drove his fingers inside my slippery tunnel. Strength pervading softness, like ying and yang, he burrowed deep—twisting and strumming—awakening the hidden bundle of nerves until they sang in pursuit of relief.

Demand surged like the sun. Blistering hot, in a blinding, shimmering light. Whimpers spilled from my lips with every stab of piercing pleasure…each drawing suckle of swelling ecstasy.

Tossed and tumbled beneath the splendor of his mouth and fingers, I reached the precipice harder and faster than ever before. My keening cries filled the room as I writhed beneath his hands and mouth. Hovering on the cusp of no return, I screamed his name. "Sam…Sir…help me, I can't…"

"No," he thundered.

Snapping his head up, Sam dragged his fingers from inside me. A mournful wail tore from my throat. The tingling numbness engulfing my fingers and toes dissipated as he hauled me back from the brink. Frustration thundered in my veins as my cunt clutched at the sudden barrenness. Every cell in my body screamed to roll beneath the waves of glory and shatter apart.

"Look at me." Sam's command boomed off the walls and echoed in my ears, like a drum.

Blinking, I forced myself to focus on his fierce gaze. Targeted my attention to the juices glistening down his chin and his plump, slick lips. God, I wanted to kiss him. Wanted to sink into the onslaught of his mouth. Feel his tongue snake with mine as he gripped my hair in his mighty fist.

He instilled the true meaning of being helpless...being totally dependent on his mercy with an onslaught of emotions that simply overwhelmed. Yet all I could do was stare at the man while I pitifully panted and writhed in need.

"You do not have permission," he whispered in wicked reminder.

"I know, Sir...but I—"

"Yes, sweetheart, I, too, know how desperately you want release. That still isn't going to make it happen. You'll hold back that blistering orgasm for me until I give you permission. Is that clear?"

"Yes...yes, Sir," I gasped, trying desperately to quiet my gnawing demand.

"Good girl. I trust you won't fail me," he taunted with an evil smile.

How could I *not* fail? I'd handed him my power and control.

Most submissives are just as headstrong and independent as you.

I never asked you to stop being you.

We wouldn't want you to be too perfect, sweetheart. It takes away the fun of keeping you in line.

Sam's words came rushing back to me in a waterfall of awakening. This confusing alternative lifestyle finally began making sense. Submission didn't mean I had to cower in the corner, spineless and weak. I didn't have to redefine my identity or conjure some other useless alter ego again. Submission was the embodiment of the woman who'd been hiding inside me all along. The woman Sam had been able to identify long before I knew existed.

Submission wasn't about Sam stripping away my strength, control, and self-esteem. It was about trusting him enough to grant me a reprieve from responsibilities and decisions. To find safety and security in the palm of his masterful hand.

A newfound sense of pride and courage filled me.

"I'll do my best, Sir," I promised with a resolute nod.

"Then suffer sweetly for me, girl."

Beneath the torturous, sublime combination of his fingers and mouth, Sam devoured me. Soaring me to the heavens time and time again before stopping and leaving me suspended in a vexing void of sob-inducing denial.

Tears poured down my cheeks as I begged and pleaded for release.

I was out of my mind with need.

"Look at you, precious," Sam cooed as he stared at me in awe. "You're so fucking beautiful. And you're mine…all mine."

"H-help m-me. Please, Sir," I pitifully pleaded.

"Soon, my sweet slut…very soon," he whispered as he nipped my clit with his lips.

At some point in my haze of frustration, Sam had moved to the side of the table. Sipping my tears as I sobbed, he plucked and pinched my nipples. Stealing the sweet carnal throb thrumming inside me, he replaced it with a wicked, biting burn. Screams tore from my lips as I thrashed, trying to escape his evil fingers. But I was pinned for his pleasure. Pinned for his pain.

Trapped.

Helpless.

At his mercy.

Bending, he laved his tongue over my fiery peaks. Chasing away the discomfort with lashes of slick, sweet pleasure. My screams morphed into moans as I rocked my hips, desperate to satiate the blaze raging between my legs.

Pulling away, he took a step back, then began stripping off his clothes.

Yes. Yes. He's finally going to fuck me, my mind repeated in an endless loop. But my gaze was locked and drinking in every inch of the sculpted flesh he revealed. When Sam kicked off his pants and slowly slid off his boxers, I wept at the sheer beauty of the man...my Sir.

"Shhh, little one," he murmured. "I'm going to make it all better for you, baby. I promise."

Fisting his cock with one hand, Sam stroked my cheek with the other. His actions were a mind-bending paradox of taunting and soothing. The old Allisinda wanted to scream, to rail at him to stop messing with me and shove his fat, beautiful cock into my cunt. But that would only leave me in a perpetual state of misery, both emotionally and sexually.

Tossing my head from side to side, I pleaded and begged. Finally he ambled between my legs once more. Pausing, Sam stared down at me, fascination written all over his face.

"Christ, Allisinda...I've never seen you like this. So fucking needy. I'd love to keep you this way...forever."

"No!" I screamed. "I can't...take anymore. Please. Help me."

"Where are you, girl?"

"I'm... I don't know. The colors are swirling. I just want you to make this fucking ache stop."

He softly chuckled. "So you want me to stop? Is that what you're saying?"

"No!" I shrieked, unable to contain any semblance of submission. Did he really think I wanted him to leave me hanging in this ungodly desperate state?

"Then tell me what you want, girl," he demanded, then pressed the crest of his cock against my throbbing pussy.

"I want you to fuck me. Please. Fuck me hard and fast."

"And who do you want fucking you, sweet slut? Your Sir or your Master?"

As his question slowly penetrated my fervid fog, the air caught in my lungs.

"My Master," I whimpered.

Pride suffused his face.

"Then beg your Master to fuck you, sweetheart," he roared.

"Fuck me, Master. Please. Fuck me like you've never fucked me before. I need you...need everything about you."

Sam's image blurred as tears spilled down my cheeks. I blinked so I could see his face clearly. Pride glowed, yet his jaw ticked. He didn't move, as if he were locked in place, struggling to gain a semblance of control...control over us both.

"Take your Master's cock, girl," he hissed as he drove himself inside me to the hilt.

Ecstasy and pain shot through me like a locomotive. Tossing my head back, I screamed as pleasure and fire ripped through my system. Sam gripped my hips, digging his fingers into my flesh, while my cunt fluttered around him.

"That's it, baby. Suck the come from my balls, like a good little slave," Sam choked.

A fine sheen of sweat broke out over his face as he held still inside me.

Bucking and writhing, to escape the burn engulfing my sex, I pressed my feet against the wooden slats and rocked my hips.

"Stop," he growled. "You don't decide when I start sliding in and out of your silky, tight pussy. I told you I'd make it better...and I will. In my own sweet time."

Using his thumb, Sam circled my enflamed clit. Pulses of pleasure zipped and sputtered. My tunnel relaxed. The burning subsided. With a slow drag, Sam pulled back, then pressed past my narrow walls. Over and over, with an achingly slow tempo, as if meant to make me feel every fat inch and distended vein. Intermittent flecks of light flickered and faded behind my eyes as I strained for control.

My control.

Swamped in sensation, the synapses in my brain misfired. Unable to string together the importance or meaning of that realization, too focused on the magic spell Sam had cast upon me.

Friction and pressure increased as did his thrusts while he urged me higher and higher toward that elusive release. Sam's heavy balls slapped against my puckered rim, sending the nerve endings there to spark and sizzle.

Like a snake ready to strike, release coiled tight.

My whimpers grew frantic.

My limbs trembled.

My fingers and toes grew numb.

The sublime and rabid pressure was crushing my will. I couldn't stave off the massive orgasm much longer.

"Master..." I whimpered in warning.

"You do not have my permission, girl." Sam shook his head. Sweat dripped from his face, and his lips thinned in a tight line.

"But I...I can't hold—"

"You can...and you will," he insisted in a gruff voice.

"I...I don't want to...to fail you," I panted.

My pulse thrummed in my ears, swelling like a cacophony of

cymbals, vibrating through my entire body. Squeezing my hips tighter, Sam plowed in and out of my pussy. He stabbed deep, slammed hard, and grunted with every stroke. With a curse, he impaled me with one last savage thrust, then stilled, buried to his balls inside me. Every muscle in his body tensed…turned to stone, while his face contorted from the strain bearing down on him. Still, he held my gaze…showing me the demand and need churning for freedom inside him, too.

"Come, sweet slut. Come for me. Now!"

The roar of his command merged with the thunder of release crashing through me. As I fragmented into a million shards of bending light, my muscles seized. I arched my hips as the most violent orgasm of my life completely and totally annihilated every cell in my body. My screams of rapture filled the room. Sam gritted his teeth as he shoved past my clutching passage and splattered my walls with his hot, slick seed. And with a deafening howl, he cried…

"Mine!"

CHAPTER THIRTEEN

Sweating and panting, our chests heaved as we struggled to draw in air. My body hummed as aftershocks quaked and rippled through us both. After several long minutes, Sam released my hips, then slowly crumpled over me. He dropped his head to the crook of my neck, and I wanted to wrap my arms around him and stroke my fingers through his wet hair. But my arms were still bound. I couldn't move. And for some strange reason, I felt more secure than ever before.

His warm breath caressed my neck as he cupped a hand around my cheek. "Where are you now, little one?" he asked in a low, sated tone.

"I need a different color to choose, because I flew past green about two hours ago. Right now, I just feel…golden," I explained on a blissful sigh.

Sam's shoulders shook in silent laughter. "You are golden, sweetheart…my beautiful golden slave."

He raised his head and studied me. I knew he was trying to

discern if the term still held negative connotations. It did, a little. I knew the weight it levied in Sam's heart. Maybe someday I'd grow to feel the same.

With a nod of understanding, Sam tugged the rope and released me from bondage. Threading his fingers through mine, he gently massaged my hands and wrists. I closed my eyes and drank in his benevolent care. Savored the heat of his naked body against mine and floated on the clouds of golden sunshine that had settled in my head.

As he eased off me and slowly pulled from my core, I mourned the loss of his warmth and safety but couldn't pull myself away from the pristine peace that hovered within. Even when Sam lifted me off the table, cradled me in his arms, and carried me to his bed, my eyes refused to open. It was as if I didn't have the energy to lift my heavy lids. I'd never experienced such profound serenity and contentment. It was as if my entire being suddenly fell silent. I didn't want to do or say anything to break the wonderful spell.

"That's it," Sam softly cooed as he slid into bed beside me and drew the covers over us. "You just keep floating for me, sweetheart. I'll be right here beside you."

With a passive hum, I curled on my side. Slinging one arm over his chest and my calf over his thigh, I snuggled in with my head on his shoulder. Sam stroked my hair and murmured softly as the enchanting haze lulled me toward darkness.

The sound of a buzzing, annoying alarm woke me from a heavy sleep. Tangled in a heap of arms and legs, Sam cursed as he tried to get free and silence the grating noise. I couldn't help but laugh when he slammed the clock down on his nightstand with a grunt.

Turning, he narrowed his eyes, but the grin twitching the corners of his mouth told me he was only teasing. "And what's so funny, girl?"

"Oh, nothing, Sir."

"Uh-huh. Come on. Let's take a shower, my saucy little wench. I would have taken you to the spa tub last night, but I wanted my seed branding you while you slept."

A shiver slid through my system, and I realized that tinges of the fog still remained, clouding my brain.

Stretching, I yawned, then rubbed the sleep from my eyes. "What time is it?"

"Five. An ungodly hour to be awake, but we have to run by your place so you can change, and we have to stop by Ian's house and pick up your car. That is, unless you want me to drive you to work instead? We can always pick it up later tonight."

"You're allowing me to decide, Sir?" I taunted.

"About your vehicle, yes. But not about the spanking you'll be receiving after work, girl."

I couldn't keep the grin from my face. "Then I vote we leave my car there for a day or two. That way, we can come straight back here tonight."

"If you're that anxious for me to redden your ass, I can do it now for you. But you'll have a hard time sitting down to do charts. I promise."

The thought of wearing a pink hue on my ass cheeks all day flipped some kinky little switch inside me. But I feared once I proffered myself over his knees, I'd end up begging for more than just a spanking.

"The shower might be safer, Sir."

"Master," Sam reminded, pointedly, before a wicked smile played across his face. "And safer for who, girl? Certainly not safer for you."

I felt immersed in this strange and unfamiliar waltz. A dance of anticipation, curiosity, and desire that swelled within, bubbling and tickling my imagination. I held no illusions—Sam had the knowledge and experience to put me through my submissive paces, but I knew he'd do so with love and patience. I couldn't wait for him to teach me more.

Inside the shower, Sam pampered me like a princess. He washed my hair, massaging my scalp with his skilled fingers before soaping up my body and showing me how incredibly talented his digits could be. As he pressed my chest against the tile, he placed the pulsating hand-held showerhead between my legs and entered me from behind. And while he didn't edge me, the way he'd done last night, Sam made me wait for his command until I was panting and pleading for relief.

He lent me a T-shirt and a pair of athletic shorts so I wouldn't have to make the walk of shame up to my apartment in a corset and thong. Even when I cinched up the drawstring as tightly as I could, his shorts still barely clung to my hips.

"It's going to be nice when you move in and take over half my closet, girl."

"Half? I only get half?" I teased with a feigned gasp. "Do you know how many clothes I own?"

Sam laughed and shook his head. "There are plenty of guest rooms. You can appropriate all the closet space you need."

"Thank you, Master." I flashed him a cheeky grin and kissed his lips. "Can I fix you some breakfast before we head to work?"

"I'd like that, sweetheart. And some coffee."

In the kitchen, Sam sat at the table sipping his coffee while I fried bacon, scrambled eggs, and made toast. Our conversation was light, with lots of playful banter. The idea of living with him, spending our mornings like this, no longer frightened or threatened me. Instead, I was actually looking forward to us sharing more time together. It simply felt right.

As I carried our plates to the table, Sam held up his hand. "Don't sit down yet, girl. I want you to go to the living room and bring me one of the throw pillows from the couch, please."

"Yes, Master." I nodded, wondering what he was up to.

After I retrieved the pillow for him, Sam placed it on the floor beside his chair.

"Kneel," he instructed.

I wanted to argue that my breakfast was going to get cold but forced the debate down and complied.

"Very nice," he softly praised as he filled his fork with a clump of fluffy eggs, then drew it down to my lips. "Eat, Allisinda."

This is certainly different...and awkward, my conscience confirmed.

Still, I wasn't going to refuse his instructions simply because they made me feel uncomfortable and prickly. Timidly, I opened my mouth, and Sam gently slid the fork over my tongue. A proud smile spread across his lips before he turned and took a bite himself.

"Feeding you is my way of saying thank you for preparing my meal. I believe a good Dom should never take a submissive's gifts for granted."

While the way Sam displayed his gratitude was foreign, if not wholly unorthodox, I relaxed and let him indulge us both.

After breakfast was through, he helped me to my feet. Sam even insisted he clean up the kitchen with me before we headed to my apartment and on to the hospital. Escorting me to the unit, he kissed me outside the double doors and told me to have a good day before heading upstairs to his office.

I felt as if I were floating on cloud nine as I began my usual morning routine. Liz came rushing in, eyes wide in question as she held up her hand.

"Let me clock in before you fill me in." I laughed and shook my head.

A wry smile curled on her lips. "Well, well. Now look who's wearing that just-fucked glow, sister."

I laughed as she gave a fist pump and raced away. When she returned, we each grabbed a cup of coffee. Since the unit was unusually quiet—a sure sign all hell would be breaking loose soon—we sat down, and I quickly filled her in on the night's events.

Pure, unadulterated happiness danced in her eyes, and it almost seemed as if she couldn't wipe the smile from her lips.

"Oh, my god, Cin. I'm so flipping happy for you. This is exactly how Masters and I hoped it would turn out."

"Don't get so excited yet," I warned. "Sam's a little ticked off at Ian right now."

Liz's smile finally fell away. "Why? Because Ian set him up to find you at the house last night?"

I blinked and giggled. "He did?"

"You bet your ass." She laughed. "You two were about the saddest little kicked puppies he'd seen in a long time. And of course, being the control freak he is—and if you tell him I said that, *I'll* beat your ass, hard," she warned, narrowing her eyes, "Ian orchestrated the whole damn thing."

"Well, when you get home tonight, tell him I said thank you. But that's not what Sam's upset about. He's mad because Ian didn't tell him that Matti never showed up."

Liz snorted and shook her head. "No. As soon as Ian explains, Sam won't be upset. In fact, he'll probably fall all over the place thanking him."

"What do you mean, thanking him?" I was totally lost.

"Duh," Liz chided. "The guys own a detective agency. James had been tailing you for days."

"What?" I gasped before slapping my hand over my mouth. "When? Where?"

"All the time...everywhere." She laughed. "He staked out your apartment, then followed you to work."

"Where was he when Darnell-dipshit came pounding on my door, drunk as a skunk?"

She cringed. "He...well, he followed you home, made sure you were inside safely, then left for a few minutes to come by the house for a—"

"A booty call?" I smirked.

"Yeah," she blushed. "James was beside himself. Oh, my god, I've never seen him so upset. I'm sorry he wasn't there to help you, Cin."

Waving away her apology with my hand, I shook my head. "Don't be. I'm a big girl. I called the cops, well, after I called Sam—which at the time I thought was a good idea, but not so much when he found out Matti wasn't there."

"The important thing is that Darnell won't be bothering you anymore now that they hauled his ass back to New York. Everything has turned out the way it was supposed to. She smiled.

"Yes. So far, so good...for now."

"Stop that," she scolded. "You and I we've been through feast and famine when it comes to men. We both are going to live happily ever after."

"Sure we are." I grinned and rolled my eyes. "You've been reading too many fairy tales, girl."

Her mouth dropped open, mockingly affronted. "Just wait and see. Then I'll get to say those four words you despise."

"What words are those?"

"I. Told. You. So." She beamed with a victorious smile.

"Don't hold your breath," I chided. "Sam and I are going to start living together. That's light-years away from white lace and promises and choking on. 'I do,' and you know it. Besides, I don't see a ring on your finger, Miss Thang."

"That's because Ian and James are still arguing about who gets to be my legal owner."

"Christ, that *sounds* awful, like you're a dog or something." I held up my hand as Liz opened her mouth to challenge my words. "I know…I know, it means something completely different. I'm just sayin'."

Liz glanced at something over my shoulder. "Looks like our vacation here is over," she announced, nodding toward the hall.

Turning, I saw Dixie scurrying our way, followed by several other nurses. "Incoming," she stated in a grim drawl. "Elementary School bus rolled over. ETA four to six minutes."

"How awful," I murmured as a lump caught in my throat.

Dixie shot me a knowing wounded expression. "Metcalf has implemented the mass casualty protocol. The entire staff is being notified as we speak. Monica is bringing in reinforcements from Social Services to give legal consent if we need it. They'll be working with the school administrators to track down parents."

I glanced at my watch. "Make sure all ancillary personnel are within earshot along with housekeeping, too," I instructed, darting a glance to the somber nurses gathered. "We've all been trained for this. We know what to do."

Reaching into my pocket, I grabbed my keys. "I'll be right

back."

I turned and raced to the supply room and quickly unlocked a drawer. Reaching in, I grabbed all the stuffed animals I could carry, then raced back to the nurses' station.

"Hand these to any child you think might need a little extra comfort."

I didn't have to tell the ladies—most mothers themselves—that the children were going to be terrified. After the plush toys had been tucked in the pockets of our scrubs, I gave a resolute nod.

"Let's make sure the trauma rooms are stocked and ready to go," I directed before leading them down the hall.

Tension hummed in the air, like strings of a violin being twisted tighter and tighter. The minutes ticked by interminably slow.

"EMTs are pulling up now," Dixie called from the communication room.

I sucked in a steely breath as the double doors exploded open. Jeb and Freddy both wore haunted, grim expressions as they wheeled in a little boy—maybe seven or eight—who was screaming in pain and terror. I knew by the look the two EMTs wore I didn't want details of the accident site. Gripping my notepad tighter, I shoved my empathy away and led the trio into trauma one.

"Broken leg, possible broken ribs, distended belly," Jeb recited from his run sheet.

The boy had probable internal injuries. A glance at Metcalf said he knew that as well. Two nurses were already moving the portable x-ray machine in place before the doctor was even able to give the order. The staff was well trained and dedicated. I knew in my heart we would weather this storm no matter what.

Another pair of EMTs wheeled a little girl covered in blood and unconscious through the door. Sam came in right behind them. He flashed me a supportive nod, then turned his attention toward the little girl.

"I've got this," he announced confidently.

I directed them into trauma room two. Vacillating, I stood in the doorway. Sam had pulled me off his team. Even though I now knew the reason, it still stung. Of course, that was before last night…before the hospital had been put on alert. Still, I didn't know if Sam had, or even planned to rescind his directive. I only knew that disobeying a direct order from Metcalf could cost me my job. I couldn't afford the luxury of fear or sappy emotions.

Slapping a layer of protection around my heart, I zipped a glance toward the hall. As Liz approached, I grabbed her by the arm and pulled her into the room.

"Here, take this," I instructed, shoving my tablet into her hands. "I need you to assist Sa…Dr. Brooks."

At first she blinked. Then understanding slowly made its way across her face. "Oh, Cin… I don't think—"

"Just do it," I instructed, then turned and walked away.

As the ER filled to capacity, Felicia—the nighttime charge nurse—and myself directed the influx of staff that had arrived to assist the overflow of patients. With Felicia's help, we were able to orchestrate each physician's orders with the lab and x-ray techs. So far, our system was working seamlessly.

Soon, frantic parents descended, demanding information about their children. Monica ran back and forth between the unit and waiting room like a track star. And soon, anxious parents and scared children were reunited.

"On it, Dr. Brooks," Felicia assured as she darted from trauma two.

"What does he need?" I asked, forcing the disquiet from my

voice.

"His patient finally came to. Brooks wants me to bring in a plastic surgeon to stitch up the little girl's face. Then he's sending her up for a brain scan. Poor little thing was out a long time," Felicia explained.

"Good. I won't keep you." I nodded.

Turning, I saw Sam standing in the doorway watching me. A look of sorrow and guilt was etched over his face. I shook my head and flashed him a weak smile, conveying there were no hard feelings. He'd make sure I was back on his team…I saw the promise in his eyes. Reaching into my pocket, I pulled out a stuffed panda bear and tossed it to him.

Jerking in surprise, he juggled the toy but caught it, then smiled. With a wink of thanks, he turned and walked into the room.

"Hey, look who I found out in the hall. She said her name is Pammy, and she wanted to know if she could come in and cuddle with you," Sam said to the little girl.

"I guess so," she answered in a tiny, fear-filled voice. "I want my mommy."

"I know, darlin'. She'll be here very soon. I promise," Sam assured in that patented calm and soothing voice.

Even surrounded in overwhelming anguish, I couldn't help but smile.

Things slowly began to settle down. The injured children were released, admitted, or sent to other departments for further care. So far, there had been no fatalities. I sent up a silent prayer of thanks.

After Sam's patient had been taken for her CT scan, he paused in the hall and pinned me with an expression of concern. "Are you doing all right?"

"Yes. How about you?"

He chuckled. "It's been awhile since I practiced emergency medicine, but it actually felt pretty good."

"Do you think your little girl is going to be okay?"

A wolfish smile tugged his lips. "My little one is amazing. I was watching you take command. Quite impressive skills you have, Nurse Noland."

I couldn't help but laugh. "Thank you, Doctor. But I meant your patient."

He was still grinning. "Yes, I think she's going to be just fine."

"All available staff to the communications room, please," Dixie called out loudly.

Sam and I joined the others crammed in the little room and spilling out into the hallway.

"Some nutjob was cooking meth in his apartment and blew up the whole damn complex." A collective moan rippled through the staff. Dixie held up her hands and shook her head. "Most of the injured are en route elsewhere, but we'll still be receiving a few. Looks like the party isn't over yet, gang."

"Well, we're here," Dr. Stevens, a young intern, said with a chuckle. "Might as well make it worth our while."

"Okay, ladies and gentlemen," Metcalf barked. "Back to work."

As the staff began to disperse, Sam stepped in front of Metcalf. "I want Noland back on my team."

Like a balloon, my happiness expanded so fully I thought I might burst.

With a sour expression, Metcalf shook his head. "Fine. But from now on, keep the drama of your love life out of my ER, Dr. Brooks."

Sam's jaw ticked. His nostrils flared.

I cringed and held my breath.

"I'd really hate to go through life being as miserable as you,"

Sam bit out in barely a whisper.

Metcalf didn't reply, simply glared at him, red-faced, before storming away.

"I don't think he likes you very much," I mumbled softly.

"The feeling is more than mutual, sweetheart." Sam grinned. "Come on, we need to get ready for round two, only this time I'll have *you* by my side."

He bent and kissed me soundly in front of god and the entire staff. Several cheers and catcalls made my cheeks blaze.

"Get some, Doc Brooks." The young intern, Stevens, laughed.

"Oh, I'm planning on a lot more than some," Sam quipped with a lurid grin.

"Sam," I gasped, my face now blazing. "You all get back to work."

Liz snorted as she sidled up beside me. "Easy, woman. You sound like Metcalf now."

"Bite your tongue," I chided.

With a laugh, she walked away.

As Sam and I worked on one of the patients from the apartment, I felt centered. Calm. As if my world had completely righted itself. Maybe Liz was right. Maybe I could find my happy ever after with Sam.

Time would tell.

Three months later...

Clad in nothing but a royal-blue corset and matching thong, I paced the small private room inside Genesis. Butterflies dipped and tumbled in my stomach.

"Will you sit down, for crying out loud?" Liz laughed, perched Indian-style on the enormous bed in her Masters' suite. "You're making me tired just watching you."

"I can't help it," I replied, wondering how much longer Sam planned to make me wait. "What time is it?"

"Three minutes since the last time you asked." Liz rolled her eyes and climbed off the bed.

"You're going to stroke out on me if you don't chill."

"No. It won't be a stroke, just a heart attack."

"Either way, Sam won't be happy if I don't deliver you conscious and in one piece."

"How much longer?"

"Ian and James will be here any minute. But, Cin…you're going to do fine. Once you step into the dungeon and see Sam, all these jitters will simply vanish. You'll see."

I nodded and took a deep breath, then raised a hand to the soft leather band around my throat. "It's just…so public. We were alone when he put his training collar on me. Why can't he formally collar me like that now?"

"You already know the reason." She frowned. "Collarings are like weddings…the whole community wants to be a part of your happiness…your future together."

"I know. I know. I'm grateful to everyone for teaching me about submission…you, Julianna, Savannah, Leagh, Mellie, Trevor, and Ebony. Hell, even Destiny stopped giving me the stink-eye and actually started being friendly. And the encouragement from all the other Dominants… It's been amazing."

"Yes. You'll be among all your friends. So why are you freaking out?"

"Because I don't want to fuck this up."

Before Liz could reply, there was a loud knock on the door. As it opened, both Ian and James strolled in. In tandem they gazed at Liz, wearing matching looks of love and lust.

Then Ian turned toward me. "Are you ready, little one?"

"I-I think so," I stammered.

"No, girl. I didn't ask what you thought," he stated, arching a brow.

"Yes, Sir. I'm ready."

"Very well. Let's go." Ian extended his elbow.

I slid my trembling hand around his forearm and swallowed tightly before we followed James and Liz out the door, down the hall, and into the dungeon.

A sea of friends greeted me, all seated in chairs...row after row. My pulse tripped in double time. My mouth went dry. Then I saw Sam standing in that knee-quaking Dominant pose before the masses. Wearing a dark suit and a serious expression, he stole my breath.

"Relax, girl," Ian whispered beside me. "You'll do wonderfully."

With a nod, I locked my gaze on Sam as Ian and I approached him. My heart slowed and my fears subsided, just like Liz predicted.

"Thank you, Ian. I owe you a debt of gratitude for interfering...err, I mean orchestrating." A round of collective laughter from the crowd interrupted Sam's speech. He waited until the uproar died down, then continued. "But in all seriousness, without your help, my stubborn pride would have probably kept me from the joy and happiness I've found with my amazing sub... Allisinda."

My name rolled off his tongue in a rich, buttery tone. A shiver slid up my spine, and goosebumps erupted over my flesh.

"It was my honor," Ian replied.

Sam reached out and opened his palm. Ian raised his elbow slightly. I removed my hand and gently placed it in Sam's. The other man stepped away. And from the corner of my eye, I watched as he took a seat next to Liz, already flanked by James.

Sam wrapped his warm fingers around mine, then helped me kneel on the pillow at his feet. A hush fell over the room. I swallowed tightly. Settling into a proper submissive pose, I placed my open hands atop my thighs. Then, taking one last long look at him, I bent my chin and cast my gaze to the floor.

"The sight of you, my sweet slut, on your knees before me like this, fills my heart with pride," Sam began. His calm and even voice worked like a balm, soothing the barbs of my tattered nerves. "Feeds the hunger in my soul.

"Not only does your submissive beauty draw me like a moth to flame. Your spirit, your strength, and most of all, your bravery make me long to be a better man…a better Dom…a better Master. Through the rough times and good, my love for you has been constant. Still, it holds no boundaries, Allisinda."

As Sam's adoring words poured over me, tears slid down my cheeks. That peaceful, serene feeling, which I'd learned was called subspace, wrapped me in its ethereal arms.

"As you've opened your eyes, mind, and heart, the growth of your submission has been beyond breathtaking. Yet there is still much I ache to show you, to experience with you, to teach you."

Sam bent and cupped my cheek. I raised my head and gazed into his sparkling blue eyes, filled with promise, hope, and love. His lips curled in a tender and reassuring smile that sent my heart skipping.

"What is it you wish to ask, my sweet slut?"

I sucked in a shallow breath. A whole host of emotions pinged and zipped through my system, but I willed my voice to be strong.

"I spent my life living in denial. Fooling everyone around me, even myself for a long time. I had everyone duped...everyone but you, Master. Had it not been for your unending patience, understanding, trust, faith, and love, I'd still be trapped and in hiding. But you took a chance with me, showed me the secrets in your soul." I couldn't help but smile. "Scared ten years off my life in the process."

Soft chuckles rippled through the crowd.

"And all the times I've stumbled...and through all the falls"—I stopped and swallowed back my tears—"you've been there to pick me up, dust me off, and wrap me in the safety of your arms. If not for all the wonderful things you've shown me, I'd never know this burning inside me...this need to serve you and bring you joy.

"I kneel humbly before you...blazing in yearning and devotion, to beg for your ownership, your continued guidance, protection...and love. Beg that I may be allowed the ultimate honor of wearing your collar as a symbol of the incredible strength and power of your Dominance, Master?"

Sam's expression, wrought with such profound and unguarded emotion, made a soft sob slip past my lips.

Without a word, he lifted me onto my feet. Staring at me with an overabundance of love, he reached behind my neck and released the leather strap. As it fell to the floor, I suddenly felt naked, empty. But Sam slowly shook his head and softly smiled.

"I free you from your training collar but not from me."

Reaching into his pocket, he pulled out a silver hoop with a filigree locket. He placed the heavy metal collar in my palms.

"Please, Sir," I softly pleaded. "Bind me to you forever.

"It would be a privilege to own you, my sweet slave."

Racked with silent sobs, Sam lifted the collar from my hands. Sweeping my hair over my shoulder, he fastened the clasp behind my neck.

"This is only the first ring I plan to place on your sexy body, my slave. The next one will be on your finger."

I sucked in a gasp of surprise as Sam pulled me to his chest, wrapped his arms around me, and kissed me breathless.

Cheers and applause broke out around us, but it barely even registered.

I was lost…lost in the sublime lure of my Master.

ABOUT THE AUTHOR

Bestselling author Jenna Jacob paints a canvas of passion, romance, and humor as her Alpha men and the feisty women who love them unravel their souls, heal their scars, and find a happy-ever-after kind of love. Heart-tugging, captivating, and steamy, Jenna's books will surely leave you breathless and craving more.

A mom of four grown children, Jenna and her Alpha-hunk husband live in Kansas. She loves books, Harleys, music, and camping. Her zany sense of humor and lack of filter exemplify her motto: Live. Laugh. Love.

Meet her wild and wicked family in her sultry series: **The Doms of Genesis**. Or become spellbound by the searing love connection between Raine, Hammer, and Liam in her continuing saga: **The Doms of Her Life** (co-written with the amazing Shayla Black and Isabella La Pearl). Journey with couples struggling to resolve their pasts and heal their scars to discover unbridled love and devotion in Jenna's contemporary series: **Passionate Hearts**.

Connect with Jenna online:
Email: jenna@jennajacob.com
Website: http://www.jennajacob.com
Facebook: http://www.facebook.com/jenna.jacob.author
Facebook Fan Page: http://on.fb.me/1sW1b1b
Twitter: http://www.twitter.com/@jennajacob3

Sign Up for Jenna's Newsletter: http://bit.ly/1Cj4ZyY

COMING SOON

BOUND TO SURRENDER

Book Seven
The Doms of Genesis

By Jenna Jacob

Release date: October 2016

BLURB:

After suffering a brutal hate crime, submissive Trevor Hammond's outward appearance projects the usual carefree demeanor his friends know and love. But inside, the remnants of his battered psyche and the ghosts of his assailants keep him bound in chains of anxiety.

While his Master, Moses Abrams, aka Daddy Drake, is aware of the devastation consuming his precious sub, he finds himself powerless to neutralize his lover's demons. Embarking on an unconventional journey, Drake is determined to find a way to heal and bring back the man who owns his heart.

Will his love be enough to draw Trevor back from the darkness?

Pre-order:
Amazon: http://amzn.to/29JN7qd
iBooks: http://apple.co/29ElyvT

EXCERPT:

Lying in bed, Moses Abram—better known as Daddy Drake to his friends in the kink community—stared at Trevor Hammond, his sleeping lover and submissive. After having rescued his sub from yet another chronic and panic-inducing nightmare, Drake rubbed his tired eyes, searching for a thread of comfort in Trevor's soft snores. Yet no relief was in sight. The clinical diagnosis of PTSD—by friend, psychologist, and fellow Dominant Tony Delvaggio—plagued Drake. He worried that Trevor would be held captive to those inner demons forever.

Lord knew it wasn't for a lack of trying. He'd attempted to coax Trevor out of the darkness in every conceivable way. But so far, nothing had worked. Still, Drake refused to give up, even as the claws of impotence and frustration ripped his control and shredded his heart.

Swallowing the lump of anguish lodged in his throat, Drake blinked back the tears blurring his vision. Dammit, what would it take to bring his lover back? He didn't know, and it made him want to pound his fist into something hard and unforgiving.

Trevor jerked and thrashed, then whimpered softly. With an inward curse, Drake sat up and gently stroked his lover's soft blond hair.

"Shhh, it's all right, precious boy," he murmured. "Daddy's here. You're safe."

As Trevor settled once again, Drake issued a soft sigh of relief. While his lover's night terrors had lessened, they hadn't disappeared completely. He remembered the times he'd find Trevor huddled in a ball in the shower, crying uncontrollably. Thankfully those times had also tapered off. The young man only allowed a handful of trusted friends to know the depths of his traumatization. The other members of Club Genesis, the local BDSM club owned by longtime friend Mika LaBrache, hadn't a clue what Trevor and Drake were actually going through. And of course, the few times he and his sub had made an appearance at the club, Trevor painted on a happy smile, pretending all was perfectly fine.

But it wasn't. Dammit.

Spying the bottle of sleeping pills on the nightstand, Drake bit back a curse. Once *he* had been the one responsible for exhausting Trevor's mind and body with his Dominant demands and sexual needs, not some fucking pharmaceuticals. And in the wee hours of the night, like this, the yearning to claim Trevor again in achingly tender or brutally rough ways all but drove Drake to the point of madness.

He missed the compelling, mystical connection they shared exploring and fulfilling each other's dark desires. Yes, he mourned the loss of his slave, but most of all, Drake grieved for the potent love they'd once shared.

He couldn't fault Trevor for the destruction of their relationship. The poor boy had been an innocent victim. Drake owned all the blame and carried that weight on his shoulders as if it were the entire universe. From the minute he opened his eyes in the morning until blessed sleep stole his thoughts, Drake lived in the same mire of guilt day in and day out…for the past six fucking months.

If only he'd gone to the convenience store with Trevor that night instead of staying with Mika and Julianna, those prick-assed fucking homophobic frat boys wouldn't have savagely attacked and beaten his precious lover half to death.

Ice. All this fucking aftermath over a worthless bag of ice, Drake inwardly railed.

He'd exacted his revenge, in a sense. Yet, arranging for Frank—a longtime friend, sadist, and skilled tattoo artist—to befriend the frat boys, roofie their beers, then tattoo gay slurs over their faces paled in comparison to the retaliation still smoldering inside Drake's soul. One day, he planned to hunt the five down. He wanted to savor their tortured screams and pitiful pleas while he unleashed a sanity-breaking brutality and a level of pain they couldn't imagine. The agony they'd inflicted on his boy had awakened a pulsing, living demon inside Drake.

Sucking in a ragged breath, he gently lifted Trevor into his beefy, tattooed arms. There would be time later for Drake to quench his bloodthirsty vengeance. First he needed to find a way to heal his lover. Feathering a soft kiss over Trevor's cheek, Drake tasted the subtle saltiness of his skin and breathed in his familiar scent.

"Tell me how to fix this for you, love. I can't stand this distance between us. Come back to me, precious boy. Please. Daddy needs you," Drake whispered, allowing several tears to leak from his eyes.

~

Floating in the peaceful darkness, Trevor finally found the respite he'd sought. All too soon, he heard the screen door slam and the loud, slurred voices of monsters behind him. Fear seized him. Somehow they'd found him again. Frantically looking around for an escape, Trevor saw tall brick towers surrounding him. No doors. No windows. Not even a light to lead him out of the black, foreboding alley.

"Look at all that pretty blond hair," one of the monsters stated.

Trevor knew what was coming next and wanted to yank the long tresses from his scalp. Prove he wasn't a girl before the monsters discovered that for themselves.

"Hey, sweet thang. Wait up. We jus' wanna talk," another demon slurred. "Come on, baby."

Panic thundered through Trevor's veins.

"We're talking to you, you stupid bitch. Don't ignore us like we're not here," snarled the one with the black eyes. The one Trevor knew was going to hurt him the worst. "Come here, you stuck-up slut. You're not deaf as well as stupid, are you?"

Then, like he remembered, a hand reached out and snatched his arm, holding him in place with a vice-like grip, and spun him around.

Face-to-face with Satan's spawn, Trevor watched as the look of disbelief widened all five men's eyes.

"Oh, that's fucking priceless." A beefy, linebacker-looking guy with short-cropped hair and crooked teeth laughed. "Way to go, Everetts. You're hitting on a fucking fairy."

"I was not. I thought this faggot was a girl," the shorter man with bloodshot eyes spat with a hateful snarl. "Where do you get off making us think you're a girl, you little sperm-burper?"

"I-I was just walking to the store. I wasn't doing anything," Trevor stammered.

"Pull out your cock, Everetts. Shove it down the faggot's throat until he gags," Black Eyes urged before inching in close to Trevor's face. "You like sucking dick. So do it."

"N-No. I was…was just getting ice," Trevor tried to explain. Panic inched up his body like leeches sucking life from his veins.

"On your knees. You know the drill," Black Eyes ordered. Gripping Trevor's hair, he kicked the back of his legs and dropped him to the pavement.

Trevor jolted against the concrete, and pain screamed through his joints as a howl tore from his lips.

"Fuck you, Robinson. I ain't letting no queer's lips near my dick," the man named Everetts argued.

"Then how about we just beat the fuck out of him instead," Robinson, the black-eyed man, suggested with glee.

Trevor didn't even have time to try and cover himself or fend off the brutal blows rocking his face, ribs, and kidneys. A kaleidoscope of agony tore through him. In the distance, he heard Drake calling out to him. Trevor tried to yell for help, but one of the monsters pressed their lips to his. Wildly swinging his fists, Trevor screamed with revulsion. Viciously biting down on the lips pressed to his, he sank his teeth in deep. The taste of copper filled his mouth as he continued to punch the oppressive weight pinning him to the soft ground.

Soft ground? What the... It's the dream again. It's only the dream, his subconscious assured. Clawing his way out of the darkness, he surfaced, blinking at the light from the nightstand that filled the room. Drake lay on top of him, blood dripping from his lip.

"Son of a bitch," Drake roared.

While Trevor was relieved that he was free from the recurring and debilitating nightmare, knowing that he'd inflicted such savage damage to his Master's lip filled him with an overwhelming blast of guilt.

Sucking in a gasp of shame, he grabbed the sheet and gently dabbed the fabric against Drake's mouth. "Oh, god. No. No. I'm sorry, Master. I didn't mean to... I was having another—"

"Another bad dream," Drake sighed grimly as he pushed Trevor's hands away. "I know."

A rolling wave of remorse drowned him in misery. Why couldn't he stop reliving the events of that horrible night and put the past behind him? He yearned to have the relationship with Drake they used to. When would these fucking night terrors ever end? Would Drake finally lose every ounce of patience and simply throw in the towel over Trevor's unpredictable mood swings and his sullen, isolated behavior?

He needed to find a way to fix things between them, but most of all, Trevor needed to fix himself. All the coping tools Tony Delvaggio gave him during their weekly sessions weren't working, leaving Trevor at a loss.

"Let me up, Daddy, and I'll get an ice pack for you," Trevor murmured, contritely.

"It's all right, boy," Drake exhaled on a heavy sigh.

With a soft caress, he pushed the hair from Trevor's face. "I tried to wake you gently, like Tony suggested. I guess I wasn't quite tender enough. It's my own fault, baby."

Trevor felt the tension and fury slowly bleed from the big man's body. As Drake stared at him with a weary gaze, he noticed the dark circles under Daddy's eyes. The sight increased Trevor's guilt even more. He swallowed the tightness in his throat.

"You haven't slept yet, have you?" he asked, already knowing the answer.

Drake shook his head as a wan smile tugged his lips.

Tears welled in Trevor's eyes. He tried to blink them back, but they spilled over his lashes. "I'm so sorry, Daddy. I'll go sleep in the guest room for the rest of the night."

"You'll do no such thing," Drake commanded before dipping his head to scrape his teeth over Trevor's flat brown nipple.

A ripple of delight danced through his system as he sniffed softly and gripped his fingers into Drake's rock-hard shoulders.

"Please...Daddy," Trevor whispered. "Please..." *Don't give up on me.*

THE EDGE OF DOMINANCE

Book Four
The Doms of Her Life

By: Shayla Black, Jenna Jacob & Isabella LaPearl

Release date: September 13, 2016

BLURB:
Now that Macen "Hammer" Hammerman shares the bond he's long craved with Raine Kendall and his best friend, Liam O'Neill, he should be looking forward to a bright future. But recent trauma has exhumed the demons Hammer thought long buried. He must confront them while Raine fights to forget her past and Liam struggles to keep their new family intact.

When a shadowy figure emerges, determined to right old wrongs, he sets in motion a plot that threatens to tear the trio apart forever. With emotions running high and forces mounting against them, can they battle their foes and bury their ghosts so they can live happily ever after?

Pre-Order:
iBooks - http://apple.co/1GLp46P
Amazon E-book: http://amzn.to/25YyE1M
KOBO: http://bit.ly/1XYaHmJ
Barnes & Noble: http://bit.ly/1S6fqKp

WINDS OF DESIRE

Book Two
The Passionate Hearts Series

By Jenna Jacob

Release Date: TBA

Made in the USA
San Bernardino, CA
20 September 2016